THE
DEEPEST
CUT

THE DEEPEST CUT

A MONKEEWRENCH NOVEL

P. J. TRACY

CROOKED
LANE

NEW YORK

Published in the United States by Crooked Lane Books, an imprint of The Quick Brown Fox & Company LLC.

Crooked Lane Books and its logo are trademarks of The Quick Brown Fox & Company LLC.

Library of Congress Catalog-in-Publication data available upon request.

ISBN (hardcover): 978-1-63910-877-0
ISBN (ebook): 978-1-63910-878-7

Cover design by Nebojsa Zoric

Printed in the United States.

www.crookedlanebooks.com

Crooked Lane Books
34 West 27th St., 10th Floor
New York, NY 10001

First Edition: September 2025

The authorized representative in the EU for product safety and compliance is eucomply OÜPärnu mnt 139b-14, 11317 Tallinn, Estonia, hello@eucompliancepartner.com, +33757690241

10 9 8 7 6 5 4 3 2 1

To PJ, always and forever the brightest
star in my sky.
And to Ted Platz, my dad in every way
that matters.

The shadows of the past are very long.

—Peter Praljik

1

The Hague, Netherlands

As GORAN STANKOVIĆ enjoyed a final cup of tea with honey and strawberry jam in his 160-square-foot cell in Schevenin-gen, he mused on irony. Examples abounded. For instance, the world's great institutions were smothered in regulations, crippled by committees of incompetent morons, and largely ineffectual because of these self-inflicted wounds. But the crude, underground prison network was as reliable as the tides and ran as smoothly and efficiently as the finest chronometer. Underpaid guards and administrators were predictably susceptible to persuasions, financial or otherwise, even in a U.N. facility in The Hague. So were politicians, lawyers, and judges, perhaps even more so. Money greased the wheels of justice, and he still had plenty of it hidden away to dispense when circumstances required it, via his network of devoted loyalists. It was good to have friends.

He heard Jan's halting footsteps approaching his cell. One of his many saviors in a long chain of them. The poor boy's right leg had been badly damaged during an incident in Amsterdam that Goran had regrettably been forced to engineer, and he might never again walk without a marked, painful limp. It was a shame, as he was quite an impressive specimen otherwise: fit, well-proportioned, and handsomely blond and blue-eyed in the way most Dutch seemed to be. A man of infinite prospects, now sadly limited by his disability. But with Jan's deeply ingrained sense of right and wrong, ensuring cooperation had required extreme measures. His simple mind hadn't been able to grasp the fact that the world was powered not by black and white, but by multiple shades of gray.

"Good morning, Jan. Do you have something for me?"

Jan avoided eye contact as he withdrew an envelope from his uniform pocket and slipped it through the bars of the cage with the shaky, sweaty trepidation of an unwilling conspirator. "A note for you, Mr. Stanković," he mumbled in English.

"Thank you for this. I'll see there's a credit to your account by tomorrow."

He looked down at the polished toes of his boots. "I appreciate that, sir, it helps with my debts."

Goran clucked his tongue sympathetically. "Yes, you were unable to work for some time. You've been through several surgeries, correct?"

He nodded.

"And yet you're still having difficulties. It's an outrage. Health-care in countries with socialized medicine is grossly substandard, so as a token of my appreciation for all you've done, I will avail to you one of the finest orthopedic surgeons in Europe with no fiscal burden on your part."

Jan quailed, but he finally looked up with expectant eyes the color of cornflowers. "But why?"

"Friends help each other. And you've been a very good one to me. So has your mother. Her jam and honey are extraordinary, please let her know how much I've appreciated her generosity."

"I will. And . . . congratulations on your release today."

"Thank you. I was unjustly convicted and it's heartening to know that the legal system isn't entirely seized by prejudice. I did nothing wrong, Jan. Nothing. It was war, but I am *not* a war criminal. I saved my people's lives. Many lives." He folded his hands together pensively. "You probably know U.S. Marshals will be waiting for me. They aim to extradite me to stand trial for financial crimes."

"I think I did hear something about that."

It took tremendous discipline not to brag about his plans for the future, which didn't include entering another courtroom ever again, not in the United States, not anywhere. "Baseless accusations, all ridiculous."

"I'm sure." Jan looked away and started wringing his hands. "I should go, Mr. Stanković, they'll be wondering where I am."

"Yes, off with you, young man. And good luck."

Jan started to turn away, then paused. "Uh . . . about that surgeon?"

"Somebody will be in touch very soon."

Goran watched him hobble away without another word, but his impaired gait seemed a little sprightlier, insofar as an impaired gait could be. He'd given the boy hope. That's all he would ever get, but most people in the world didn't even have that.

As Jan's footsteps receded, Goran retreated to a corner of his cell, his back to the camera that was always watching through a cold, unflinching electronic eye. With trembling hands, he tore open the envelope like a spoiled child on Christmas morning. On a single sheet of paper was a long, beautiful series of numbers and letters. He was stunned by the onslaught of emotion that took his breath away; the joyful tears stinging his eyes.

He was finally going to get his goddamned money back. All he had to do was torture a few additional pieces of information out of Wolfgang, one task he wouldn't delegate. The pleasure he would derive was well worth the risk of reentering the United States, which he would very soon. There was a plane waiting for him.

2

Dundas County, Minnesota

Danielle Rieger was watching nature rage outside the front doors of Gustavus Adolphus Security Hospital. Monolithic raindrops exploded against the windows like liquid projectiles, driven by a screaming wind. Lightning strobed incessantly in the night sky, making the world look like a stuttering, overexposed photograph; the thunder was constant and so loud she could feel it in her gut and bones. She couldn't remember a spring storm so fierce. Even the one that had ripped all the shingles off her parents' barn roof in 2016 seemed placid in comparison.

Above the clamor of wind and thunder, she heard a crash somewhere in the surrounding woods—a tree had succumbed to the violence, likely one of many botanical casualties that would be sustained before this system passed. When the sun rose in two hours, the totality of the damage would be revealed. She was glad to be a guard and not a member of the grounds crew, because the place was going to be a mess.

"Heck of a storm," Brian commented from his post at the security desk, tapping at his phone's screen. "According to this big red blob on the weather radar, it's right on top of us."

"I'm glad you told me, otherwise I would have never known."

He didn't register the sarcasm. "At least it's too cold for tornadoes."

Danielle turned away from the hypnotic show and returned to her station. "Who said it's too cold for tornadoes?"

"Some meteorologist from Channel 9."

The blond, fresh-faced kid had only been on the job a week, which was long enough to know he was obsessed with the weather. Most Minnesotans were, but Danielle didn't pay it much mind. It was just a part of life—anybody who'd grown up on a farm knew that. There was nothing you could do to change it, so why fixate on something that just stressed you out? It was like watching a Vikings football game. "Put away the phone, Brian, and pay attention to the camera feeds."

"I've been staring at them all night. Nothing's going on."

She stifled her irritation because he was still in training. If he didn't shape up after his probationary period, *then* she could abuse him. "It's your job to stare; things can change here in a heartbeat. I'm going to make a round of the wards and when I get back, I don't want to see your phone. You know personal use is against regs. I'll let it slide this time, but don't let me see it again."

He bobbed his head in apology. "Sorry, I was just kind of worried about the storm. Why are you rounding the wards? Isn't that the orderlies' job?"

He was asking questions—a good sign that there was hope for him. "Because it's a skeleton crew tonight and an extra set of eyes is insurance that things stay calm. Some of the patients get very agitated during storms, and it's contagious."

Brian considered this while he unwrapped a Snickers bar. "So? They're all locked in their rooms, they can't hurt anybody."

Her irritation flared into anger, but she tamped that down too. Brian probably didn't have a schizophrenic brother who'd jumped out a third-floor window and broken half the bones in his body attempting to escape the demons that hunted him mercilessly. "They can hurt themselves," she said sharply. "These people are very sick, Brian, with terrors in their heads we can't imagine in our worst nightmares. No matter what you think of them, they don't deserve to suffer. You ever hear of the Eighth Amendment?"

"Didn't pay much attention in math class."

Was that a joke? Was he smart enough to have a sense of humor? "I'm talking about the Constitution. The Eighth Amendment protects citizens from cruel and unusual punishment. Trust me, you never want to hear an entire ward screaming and howling and throwing themselves against the doors, trying to get away from imaginary tormentors. It will scare the hell out of you and break your heart at the same time."

His blue eyes doubled in size. "That happens? Even with all the meds they're on?"

"Sometimes."

"They didn't mention that in orientation."

"Sure they did, you just weren't paying attention." She jumped when a wall-shaking clap of thunder momentarily deafened her. The lights flickered like they were about to give up the ghost but didn't.

Brian's ennui was deteriorating by the second. "The cameras just went offline."

"Probably a power surge—reboot everything."

"On it. Uh . . . what happens if we totally lose power? I mean, the locks on the doors would still work, right?"

"Not without electricity, but the generator automatically kicks in."

There was an ominous whine—the precursor of a lightning strike close enough to singe your eyebrows if you were out in the elements—then another earsplitting crash. The lobby was plunged into blackness, punctuated only by anemic, battery-operated wall sconces. Danielle clicked on her flashlight and waited for the generator to take over. After a minute, she started to get anxious.

"Does it usually take this long?" Brian asked.

No, it didn't. The switchover was supposed to be seamless and nearly instantaneous. "Something's wrong. Call in a maintenance emergency, then report the outage and get ahold of Dr. Drexler. I'm going to the basement to check it out."

"If the keycards don't work without power, how are you going to get down there?"

Maybe he wasn't as simple as she thought. That cheered her slightly, and she found a smile of reassurance for him. "I'm the boss, I have a master override key. Sometimes you have to go analog."

He grinned back timidly. "Nice."

"Hold down the fort, Brian, and make the calls."

"Yes, ma'am. What about the computers—should I shut them down?"

"Not now, the backup batteries have about thirty minutes. If I'm gone for twenty, then you can shut them down. But the generator probably just needs a reset like the cameras. Are they up yet?"

"They're still rebooting. I hope the computer's not screwed up."

Danielle felt a flush of regret that she'd judged him too harshly. Brian wasn't a dolt, he was just young and inexperienced. She'd been on the job too long to remember what it was like during those first weeks and months when she'd been uncertain and afraid too. "Don't worry, it can take some time. I'll be right back."

As she made her way past the security doors of Ward B, she heard the murmurings of an unsettled population, which put her on edge again. She paused to peer through the steel-meshed window. To her great relief, an orderly was on the floor. She tapped on the glass. "Everything okay in there?"

"Good so far."

"Call if things change. I'm going to see about getting power back, but Brian Gunderson is at the security desk if you need assistance."

"Appreciate it."

Danielle almost wished there had been a distraction that would delay her journey to the dungeon. But you always had to be careful what you wished for. She paused at the basement door, then keyed herself in and started down the stairwell. She hated this place, hated the way it seemed to swallow up sound. It took a lot of mental energy to dispel the unnerving sense that she was descending into a tomb.

Gustavus was over a hundred years old, built into solid rock by a despairing lumber baron whose daughter had been institutionalized in a horrific snake pit out east, the standards of the day. Enraged by the conditions, he built a sanitarium on a cliff that would become the benchmark for humane treatment of the mentally ill decades before the term had even entered the language.

The building was of historical import, so the exterior had been preserved, but the interior was now a state-of-the-art facility. The budget hadn't allowed for modernizing the basement, so the original low stone ceilings and narrow passageways remained much as they had been a century ago. The creep factor was amplified by the darkness. There were anemic, battery-operated sconces down here too, but their feeble light made everything seem even more sinister. Danielle believed that the Lord was her shepherd, and He was looking out for her, but down here, the concept of divine love and protection seemed very distant. It felt more like the devil's playground in this cold, clammy place from another century.

When she heard a furtive rustling in the corner by the generator, all the hairs on her arms stood at attention. She spun and trained her flashlight toward the sound with trembling hands, her mind playing scenes from every horror movie she'd ever seen. *Don't be ridiculous, it's just a mouse or a rat.* But if that was true, then why did she sense a skulking presence?

"Stop it, it's just nerves," she said aloud with false bravado, willing her stubborn feet to keep moving forward. Just like every stupid heroine did before they got slashed to ribbons by a psycho in a hockey mask.

The generator's electronic display was dark, which puzzled her. That had a battery backup too, so it could be reset in cases like this. Maybe the power surge had fried the circuitry. Whatever the problem, this was something beyond her scope of knowledge.

She hurried back to the stairwell, anxious to be out of there, but just before her foot hit the first riser, something hard collided with the back of her skull, and what little light there was retracted into a pinprick and disappeared.

3

L EO MAGOZZI PAUSED in mid-shave as he caught his eyes in the
bathroom mirror. They didn't look any different than usual,
but shouldn't they? For the last decade, those putative mirrors to
his soul had belonged to a Minneapolis homicide detective, but
tomorrow they would belong to a *retired* Minneapolis homicide
detective. The last gunshot wound, courtesy of a warped freak
named Wolfgang Mauer, had expedited that. The incident hadn't
disabled him physically or emotionally, but it had roused unremit-
ting thoughts of his little daughter growing up without a father,
and that scared the hell out of him.

You retire early from this job, Billy—

I'm Leo, Grandpa.

*Don't interrupt me, son, this is important. If you don't retire
early, you end up dead. There's a point when even the best cops start
making bad choices. Maybe you get scotched by a shitheel with a gun
because you're not as sharp as you used to be, or your luck's just plain
run out. Or maybe it's because your liver looks like a lava rock because
you're drinking away bad memories. If you don't have the sense or the
chestnuts to do it for yourself, do it for the ones you love. And goddammit, don't ever take a desk job or join the brass once you get out of
the action, it'll crush your soul. Did I ever tell you about Jerry*

Wasserman? He made deputy chief after a skel with a bigger gun benched him, then he hung himself a year later and never got to meet his grandkids. You can be dead while you're still breathing, Billy, remember that. When it's your time, make the right choice.

Uplifting, inspirational words of advice from his retired cop grandfather, spoken on the day Magozzi told him he was going to enroll in the academy. Alzheimer's had taken his grandfather before graduation day, but the passionate, unfiltered sentiments of a waning mind had lodged in the deepest recesses of his, mothballed for later access.

As far as anyone in the family knew, Billy wasn't a specific person, just a random name that represented all the young cops Grandpa had mentored over the years. At a certain stage of the disease, you couldn't remember your grandson's name or how to dress yourself, but parts of the past became a crystal-clear present. He'd made some salient points despite his deteriorating condition, although Magozzi hadn't realized it at the time. Wisdom was lost on everybody but the wise.

So, on this otherwise inauspicious spring morning, at the tender age of forty-two, he was facing down not only his own reflection but a different life, a different identity, and a new future. Tomorrow he would be shaving his whiskers as a full-time father to Elizabeth and house husband to Grace MacBride, although that last designation was a reach, because they weren't married and probably never would be. Sure, he still thought about it occasionally—it was a hypnic jerk of generational memory rooted in his Italian-Catholic background. But Grace wasn't the marrying kind, and he'd learned to live with that.

From the Big Decision to the Big Now, the impending change hadn't bothered him one bit. In fact, he was thrilled about it. Staying home—either here at Grace's little fortress in the city or at his lake place an hour north—and doting on the cherished women in his life was a dream come true. And it was a new mission that would never entail mucking through the blackest, most depraved depths of the human soul on a daily basis. Hell, he might even learn to enjoy cooking, yardwork, and fishing, though he doubted it. He would find other ways to make himself useful, like grocery shopping and changing light bulbs.

What *did* bother him was that such a dramatic milestone could pass so languorously, without affecting at least some sort of physical manifestation. If eyes truly did reflect the depth of the human soul, his were either incredibly lazy or in complete denial.

Grace appeared in the mirror behind him with a mug of coffee, stopping his heart. It happened every time he saw her. He'd been certain the visceral impact of her beauty would eventually diminish with familiarity; now he didn't think it ever would.

He turned and gave her a goofy grin, happy to shift his attention from his onerous thoughts and boring brown eyes to her dazzling blue ones. They always reminded him of the sparkling water of a lake or ocean, just beginning to darken before a dangerous storm.

"Wow, coffee delivered to the bathroom? I'm getting some vibes . . . yep, very distinct vibes. You want to take a shower and you need me to scrub your back. I mean, I already showered, but—"

"Magozzi."

"You'd rather take a bath? I'm okay with that too." He saw the corner of her mouth twitch, but her expression remained impassive. Damn, she was hard to crack.

"Finish shaving, you missed half your face."

He watched her plunk the mug onto the vanity unceremoniously. No verbal acknowledgment that this day was unlike any other. In Grace's interior world—one shaped by a terrifying, tragic past—there was no room for indulgent rumination or sentiment. Whatever happened, you just got on with the business of life and carried two guns just in case. The most basic tenets of survival. But the hardships she'd suffered had engendered compassion instead of bitterness, which made her an extraordinary mother and almost-wife. No man could conjure such complex perfection, even in his wildest fantasies. It would never be easy with her, but every moment was a gift.

"I don't know, Grace, I kind of like the half-shaved look. Duality of man and all that. What do you think?"

She fought her burgeoning amusement hard, but her eyes betrayed her, just like the twitch of her mouth had. Grace and smiles had always been antithetical, but during the pregnancy, and especially after Elizabeth's birth, her mouth and her psyche were getting friendly with the unaccustomed expression. Of course, most of the smiles were reserved for the little cherub, who had recently matriculated to the dreaded Terrible Twos, which weren't so terrible. But as a habitual scowler, Grace instinctively tried to stifle smiles when it came to adult interaction, even though it was getting harder with each passing day. He suspected it was part stubbornness, part artifact from darker times. You could always trust kids, but you could rarely trust adults, and vulnerability could get you killed.

"I don't think Descartes was talking about a sloppy shave, Magozzi. Finish up and come down for breakfast. Elizabeth is waiting for you and so is French toast."

His stomach growled rudely. "My favorite? Soaked in melted vanilla ice cream?"

"I added some rum this time. It seemed appropriate for today, whether it's a celebration or a wake."

He was excessively pleased that she'd actually referenced the "R" word. "I'm not in mourning. Far from it."

She tipped her head, assessing him as a clinician might scrutinize a mendacious patient. "You might be later, at least for a while. Personally, I'm celebrating. Gino will be here in half an hour, so shake a leg."

Magozzi's newly introspective thoughts, endemic during a major life change, rewound to fond memories of 80s rock. By the time he'd hit junior high a decade later, all the cool kids were wallowing in Seattle grunge and entertaining idealistic visions of heroin addiction, but he was still dreaming of shredding a Gibson SG through a gigantic Marshall stack like Angus Young. Why hadn't he ever learned to play guitar?

"'Shake a Leg' is one of the greatest AC/DC songs ever, even though it's considered a deep track. I didn't know you were a fan."

She gave him a long-suffering look. "I'm not. You do realize the saying didn't originate with AC/DC, right?"

"Now you're just insulting the gods of rock and roll." Her latent smile finally emerged, and he ticked off a victory point in his column. He was breaking her down one ridiculous comment at a time. Damn, he was good.

"It was a Civil War triage strategy. Stretcher bearers would jostle the legs of wounded men to elicit a response so they could ascertain whether they were dead or alive. But the original meaning is lost in the modern lexicon."

"That might be a bigger buzzkill than Grandpa Magozzi's fatalistic thoughts about being a cop."

"It's good to know where things come from. It's also a good time to look back. You'll have to tell me the Grandpa Magozzi story sometime."

She disappeared as quickly as she had materialized—a cipher, a sylph, a siren. Magozzi hacked at the other side of his face, thankful for the invention of safety razors so he didn't bleed out before breakfast, then dressed hurriedly in his new suit and tie. After a final check in the mirror—eyes still unmoved, but suit and tie looking fantastic—he charged downstairs to wolf down booze-soaked French toast and usher in a new life.

4

ANDY FARRIS WAS jogging the high river bluff trail through trees just beginning to show the pale haze of unfurling leaves. There was nothing better than spring in Minnesota. It was a time of new beginnings, and it seemed miraculous to him that life could so suddenly, exuberantly burst forth after so many frigid months of dormancy. The scents of damp earth and flowering dogwood were intoxicating—the first indicators of a waking world after a long, dark winter—a season that didn't smell like anything at all in his opinion. Some folks swore they could sniff out a coming snow, but how was that possible? Your nostrils, along with your olfactory glands, froze the second you stepped outside.

He paused to stretch against a giant maple whose canopy was furred with tiny red flowers. A lot of people didn't realize maples bloomed, because they weren't paying attention to the natural world around them. He'd been ignorant himself until he'd moved to the country and discovered little miracles everywhere, in every season. You just had to look.

Once his hamstrings were loosened up, he began his descent into the valley, where a greening meadow opened before him, brought to vivid life by last night's storm—another little miracle. Sagging onto a bench, he sipped Gatorade and basked in the prickling heat of morning sun on his winter-blanched face, his reward for the hour he'd spent navigating the shaded, treacherous paths above.

The view from this spot was stunning, flawed only by the forbidding stone citadel looming on a distant hill. It had always unsettled him that this beautiful park crouched in the shadow of Gustavus Adolphus Security Hospital, which was the politically correct term for a prison for the criminally insane. He always wondered if the cells had windows, and if so, did the inmates look down on the people hiking and jogging and picnicking and fantasize about murdering them horribly? Fortunately, it was a good mile away, and no one had escaped since 1974—some consolation.

He waved to a trio of fellow joggers as they passed, the only other people he'd seen this morning, then cursed himself when his legs suddenly seized with cramps. The treadmill and elliptical machine at the gym helped him keep up his strength during the cold months, but they were a sorry substitute for the real thing. Like all fitness-minded Minnesotans who let the euphoria of spring override common sense, he'd overdone it.

There was a nasty voice that hunched in the back of his mind like a sleepy troll, one that sounded very much like his ex-wife. It had been silent for months, but it was wide awake now.

Get over yourself, Andy. You're not young anymore, and if you don't snap out of your denial, you're really going to hurt yourself one day.

That ongoing dispute hadn't ended the marriage, it was merely one of the thousand tiny cuts that had eventually bled it to death. He wasn't a total idiot—there was truth to what she'd said—but he wasn't ready to give up the fight against time just yet.

He took it easy on the way back to the car, focusing on the jubilant bird chatter and the droning chorus of peepers celebrating their liberation from the frozen mud. Soon they would be able to enjoy their little froggy lives swimming in warm water. Ten minutes later, he caught up with the joggers, but only because they were clustered together on the side of the trail, staring at their phones. Another war? Another mass shooting? The world really was going to hell, and the giddy optimism that rode in on warmer breezes couldn't entirely banish that reality. The human race was losing its collective mind and soul.

"Is everything okay?"

"A patient escaped from Gustavus," the young woman with an auburn braid said anxiously. "They're telling people in the area to shelter in place or stay home."

So much for the fifty-year track record of keeping the beasts on the hill. His empty stomach spasmed as he thought about all the excellent concealment Dundas County Park offered. No way in hell he was sheltering in place here. "Let's all stick together until we get to the parking lot, just to be safe. But I'm pretty sure whoever escaped is long gone. They'd be anxious to get as far away as possible." He wasn't sure of it, not at all, but it sounded good.

She let out a relieved sigh. "That's a good idea."

"Only thing is, I'm cramping, so I can't run."

"Don't worry, we'll stay with you. My name is Lily, this is Luke and Sasha."

The Gen Z, man-bun duo forced vapid, disconnected smiles. It was clear to Andy that they couldn't conceive of anything bad happening to *them*. They'd been coddled into perfect prey. No worries that a deranged killer might be lurking in the brush a few feet away, ready to gut them with a shiv. But Lily had the healthy, instinctive fear of a woman.

"I'm Andy, nice to meet you. Do you guys live in town?"

"On Pine Street, in the student housing complex. We're seniors at Sigsimund."

So many complicated Scandinavian names in Minnesota. Even the colleges presented linguistic challenges. "Then we're sort of neighbors. I'm on Mulberry."

"That's such a pretty street!" Lily effused. "Do you live in one of those cute Victorians?"

"I don't know how cute it is, but it definitely has Victorian plumbing." Lily seemed to appreciate his lame attempt at humor, but Luke and Sasha pointedly ignored him. They obviously weren't happy about a slightly overweight, middle-aged man with cramping legs interfering with their routine—and Lily, he suspected.

She'd put her trust in a stranger instead of them. Little wonder—they weren't offering any solace, and he uncharitably considered that they had been gelded at birth.

Like all nice Minnesotans, they made small talk as they hiked the mile to the lot, but it was punctuated by uncomfortable, protracted silences. Andy had never been a sparkler, and his much younger companions were paying more attention to their phones than anything happening around them. But halfway there, they were startled out of their digital trances by the sounds of distant shouts and dogs barking and baying. "That must be a search party. Maybe they found him," Andy offered as a morale booster, mainly for Lily, who was twisting her braid and worrying her lower lip with her perfect teeth.

"Of course! There are probably tons of people scouring this whole area." She giggled nervously. "This is like that *Halloween* sequel when Michael Myers is being transferred from the loony bin and escapes."

Andy had seen every *Halloween* movie made, and he didn't think that was funny because he knew what happened next. But he chuckled to be polite. And because Lily was sweet and pretty and trying to be brave. Chivalry wasn't entirely dead in the twenty-first century.

When the parking lot was finally within view, his young charges became more voluble. Nothing bad was going to happen, they were almost to their cars, this was going to be an insane Tik-Tok post, let's meet up at the Chickadee Café, blah blah blah. But Andy had age and wisdom on them, and the reasonable sense of paranoia that came with it. People really were out to get you sometimes, so he remained vigilant, eyes coursing his surroundings. Without the magnified awareness, he never would have noticed the carcass of a deer in the brush.

Only it wasn't a deer.

5

Dundas County Sheriff Iris Rikker kept her eyes fixed on the narrow, storm-littered road that corkscrewed up to Gustavus because it would have been suicidal not to. But her ears were honed to the subtleties of Lieutenant Rich Sampson's grunts and incomplete sentences, as if she could miraculously divine some meaning from his one-sided conversation. According to the dashboard clock, he'd been on the phone for almost five minutes and hadn't uttered a single intelligible phrase. Men had a secret, prehistoric language in this rural county, and it rarely included any lucid verbalization. "Me Tarzan, you Jane," she muttered irritably.

"What?"

She could see in her peripheral vision that he'd hung up and was staring at her with an amused expression. Which meant he'd heard her.

You're not home alone, conversing with your geriatric cat. You are on duty, in your official car in your official unflattering brown uniform, on the way to investigate the escape of a homicidal maniac. Get it together and stop talking to yourself before you end up in Gustavus.

"Please tell me they found him."

"Nope, but some joggers found a body in the park. Fresh. Stripped down to his underwear. Neville was the first responder and he's securing the scene. Good news is, he found a Gustavus jumpsuit stashed in the underbrush, so now the dogs have something to track."

Iris felt her blood drain to her feet. Dundas County had only had one homicide during her two-plus years on the job, and she was hoping it would be her last. She still saw the victim's face in nightmares—the opaque cataracts filming his eyes, the ghastly white of his skin, the frozen blood crusted around the hole in his head. Then there was the anger and sorrow and disbelief that human beings were capable of such carnage, for the pettiest of reasons.

Without Neville and Sampson, you would have been a corpse too.

She shivered and tried to stuff away the black memories that still lurked too close to the surface to reliably keep at bay. "He killed for a change of clothes."

"And a wallet, phone, and probably a car. Everything we need to find out who this poor soul is."

"So the escapee could be on the road already in an unknown vehicle—that's not good. The witnesses didn't recognize the . . ." *Corpse? Dead body? DB?* "Deceased?"

"He's face down. And the scene is bloody, just so you're prepared. Guess they scattered pretty quick to puke in the bushes."

Iris hoped she could keep the bruised banana she'd eaten for breakfast where it belonged once she got there. "Have Neville print him. Maybe we'll get lucky."

"He already thought of that. The victim isn't in any databases."

She slowed and pulled onto the shoulder because she couldn't safely work out the sudden burr in her thoughts while negotiating a tangled strip of road with no guardrails between her and the steep drop-offs of sudden death on either side. She would have to do something about that when there weren't escaped killers and dead bodies to worry about.

"What's wrong?"

"The park is miles away from anything, you have to drive there."

"Right. And?"

"I run there sometimes before work, and there are never more than a few cars in the lot this early. One of the witnesses could have seen a vehicle that was there when they arrived but isn't now. And maybe the person who owns the vehicle never made it home or to work after their walk or run."

Sampson grunted again, briefly reverting to his native language. "You might have something there."

She put the car in gear, checked her mirrors, and executed a U-turn.

"Where are you going?"

"To interview the witnesses?" Why had she phrased that as a question? Self-doubt was not a good look for a sheriff, even if she was still green as a sapling.

"Neville is more than capable of that. I'll let him know."

Iris pulled back onto the shoulder and gritted her teeth in frustration. Of course he was capable of interviewing witnesses, far more capable than her, most likely. She was micromanaging again. She'd done it her entire life, and old habits were stubborn things.

Sampson nudged her arm. "You're a good sheriff and a good cop, Iris. I hope you're finally starting to believe that."

She *had* made some progress since she'd been a substitute English teacher and a freshly minted deputy working the graveyard shift on the dispatch desk. Two months in, she'd put her name on the ballot on a whim and won. Nobody had been as shocked as her when she'd unseated her predecessor, but it never would have happened if Sheriff Kenny Bulardo hadn't been a corrupt, wife-beating, homicidal dirtbag. Not a great confidence booster.

Her hand instinctively went to her chest to cover the scar his big gun had left. It was an ugly, puckered thing, but the unseen scars were the worst, haunting her dreams and gnawing away at what little self-esteem she'd gained during her tenure as sheriff. Deep in her little insecure heart, she would never believe she was up to the job. And like homicides, manhunts were way over her head. By fathoms.

Sampson signed off his call. "Neville's going to talk to them now."

"How long until the BCA can get a response unit down here?"

"About an hour, give or take."

Thank God for the Bureau of Criminal Apprehension. They provided support for all the state's small forces not equipped for crime scene investigations. She was definitely not equipped, and this was a high-profile case that required experience and expertise—more lives might depend on it. "We have to find this slimebag before he kills somebody else."

"There are answers at Gustavus, and the sooner we get there, the sooner we find him. Dr. Drexler is waiting for us. He's the administrator and head psychiatrist."

Great, another visit to another shrink. At least she wouldn't be the subject this time. Or would she? Psychiatrists probably picked apart everyone they met like a crab. The compulsion had to be as innate as the mammalian diving reflex, totally beyond their control. She reversed her U-turn and felt the rear tires skid on the gravel as she over-accelerated away from the sudden-death drop-offs.

"Thanks for keeping me from making a rookie mistake."

"Responding to a dead body first is instinctive."

She was about to protest but didn't. Sampson always made her look good, even when she didn't deserve it. Maybe she should go to night classes—did they have night classes for inexperienced, unqualified, traumatized sheriffs?

"You've got a little lead in your foot, never noticed that before."

"I'm a closet Formula One fan."

"No kidding?"

"God's truth."

Sampson smiled and gazed out his window at the forested landscape flashing by in jittering frames of brilliant sunlight. He saw the pale raw wounds in mature trees that had lost limbs, and hoped they were old enough to survive the amputations. Hoped Iris would survive her wounds too. "How are you doing? This has got to bring back memories."

I'm just peachy, thanks. Never better. Not at all afraid and insecure. "It does, but I'm fine. What doesn't kill you makes you stronger, right?"

"You're the strongest person I know, but healing takes time. Bulardo is going to die in prison thanks to you, so hang on to that."

"I don't want to hang on to anything from that case."

"I hear you, but it will always be there, so focus on the victory and the victories to come, not the loss. You have every right to be mad as hell about what he took from you, but you won. Be proud of that."

Yes, mad as hell. Indignant. Proud, and fighting for the victories to come.

"How's Puck?"

"Huh?"

"Puck. How is she?"

Now he was speaking in non sequiturs. A man of many verbal stylings. Sampson had only met her cat a few times, but there was mutual affection there, and it touched her that he'd asked. "She's good, but the vet said her kidneys are starting to fail, so I have to give her this special wet food twice a day. I guess it's common for a sixteen-year-old cat."

"I'm sorry to hear that. I'll stop by one day and visit her. She's very fond of me, you know."

They'd been dipping their toes in dangerous waters for a while, skirting another type of mutual affection. But *if* she decided to run for sheriff again, there was no way she would get reelected, night classes or not, so the conflict of interest wouldn't last much longer. "We'd both like that."

*   *   *

Deputy Jason Neville panted as he slogged the long, muddy mile to the parking lot. He'd put on forty pounds since he'd gotten his badge, and if he ever had to chase a suspect on foot, he'd probably drop dead of a heart attack. It was past time to get serious about making some changes. He owed it to himself, his wife, and Sheriff

Rikker, who hadn't called him out after the last department physical, even though she could have. Classy lady, brave lady, that one. Tiny as a peanut but tough, and smart too. Asking the joggers about a car was a fine idea, and one he wouldn't have ever thought of.

He finally reached the clearing that opened onto the parking lot. The joggers were in a pathetic, shell-shocked cluster next to his squad, their faces still white as fish bellies. Couldn't blame them, especially the youngsters. Andy Farris was pulled together, though. He hadn't even puked, which was more than he could say for himself, although nobody had been around to see it, thank God. He paused to catch his breath and mop the sweat from his brow before approaching.

"How are you folks doing?"

"We've been better," Farris admitted. "Any news on the escapee?"

Neville hitched his sagging utility belt up as far as his gut would allow, feeling shame as he faced this athletic group who clearly prioritized health. "Nothing yet, but don't worry, we'll get him. Just a couple more questions, then I can cut you loose."

They nodded anxiously in unison.

"When I got here, your cars were the only ones in the lot. Did any of you notice another vehicle when you arrived?"

The three students shook their heads, but Farris's brows lifted. "I did, Deputy. I got here at sunrise like I usually do, and there was only one other car. A red Nissan Pathfinder . . . well, not red, more maroon. I noticed it because one of the tires was almost flat. There's a lot of debris on the roads this morning, I figured the driver punctured his tire and didn't even realize it. I left a note on the windshield in case they needed some help."

"Did you happen to catch a plate number?"

"No, sorry."

"Thank you, Mr. Farris. This could be helpful, even without a plate number."

Lily lifted her downcast eyes shyly. "Do you think that was his getaway car, Deputy?"

"It's a possible lead we didn't have before. You're all free to go now. I have your statements and contact information in case we need any follow-up. Thanks for your patience, and take care."

Neville watched them disperse to their own vehicles, their spirits visibly burdened by something they could never unsee. He knew the feeling.

6

W HEN MAGOZZI ENTERED the kitchen, he wasn't surprised to see that his partner and best friend had arrived prematurely, and his mouth was full. Gino Rolseth's existence was predicated on food, and if Grace was cooking, nobody beat him to the table. His sainted wife Angela was the undisputed queen of the Italian American kitchen, but Grace operated in a different, more sophisticated milieu. Her first triumph was getting Gino not only to eat but to love fiddlehead ferns, launching the expansion of his culinary horizons.

He had already inhaled most of a plateful of French toast and sausage, chortling between bites as Elizabeth amused herself by smearing syrup on his face. Kids had absolutely no sense of propriety, which was one of the great things about them. It made up for potty training and crimes against food, and without the charm factor the human race would have become extinct centuries ago.

Grace's tailless mongrel Charlie was planted at Gino's feet, his pink tongue lolling; there was love, devotion, but mostly chicanery in his eyes. He knew ass-kissing dogs got table scraps. Soon Elizabeth would hone her skills of manipulation too and quickly surpass the formidable proficiency of her canine mentor.

As per Charlie's master plan, Gino executed a clandestine move and dropped a sausage on the floor. "Hey, Leo, looking sharp. New suit for your swan song?"

"And tie."

"Are those guns?" Gino was squinting at the tiny pattern. "Those *are* guns. And blood spatters? Who's the genius behind that?"

"Harley got it for me." No further explanation was necessary. Harley Davidson was the most boisterous and irreverent member of the Monkeewrench Software crew, comprised of Grace's three best friends and cofounders. He always managed to find the perfect gift with just the right amount of derangement to suit any occasion.

"Of course he did. I am so pissed I didn't think of that myself."

"You're not as bent as Harley, so don't beat yourself up." Magozzi kissed Elizabeth and was rewarded by a babbling, syrupy caress on his cheek. Best aftershave ever.

"Pissed!" she chirped merrily, and Gino tried to disappear into his chair, avoiding Grace's eyes.

Magozzi ignored the silent dialogue between two people he loved and enjoyed Charlie's warm, soft tongue on his hand, the dog's weight settling on his foot. It was no coincidence that he'd refocused his adoration just as Grace had dropped a loaded plate in front of Magozzi. He wasn't deceived, but since competition for the dog's affection was fierce, he caved and snuck him a sausage too. Did they make statins for dogs?

"The next person who gives Charlie a sausage gets bounced," Grace said tartly, but there was mirth underpinning her words.

"This is the best French toast I've ever had, Grace," Gino deflected sweetly. "What's the secret?"

"It's Magozzi's recipe. Melted ice cream soak, but I added rum. And a little malt powder."

"You two should open up a breakfast joint now that Leo's going to be jobless and on the dole." He laid down his fork with an earnest expression. "Leo, I don't want to scare you, but McLaren has been talking about jumping out of a cake for you in a leopard-print thong. Who can tell when that skinny little sh . . . punk is joking? But I just want you to be prepared for anything."

Magozzi choked on his first bite of food. The thought of a nearly nude Johnny McLaren squelched his appetite, which was infuriating because the French toast was spectacular. "Then I'm not going into the office."

Gino winked. "Just kidding. But anything can happen, right?"

Had Grace just snickered? Did she know something he didn't? "Isn't retirement supposed to be a dignified affair? You sit and listen to people say good things about you, then ride off into the sunset quietly?"

Gino leaned back in his chair with a snort and draped his hands over his well-fed, ever-expanding belly. "No, you sit and listen to people tell embarrassing stories about you while you suffer through a plastic cup of punch spiked with cheap rail pour. Then some idiot like McLaren does something wildly inappropriate and people start dancing on desks. Nothing about this job is quiet, Leo. Not even retirement."

Grace *did* snicker for sure this time, and it was infectious. Still, Magozzi wished Gino hadn't said that last part, because even as he got a chuckle at his own expense, Gino's words formed a barbed wire ball in his stomach. It was totally irrational, of course. Just nerves, emotions, and the decades-old, doomful proclamations of his demented grandfather. There was plenty of superstition in the brew too. Every precinct in the country abounded with anecdotal, cautionary tales about cops getting waxed on their last day. Even detectives who'd been unofficially scoured from the duty roster a week earlier by generous, appreciative chiefs like Malcherson.

Just ghost stories . . .

He started when Grace's hand landed gently on his shoulder— taciturn, all-knowing, all-seeing Grace. She'd obviously divined trouble lurking beneath the jollity, just like she'd known he and Gino were sneaking sausages to Charlie, even with her back turned. "It's going to be a great day, Magozzi. Just don't drink the Kool-Aid. It will blow out your palate, and you won't be able to appreciate the big boys Harley pulled from the wine cellar for your party tomorrow."

"Leo is in good hands. I won't let him touch that swill," Gino promised, clearing and rinsing the plates to further engender some goodwill after his slip of the tongue.

Magozzi covered Grace's hand so she couldn't reclaim it just yet. "When are you going to Harley's?"

"Soon. We have some glitches in the new software to work out, then I'm bringing Annie to her designer's studio for a fitting. She had some last-minute wardrobe issues."

Magozzi wondered what a designer would think of Grace's perennial black armor of jeans, duster, English riding boots, and SIG Sauer. It wouldn't surprise him if shoulder holsters were the latest fashion craze. It would make sense in this world. "Annie has never had a wardrobe issue in her life."

She shrugged. "I don't know the details, I only know she'll die if everything isn't perfect for your party."

"She'll steal your thunder, Leo, even if she's in a burlap sack," Gino commented from the sink.

"Yeah, well, you don't know what I have planned for my wardrobe."

Gino turned and grinned. "Leopard-print dick suit?"

"Dick suit!" Elizabeth parroted.

Gino winced and slunk back to the table. "Man, would you look at the time? It just flies when you're eating the most magnificent breakfast ever cooked." He bent to give Elizabeth a loud, liquid smooch on the cheek that sent her into a paroxysm of giggles. "Don't give your mother a hard time. C'mon, let's hit it, buddy, before Grace shoots me. We've got places to go and people to see before you turn your back on Homicide's vale of tears."

7

Annie Belinsky was in a state of high pique, a result of the many hardships that had befallen her this week. There was a glitch in the code she'd been writing for the latest Monkeewrench program, which hadn't happened since Moby Dick was a minnow. Then she'd found an unmendable tear in her gold lamé gown, and a scuff on the four-inch heel of one of her metallic python sandals, which left her a very small window to pull together an equally magnificent outfit for Magozzi's party. Her designer promised she would come up with something, but time wasn't on their side.

To add insult to injury, her scale had informed her just this morning that she'd somehow lost three pounds, an absolute disaster for a proudly Rubenesque Southern belle. The first things to go were the boobs, and damned if her bra didn't feel just a tiny bit looser.

She felt painfully guilty for being in a kerfuffle over such insignificant, superficial things when people all over the world were truly suffering. She'd known that kind of life longer than she'd been successful, and her empathy was deep. But focusing on petty, first-world problems distracted her from the real source of her vexation: Harley's inexplicable, persistent moping, which was genuinely alarming. He was an outsized man with outsized passions, but something had leached every bit of joy from him. Life-force-sucking aliens came to mind.

She was surreptitiously watching him from the corner of her eye as she arranged flowers in a monstrous and monstrously ugly bronze urn that had cost him a fortune. He was listlessly polishing the crystal goblets lined up on the walnut buffet, his massive, leather-clad shoulders sloped under an unseen weight. It was just plain wrong, and enough was enough.

"What is your problem?" she finally snapped. "You've been sulking for days, listening to the *Tannhäuser* overture on a loop—which, by the way, is the saddest piece of music ever written—and now you're having me arrange black roses in a hideous Etruscan funeral urn. Do you really think Magozzi wants a goth-themed retirement party? Are you going to have tattoo and body piercing stations too?"

He continued polishing the goblets mechanically. "The *Tannhäuser* overture is *not* sad, it's triumphant. And those roses aren't black, they're deep burgundy. 'Midnight Chocolate.' It's a new hybrid from Australia."

"Don't try to talk your way around this. You haven't insulted Roadrunner for days, and as much as I loathe your vulgarity, you haven't said one disgusting thing to me in recent memory. It's disturbing."

"I told you I wanted to lick your dress off—"

"Last week, back when you were your normal, pestiferous self. God help me, but I miss the infuriating you."

He shrugged. "Sometimes a man needs to reflect."

She expelled a genteel but very aggravated puff of air through her nose. "Reflect on what? How stupid you were to throw away good money on this creepy vase? You're depressed, and you're going to tell me why."

"I'm not depressed—"

"Spill it, sugar, you know better than to try the patience of a woman who stabbed a man to death when she was seventeen." That got his attention, and she was pleased.

"You never talk about that."

"It was the only way I could think of to snap you out of your self-indulgent funk." She abandoned her botanical endeavors and sat down on one of the twenty dining room chairs he'd had reup-holstered in custom fabric, woven with images of crime scene tape for the occasion. "Tell me what's wrong, Harley. Everybody's worried about you."

"You're talking behind my back?"

She threw up her hands in frustration. "We don't have to talk, it's obvious to everyone who knows you that your mind isn't right. Mercy, Harley, we're *family*, the only family any of us has ever had. We spent ten years of our lives running from a serial killer, and we survived because we had each other. You can't shut us out."

His eyes widened in horror. "I am not shutting you out. I wouldn't do that."

She drummed her long, rainbow-lacquered nails on the table impatiently. "I'm not moving a single inch until you start talking, and I can wait here all day."

Harley took a seat across from her and dragged his fingers through his long black hair. "You're not going to let this go, are you?"

"Oh, hell no."

He let out a pained sigh. "Everything's changing, Annie, and it snuck up on me. Magozzi is turning in his gun and shield, Elizabeth is already two, she'll be in school before we know it, and Roadrunner is in love, which none of us ever thought would happen."

"Change is a part of life, fool. And isn't it wonderful? The people we love are happy and flourishing. Moving forward—"

He stabbed a finger into the air to emphasize his sudden revelation. "Exactly! Everybody's moving forward but us. Don't you feel like life is passing you by sometimes? Like we're just voyeurs watching other people grow and evolve while we're stuck in idle?"

Annie had never felt that way, not ever, but she knew exactly what his problem was now, and why hadn't she realized it earlier? It was so obvious. "This is about Roadrunner and Petra, isn't it? You two were always inseparable peas in a pod and you miss having him around all the time."

Harley scoffed. "I'm happy as hell for him. He actually has a life now, which is a frigging miracle. And Petra is a crown jewel. Way out of his league, you ask me."

"You didn't answer my question."

He averted his gaze to the bay window that framed the newly verdant back lawn of his Summit Avenue mansion. "Yeah, I miss having him around all the time. I miss sneaking anchovies onto his disgusting vegan pizza and pulling all-nighters to save the world from evil assholes with the software we wrote together."

"You know perfectly well that Roadrunner is still the first to arrive and the last to leave. And our software is still solving crimes and saving the world from evil assholes, especially since Petra brought it to the war crimes division of ICE. Their success rate apprehending monsters like Peter Praljik has doubled since the implementation. She's part of our team now, like it or not."

Harley leaned forward and thumped his hand on the table petulantly. "I don't just like it, I love it, and I love *her*, because she gave Roadrunner something none of us ever could, something he deserves." He receded back into his chair, docile and introspective again. "I guess the crux of it is, he was always like the Monkeewrench kid, even though he's the same age as the rest of us. A six-foot-seven, antisocial dork who only wears Lycra biking suits and thinks he's going to win the Tour de France someday. But he's all grown up now, and it feels weird. Jesus, he might even get married and procreate and start wearing real clothes. I don't know if I can take that."

Annie had an epiphany of her own. What Harley said was true, but she'd never thought of it quite that way. Roadrunner was smarter than the rest of them put together, but he'd always been childlike, and they'd all doted on him in their own ways—Harley more than anyone.

"So you're a parent going through empty-nest syndrome. Get over it. Magozzi and Gino analyze people's behavior for a living, and if they see you like this, they'll probably have you committed. If they don't, I will." She saw a spark of mischief in his eyes and a slice of smile slashing his beard for the first time in days.

"You are a woman of astounding compassion."

"I am a woman of astounding pragmatism. We have a grand fête to prepare for, so stop lamenting over the natural course of things and start setting the table so I can supervise. You don't know a salad plate from a baboon's butt."

He bristled indignantly. "I spent *three* hours on the Emily Post website last night, I know about salad plates. And bread and butter plates, silverware placement—"

"Yet you'll still manage to screw it up without proper oversight. Now stop trying to rub that crystal back into sand and make yourself useful."

Harley shrugged off his biker jacket, exposing enormous arms covered in tattoos. "It's hot in here."

"It's perfectly comfortable. You're not sick, are you? You can't get sick, the party is tomorrow."

He tipped his head, examining her sheath dress appreciatively. "Sick with lust as I gaze upon that silk bandage barely restraining your luscious curves—"

"Oh, dear God in heaven, I hope you've never actually used that line for real."

"Did I mention how fetching you look in pink? Like a big, beautiful Easter egg?"

"Of course you didn't, you've been brain-dead."

"Eggs are a sign of fertility, you know. Wanna crank out some kids? It's one sure antidote to empty-nest syndrome. And those child-bearing hips are just crying out for the opportunity, what with your biological clock ticking."

She let out a long-suffering sigh and rolled her eyes up to the soaring, coved ceiling, where a fresco of Bosch's *Garden of Earthly Delights* hovered. Another twisted, ill-advised waste of money. "I liked you better when you were depressed and not completely delusional. But welcome back, all the same. Where *is* Roadrunner, anyhow?"

"He's helping Petra make some fancy Eastern European pastry for Magozzi's shindig. I guess you have to stretch out the dough over a huge table until you can read newsprint through it. He said he'll be here by noon."

She shook her head in amazement, trying to imagine Road-runner making pastry or anything edible for that matter. He could barely peel a banana, which accounted for ninety percent of his diet. The love of a good woman surely could summon miracles.

8

Iris was gazing at all the framed diplomas and academic awards hanging on Dr. Drexler's office walls. The sports trophies and photos of adventure travels on bookshelves behind his desk. Admittedly, he was a fit, handsome older gentleman with a thick shock of silver hair, but the shirtless jungle shot was a little too Tinder for the workplace. If he'd gotten into psychiatry for self-help, it failed, because he was obviously an unreformed narcissist. But he wasn't so full of self-adoration now—his professional life was falling apart and the additional bad news of the dead man in the park had taken another bite out of his ego and composure.

He rubbed his temples, trying to massage away a nightmare. "This is all just so horrible. Unthinkable."

"It certainly is. Let's continue with the timeline, Doctor, and please be detailed. You said you were contacted by Brian Gunderson at approximately four AM. What happened after that?"

"He informed me that there was a power outage and a generator failure. I arrived half an hour after that and learned that Danielle Rieger had been found unconscious in the basement mechanical room. She's at Mercy and I just spoke with her. She has a serious concussion, but thank God she's going to be okay."

"That's excellent news."

"Was Ms. Rieger armed?" Sampson asked.

"Our guards don't carry guns, but her baton and pepper spray were taken, along with her master key."

"That's how Wolfgang Mauer escaped?"

"It's the only way he could have. Every door in the facility requires a keycard or a master key to get in or out."

Iris frowned. "Then how did he get out of his room and down to the basement?"

"The cameras stopped recording around the time the power went out so I don't have a definitive answer to that yet, but some of the locks on the patients' doors also malfunctioned."

"You didn't report him missing until six AM. Why?"

Drexler's face bloomed. "There were patients loose, Sheriff. It was chaos and required the attention of everyone on duty. It was only after the situation stabilized that we noticed he was absent."

Mauer had at least a two-hour head start. If he had a vehicle, he could be anywhere by now. "Were these malfunctions a result of the power outage?"

"I assume so, though it should never have happened. We're a hospital, yes, but we're also a prison, and we have multiple redundancies in our security system. I assure you, we're conducting a thorough investigation as we speak."

"Did you find anything of interest in his room?"

"Nothing. Nothing at all, but that's to be expected. The patient rooms are checked daily and the opportunity for contraband or conspiracy is virtually nonexistent here, unlike in a traditional prison setting."

"Why is that?"

"We house some of the most troubled individuals in the state, Sheriff. Many of our patients are impaired to the point where they are unable to engage in an open ward setting. For some, leaving the safety of their rooms is too terrifying. For others, we don't allow interaction because they're too dangerous. Safety is our primary concern."

Hence the name "security hospital," but there had been an epic failure somewhere. "Where is Mr. Mauer on that spectrum?"

"The latter. Very definitely the latter." His desk phone rang, and he lifted a finger. "I'm sorry, I have to take this."

Iris shifted in her straight-backed wooden chair and felt a zing in her sciatic nerve. Back in her wholesome youth in southern Minnesota, she'd been at church basement potlucks that had cheap metal seating more comfortable. If you were on the precipice of a mental health crisis, the furniture might take you all the way. Maybe that was the plan. Job security.

Drexler didn't do much talking, but his previously pink face suddenly bleached white as bone. Not good news for him; maybe not for them, either. He finally placed the receiver back in its cradle. His eyes looked like black craters against the pallor of his skin. "That was IT. There were no power outages in our area this morning, and the generator was tampered with. They tell me we were hacked."

Sampson leaned forward. "Do they know who did it?"

"Not yet, but they'll be working around the clock until they do. They say the attack was very sophisticated, so I'm positive Mr. Mauer is behind it somehow. He's a computer scientist, and his prior crimes involved very high-level hacking." His expression soured. "Among other things."

"Could he have accessed a computer?" Iris asked.

"Impossible. None of our patients have access to computers with internet connectivity. We only use them for therapies."

"So he has an ally and he had to communicate with them. How?"

"It's inexplicable."

"Is there any chance Danielle Rieger was involved? Perhaps helped facilitate the escape by staging her assault?"

His eyes widened in horrified disbelief, which made her feel bad for asking. "Absolutely not! She's been our security chief for eight years and has an exemplary service record. She's also a very good person. And security personnel don't interact with patients unless the medical staff needs assistance with an incident, so I doubt she's ever even seen him before. Mauer wasn't a troublemaker because we never gave him the opportunity to be one."

Iris made a few notes in her clearance rack notebook, which had a basket of puppies on the cover. She really should get something more professional, something that didn't make her look like a grade schooler, but she loved a bargain. And baby animals. "Did Mr. Mauer have a roommate?"

"Certainly not. He had no contact with anyone but the medical staff, which is highly regulated, supervised, and logged. He is one of our highest security patients."

"Visitors?"

"Only a nun from St. Bridget's. Sister Lucia."

"He's a religious man?" Sampson asked curiously.

Drexler folded his manicured hands on his ornate oak desk. "Some patients have delusions and fantasies of a religious nature; some have been devout their entire lives. I can't speak to Mr. Mauer's beliefs because he wasn't particularly cooperative during our sessions, but he did request regular visits, so I assume so. I took that as a positive sign."

Iris flipped to a new page in her puppy notebook. "Do nuns come here often?"

"Two or three times a month. We have an arrangement with St. Bridget's. They're interested in saving souls and I'm interested in helping these people in any way I can, so I welcome their visits."

"Tell us more about Wolfgang Mauer and why he's so dangerous."

"Patient-doctor confidentiality prevents—"

Sampson interrupted. "Doctor, a violent felon attacked one of your guards, escaped your facility, and killed a man all in the space of a few hours. It's our job to bring him back. We need every scrap of information you have on him."

Drexler's eyes narrowed slightly, and his mouth curved down in a moue of distaste. "He's an unrepentant murderer, extremely calculating, extremely intelligent. He has the highest score on the SD-4 I've ever seen."

Why did some doctors assume you were fluent in medspeak? "SD-4?" Iris asked, trying to keep the irritation out of her voice.

"Short Dark Tetrad test. Dark Tetrad isn't a mental disorder but a confluence of negative personality traits: narcissism, Machiavellianism, psychopathy, and sadism. SD-4 isn't predictive, it's merely an assessment tool, a snapshot of where a patient is at the time of the test. Whether Mr. Mauer possessed these tendencies early in life, we'll never know, but his childhood and upbringing are by far the most compelling factors in his antisocial behavior."

Iris marveled that murder was now blandly considered antisocial behavior. Everything was nestled in cream puff filling these days, and God help you if you didn't get your phrasing right. "Go on, Doctor."

Drexler rubbed the gray stubble on his chin. No time for a shave at four this morning with all hell breaking loose. "As I mentioned, he was largely uncooperative in therapy sessions, so much of the information we have on him is from police files. We do know he was an orphan of the Balkan wars and came under the care of a sadist who raised him from the age of five—a man who saved his life and ruined it at the same time. He became a powerful father figure, an idol really, and Mr. Mauer never left his side. The only thing that separated them after nearly three decades were their arrests for the joint kidnappings, torture, and killings of women last year. It rocked the art world and was very high-profile, you must remember."

Iris took a sharp breath. Magozzi and Gino's case. "The artist Rado, aka George Bormann, aka Peter Praljik, the war criminal."

Drexler nodded. "Yes. Praljik died in police custody—a bad heart—but Mr. Mauer blames the authorities for his death. His revenge fantasy was really the only thing he spoke about at any length. He harbors intense anger and hatred for anyone who helped facilitate justice, including witnesses at his trial."

Iris didn't bother to conceal her disgust. "That's ridiculous. Praljik wouldn't have died in custody if they hadn't tortured and murdered women."

"Mauer has a badly warped perception of reality and a deeply rooted persecution complex."

"Do you think he might act on this fantasy?"

The psychiatrist's expression was grim. "If he can evade capture long enough, I absolutely believe he will try. He told me he had a hit list—he called it the Eight. He refused to share names, but he's obsessed with these people. I wouldn't dismiss the possibility that his escape was primarily motivated by revenge, not freedom."

9

Travis Dunbar was shivering in his bed, the smelly charity bin blanket pulled tightly over his head to drown out the sounds of anger. He was used to his parents' violent fighting and their scary, erratic behavior. He was even used to getting knocked around for no reason. But when the shouting escalated into screaming . . . that's what he couldn't take. The sound drilled into his brain and made spiky white stars flash behind his eyes until he thought he'd go crazy.

Sometimes it helped to hum, but it wasn't helping this morning. If he had a phone and earbuds like his friend Malcolm, he could play his favorite metal bands really loud and drown everything out. But he didn't have a phone or earbuds. He didn't have anything except an old gun he'd found in a moldering box in the barn. It was half-eaten by rust, and there were no bullets, but it was something real, something concrete he could call his own.

It's just an old piece of junk, Trav. It's probably a hundred years old.

I'm gonna fix it one day, just like I'm gonna fix the stars behind my eyes.

Malcolm had given him such an astounded look, maybe even a frightened one, that Travis had laughed it off as a joke and never mentioned it to him again. The stars weren't normal, that much was clear.

But a few months later, in a moment of weakness, he'd made the mistake of telling the school counselor about them. Mrs. Christianson was nice, but she had piercing, probing eyes the color of violets that spooked him and made him feel naked.

Have you seen a doctor about this?

Uh . . . yeah, he says everything's okay.

He'd been too ashamed to tell her he'd never been to a doctor in his life, at least that he could remember, that he hadn't broken his arm falling out of a tree, and that his black eyes weren't from baseball games or rough play.

But Mrs. Christianson knew, because a lady from child protection had shown up two days later. Nothing had come of it, because his mom had been on the wagon for a week and was making homemade chili instead of burning fish sticks and sucking on a pipe that didn't look anything like the one Grandpa Dunbar smoked cherry tobacco out of when he was still alive. She'd even put out a dish of Oreos and offered the social worker coffee or tea. Travis still couldn't decide if he was relieved or disappointed, but it didn't matter. Wherever he ended up, he would be on his own. He always had been.

Travis pinched his eyes shut and pressed his hands over his ears when the screaming reached a new pitch, fighting the spiky stars and the icky feeling that something inside him was coming apart.

Stop stop stop stop!

And suddenly, it did, as if his thoughts had the power to mute the horrific soundtrack of his home life. Malcolm was always rambling on about people who could bend spoons with their mind, see into the future, and control events. What if Malcolm wasn't totally full of shit? What if some people really did have special gifts?

Travis popped his head out cautiously, like a turtle emerging from the safety of its shell. His arms bristled with goosebumps, not just because it was cold enough to turn his breath into frosty balloons, but because the silence felt ominous. Their fights usually lasted a lot longer, until one of them passed out.

He listened until his ears hurt from the deadness of the air, but there was nothing to hear. They must be really messed up this morning. He retreated back into the relative warmth of his dingy cocoon. The boiler was broken again, and Mom said they couldn't afford to fix it, just like they couldn't afford to fix the washing machine because Dad was a worthless piece of shit. But wasn't she a worthless piece of shit too? At least his dad sometimes took shifts at Centennial Cement, but as far as he knew, she'd never worked, she just burned fish sticks and slapped him when he told her he was hungry. Malcolm's parents both had full-time jobs and they always had heat in their house and ate pizza from Frankie's Pasta and Pies every Friday.

He considered the possibility of special gifts again and prayed to God and the universe and anybody or anything else out there listening that any abilities he might possess would come out from wherever they were hiding. Most of all, he wanted to be able to see into the future, so he could find out what the next winning lottery number was and run away to someplace warm, where there was always a full refrigerator and a giant TV in every room. And maybe before he ran away, he would burn this crumbling farmhouse down, and his parents along with it.

That last thought brought on a powerful wave of nausea, so he filled his mind with plans for his lottery winnings. He would buy his own tropical island and build a mansion right on the beach. Next door, he'd build a Frankie's Pasta and Pies that only served his favorite, extra-large pepperoni and sausage. Malcolm would come to visit, and they'd ride the ocean waves in his speedboat before pizza and video games.

Finally, he began to drift off to a cozy place where he had control of his life. But all the cozy iced up and shattered when he heard the garage door squeak open, then the loud coughing sound of the old Ford's engine. It didn't make sense. His parents were unconscious, so who was taking the truck?

Travis bolted out of bed and pulled on worn sneakers and a sweatshirt five sizes too large for him, another scavenged charity bin find. He peered out his window and saw the battered red truck backing down the driveway. "Wait!" he yelled, knowing the driver couldn't hear him. Nobody could because the nearest neighbor was a mile away.

He ran down the hallway, tripping over empty cans and bottles, and burst out of the sagging front door, waving his arms. If it was a car thief and he got shot and killed, it really wouldn't matter much, he supposed. Sometimes he wished he was dead anyhow, especially when he thought about killing his parents.

*   *   *

Son of a bitch. First, the flat tire, and now this.

Wolfie was clenching his jaw so tightly, he thought his teeth would shatter. Where the hell did this skinny, raggedy kid with windmilling arms and a black eye come from? A few seconds ago, he'd had a different vehicle and phone that couldn't be connected to him. He'd even discovered a fat roll of twenty-dollar bills in the glove compartment, something he hadn't anticipated from a horror show like this place. But suddenly, everything good had been quashed by a most unlikely adversary.

He really didn't want to kill this poor, innocent victim of squalor and evil dissolute parents; it would be so wrong. But if he let him live, the cops would be called. And his plans would be ruined, something he couldn't let happen.

A young man of your brilliance and ability will always be able to imagine at least one alternative solution to a difficult problem. It merely requires serenity and focus, my dear son.

With Peter's unyielding faith and support, he'd proven the prognostication time and time again, up until the last difficult problem. He'd failed miserably because he'd refused to believe that Monkeewrench could possibly be smarter than he was. And now the only person who'd ever mattered in his life was dead. He owed Peter vengeance, but he also owed him penance. He had to save the boy if he could, just like he'd been saved, to balance the scales.

Wolfie focused on the serenity Peter had valued above all, and it freed his mind to calculate the outcomes of multiple actions and scenarios. The blizzard of electrical impulses that streaked across neurons took less than a second to reveal a simple truth: the boy might be useful in any number of ways. He might even become like a son to him.

He put the truck in park and opened his window.

*   *   *

Travis stood absolutely motionless on the spongy spring earth, eyes closed, waiting for his fate. A red-winged blackbird pierced the quiet with a burbling call that sounded like the steel drum he'd heard on a song from Malcolm's iTunes playlist, but there were no gunshots, no hail of bullets. He lifted his lids a fraction and saw a handsome, smiling man in a Nike windbreaker leaning out the truck's window, arms draped casually over the steering wheel. Travis took a step back, bewildered.

"Good morning, young man. Do you live here?"

The politeness confounded him further. Robbers weren't supposed to be friendly, they just took their loot and ran. "What the fuck are you doing in my parents' truck?" he blustered weakly, not at all sounding like the movie-screen, tough guy of his imagination.

"I'm repossessing it. They missed six payments. I'm sorry, but that's my job."

Travis felt his heart start to stutter manically, an incessant double-bass beat like Lars Ulrich from Metallica was right inside of him. Something wasn't adding up. As far as he knew, Uncle Ray had given Dad the junker two years ago. "I think you got the wrong house."

"I have the paperwork right here."

"I better wake up my folks."

"It's best they don't know. I heard them fighting like pit bulls when I got here, and I don't want any part of that. I've been shot at before doing this job."

Travis looked around the empty yard and the empty, muddy dirt road beyond. He remembered a movie he'd seen, where the main character was repossessing a car, but he came with a tow truck and a couple other guys. "How did you get here?"

"My boss dropped me off."

"If your job is so dangerous, why don't you have anybody with you?"

"We're understaffed today."

"Where did you get the keys?"

"They were in the ignition." The man chuckled. "You're pretty smart. What's your name?"

He'd never heard from anybody, ever, that he was pretty smart, and felt an unfamiliar sense of pride filling the emptiness inside. "Travis. What's yours?"

Wolfie considered briefly and decided a pseudonym would be most prudent at this point. The perfect one came to mind immediately. "Peter. Peter George."

"You have two first names."

His smile expanded into a grin. "I guess I do. You're what, about ten years old?"

Travis straightened and puffed his chest out. "I'm almost eleven."

"How come you're not in school?"

"It's spring break. I don't have to go back until Monday."

"Do you have any brothers or sisters?"

"No, but I wish I had a big brother."

"I always wished that too. Do your parents always fight like that?"

Travis looked down and scuffed the toe of his sneaker into the mushy ground. "Pretty much."

"Looks like you have a shiner that's just healing up."

"I got hit by a baseball," he mumbled to his feet.

"I had it pretty bad growing up myself, until I got adopted."

He finally looked up and saw empathy in Peter George's eyes. He understood. He *knew*. "You were an orphan?"

"My parents were killed when I was very young."

"Oh. I'm sorry. Is your new family nice?"

"My dad was the best—very rich—but he died recently."

Travis considered this tantalizing bit of information. "I'm sorry. Did you get any of his money?"

"I'll be getting it all very soon. Probably by tonight."

This was even more tantalizing. "Then you won't have to repossess cars anymore?"

"No. And I won't have to live here, either. I hate cold and I hate snow."

"I bet I hate it more than you. If I win the lottery, I'm going to buy a tropical island and build a big mansion right on the beach."

"That's my plan too once I get my money. I just have to finish some important business, then I'm gone. You and I think alike."

"What kind of business?"

"There are some people I need to take care of."

"You're going to give them some of your money?"

Wolfie smiled. "Something like that."

"That's nice." Travis looked up at a distant thumping. "A helicopter, cool! We hardly ever get them around here." He smiled at Peter George, but he didn't look so happy anymore as he put the truck in gear.

"I'd better get out of here before your parents wake up. Are you going to be okay?"

Travis hadn't even realized he'd spoken until the words were already out of his mouth. "Take me with you."

Wolfie was pleased his manipulation had yielded the outcome he'd hoped for, but then the truck squealed, coughed out a last, dying gasp, and went silent. Cruel fate had just stripped away the boy's only chance of survival. His own wasn't looking so good now, either. "I'm so sorry, Travis, but I'm afraid that's not going to happen."

10

GINO WAS BEHIND the wheel of the Insipid Department-Issued Sedan—an official title—driving as fast and as dangerously as possible through a warren of side streets. A few years ago, there had been a shortage of fleet cars, so for a brief and blissful moment in time, he and Leo had been assigned a seizure from a drug bust until their permanent nag was delivered. It had been a bells-and-whistles custom Cadillac with buttery leather seats capable of more positions than the *Kama Sutra* described, as he'd told Leo on more than one occasion. It had a super-charged engine that could take the paint off the walls of any house it passed with the right driver behind the wheel. He was the right driver.

Then darkness had settled upon the land when the Insipid Department-Issued Sedan finally arrived and the Caddie went up on the police auction block. He'd never stopped mourning the loss and had never stopped trying to recreate those splendorous days of yore. Maybe he should have been a drug dealer . . .

"Squirrel, Gino!"

He slammed on the brakes and watched the fat, indolent rodent amble away unscathed and unruffled. "Look at that arrogant son of a bitch. Do you think they really taste like chicken?"

"Like everything else that's not a chicken? No, I don't. Slow down. There's a school coming up, and students probably don't taste like chicken, either," Leo grumbled.

"It's spring break."

"That's not the point."

"You don't care when Charlie chases squirrels at the lake."

"Car versus squirrel is unsportsmanlike conduct."

Gino grunted. "Seems like natural selection to me. God, I miss the Caddie."

"So you say every time you drive, but you're doing just fine without it. I used to think the Caddie made you drive like an idiot, but now I realize it's something that comes from deep inside."

"Go ahead, Leo, besmirch the sacred bond between man and machine."

"I told you to buy it at auction, but you didn't listen."

"Of course I didn't listen. You were a bachelor back then, without a family or college tuition to worry about, and no beautiful wife who would have neutered you. It was the Caddie or my manly parts. Easy choice."

"Angela wouldn't have neutered you."

"Oh yeah? Just ask her. I did, and she was convincing." He glanced over at his partner. Tomorrow that seat would be empty, and it already bedeviled him like a ghost limb. He knew the loss would be a million times worse than the Caddie, but getting drunk at the retirement party Harley was throwing would kill the pain and postpone the blow. Especially with the big guy's infinite cellar of rarities Gino couldn't pronounce and couldn't afford, not in several lifetimes. It would be worth the hangover, but according to the gospel of Harley, the more expensive the booze, the less pain the next morning. Gino was anxious to test the hypothesis.

Angela was coming too and had given him carte blanche to get as stupid as he deemed necessary. God bless her sweet soul, she got it. Maybe even more than he did himself.

"Gino, you missed the turn to the freeway."

"Did not. I'm taking you on a tour of all the dives where we had our best epiphanies, for old time's sake. The Pig's Eye, for starters. You didn't actually think we'd be working today, did you?"

"No, but I thought we were going to city hall so I could be feted, ideally before McLaren does something stupid, then go to Grundy's and get drunk on Wild Turkey shots by noon."

"Grundy's is next, right after Pig's Eye. But I promised Grace I wouldn't let you blow your palate, and I'm a man of my word." He tapped the steering wheel with a wistful sigh. "Man, we really messed with Chief Malcherson and the feds at those places. And we were always right, no matter how crazy we sounded. Glory days, buddy." He shifted uncomfortably and cleared his throat. "As long as I'm getting sentimental, I need to say something before this day starts."

"That sounds vaguely ominous. Go ahead."

"I'm happy for you, Leo, everybody is. You're doing the right thing. But it's going to suck without you. I love my job, but it's going to lose some luster when you're not around to shoot down my brilliant theories that are always right."

Magozzi snorted. "Occasionally right."

"Come on, my track record of incisive thinking is pretty much pristine, factoring in some very minor adjustments on your part. I go places you won't, which is why we're the best crime solving team on the planet. You know I speak the truth."

"I promise I will always be happy to shoot down your crazy-train theories, day or night. I don't need a detective's shield to do that."

Gino sucked his cheeks thoughtfully. "Although, it might be refreshing to have a partner who admires and respects my unconventional thought process. Maybe even worships my dazzling intellect."

"Someone young and inexperienced and susceptible to complete bullshit?"

"Now you're just being mean."

They both kept straight faces for roughly a millisecond, then started laughing in perfect unison. It hit Magozzi squarely in the gut and made him realize all his mental wanderings of the morning were creeping up on a reality he hadn't been able to define until now, or maybe had been unwilling to. His job, his seamless partnership with Gino, had defined the best and most important part of his adult life until Grace and Elizabeth. It had shaped him as a cop and a man.

Gino had his own beautiful family, but he still had his job, even though it would look a lot different now. In their own ways, they were both facing loss—not of friends but of parts of themselves. Why hadn't he thought of that until now?

As Gino maneuvered up to the curb in front of the Pig's Eye, Magozzi was astounded to see Chief Malcherson standing at the entrance like a stern Swedish bouncer, his white hair glowing like a halogen bulb in the spring sun. Like Grace, his mouth rarely betrayed emotion, but his spooky, pale blue eyes did have their moods if you'd known him long enough to read the colors. This morning, they were more melting glacier than hard Antarctic ice.

Magozzi swallowed the unexpected emotion that was clutching at his throat and got out of the car. "It's good to see you, Chief. I didn't realize you frequented the Pig's Eye, but I understand why—the cinnamon rolls are worth the drive."

His expression remained a study in granite. "I most certainly do not frequent the Pig's Eye, or any of the other establishments of questionable repute you and Detective Rolseth have summoned me to over the years. I'm here for you, Detective Magozzi, but I'm sure you've already ascertained that with your extraordinary insight and skills of detection."

Magozzi side-eyed Gino, who just shrugged innocently. "It's kind of you to be here, Chief. Thank you."

"I was quite certain I would lose my job many times because of you."

"Uh . . . I'm really sorry . . ."

"But I don't regret it."

"That's good to hear. And you outlasted me, so that's something."

Malcherson's eyes thawed further, and he offered his hand. "That is something I do regret. Don't be a stranger, and tell Monkeewrench the same."

"You can tell them yourself at my party. It's going to be the social event of the season, and Harley is raiding his wine cellar."

Malcherson tipped his head and offered the faintest hint of a smile before he extinguished it to save his reputation. "I've enjoyed treading murky waters with all of you, at least after the fact. Serving justice takes on many hues these days. It's been an education."

"And none of us are in federal prison, so that's something, huh, Chief?" Gino said artlessly, earning a sharply disapproving glare. "Can we buy you a beer, sir?"

"Absolutely not. The beers are on me, and I look forward to toasting with a watery, unpalatable glass of tap."

They both gaped at him. "You're going to drink in the morning? I mean, we weren't even going to drink."

"The day demands it."

11

T HE INTERIOR OF the Pig's Eye was predictably dark and gloomy. The single exception was a finger of hopeful sunlight seeping in from an east-facing window, but it didn't illuminate anything but a dense trail of dust motes whose DNA probably dated back to the early twentieth century. The air was a miasma of stale beer and fryer oil, nuanced with a base note of cigarettes—an olfactory ghost from long ago, when smoking in bars wasn't a capital offense.

In spite of the seedy, foul atmosphere, a warm rush of nostalgia overrode Magozzi's instinct to hold his breath until he passed out. He and Gino had indeed messed with Malcherson and the feds here on more than one occasion, and there was nothing to love about the place except those good memories. And the cinnamon rolls, of course.

There were only a handful of patrons this early, most nursing their liquid sandwiches at the bar. The bartender was a thin, grizzled gent with the wary eyes of someone who was used to trouble. He nodded in acknowledgment and gestured around the room in a brusque invite to sit anywhere.

Magozzi selected a corner booth near a window that offered a view of an unlovely intersection in an unlovely neighborhood in St. Paul. The cracked vinyl upholstery was less than charming, but at least the table had been recently disinfected, evidenced by the strong smell of bleach. Then again, maybe someone had been murdered here recently. It was the kind of place where that might happen on occasion.

The tender plodded over and eyed their suits. "You're cops."

Magozzi thought it sounded more like an accusation than an observation. "What tipped you off?"

"Your suits, but mostly your guns."

Gino raised a brow at him. "We could be mobsters."

"They don't get up this early. What can I get you?"

"A pitcher of your finest swill. My buddy here's retiring. And three cinnamon rolls, the ones with raisins."

The bartender gave Magozzi a crooked smile. "Congratulations."

"Thanks."

"That's one hell of an excellent tie. Makes me wish I had a suit."

The place started to fill up as they enjoyed their suds and cinnamon rolls, and after his first glass, the chief did the unthinkable and loosened his much more conservative tie. Magozzi had to smother a gasp. Apparently, nothing but watery, unpalatable tap could slacken the man's rigid sartorial standards. The moment was so extraordinary, he ignored his phone when it buzzed in his pocket. A call from Grace always rang through, so whoever it was, they could wait.

Unfortunately, Malcherson's phone interrupted shortly afterward, and he didn't have the luxury of ignoring it. He reverted to type and slid the Windsor knot back to its proper place, as if the caller might deduce his transgression by the tone of his voice.

"Excuse me, gentlemen, I'll be right back."

Gino took a deep, contented drink and wiped foam from his upper lip. "God, this is great. I didn't even know Malcherson drank, let alone crappy beer."

"He was a cop before he was a political animal. He probably still eats doughnuts in secret too."

"Have you ever seen his tie loose?"

"I've seen it crooked once, but that was when he found out one of his best friends was murdered." Magozzi slid his glass across the table for a refill.

"I have a feeling that call is bad news, Leo."

"You're singing the dark song already? It could be his wife or one of his kids or his drycleaner, who he's going to need after this stop."

"He had that look when he saw the caller ID."

"What look?"

"The kind he gets when Paul Shafer calls."

"I sincerely doubt the FBI is calling, Gino. You're overestimating your ability to read Malcherson, or else you're drunk already."

"There you go again, questioning my unimpeachable judgment."

When the chief returned, his pale face was just a bit paler.

"That was Shafer, wasn't it?" Gino asked confidently.

"No. Why would you think that?"

Magozzi gave his partner a smug glance. "Any news we need to know about, sir?"

"That was Sheriff Iris Rikker."

"No kidding? She doesn't have another body in a snowman, does she?"

Malcherson scowled. "Wolfgang Mauer escaped from Gustavus sometime early this morning and is still at large."

"How did that freak get out?" Gino fumed. "Gustavus is like Fort Knox times ten."

"Apparently, their system was hacked."

"Son of a—" Gino checked himself. The chief hated cursing more than Grace. "This has to be his brainchild, and he had to have had outside help."

"That's the consensus, and he's already killed again. There's a multiagency search response in progress."

Gino nodded in satisfaction. "He's living on borrowed time. So, was this just a courtesy call to let us know the scumbag who shot Leo is on the loose?"

"You have the misfortune of knowing him better than anyone, so she's interested in your case files and your opinions in the hopes that might give her an idea of who his accomplice might be or where he's going."

Magozzi pushed away his beer, feeling a psychosomatic ache in his injured shoulder. "We'll call her back and help in any way we can, but sociopaths are lone wolves. We never found anyone connected to him but Praljik, and vice versa. Neither did the feds or Monkeewrench, and they were all deep into their digital communications, tracking down their cybercrimes."

"But when Praljik was playing the role of Rado the artist, he had rabid acolytes," Gino pointed out. "Their largesse would extend to Mauer when they found out he was his son. Air quotes."

Magozzi's jaw slid open is disbelief. "Anybody with a soul would have torched his sculptures when they found out his 'work' was a paean to his rape camps and the massacres he ordered. And the women he tortured and killed *with* his son. Air quotes."

"I'm not talking about a person with a soul. Madeline Montgomery comes to mind."

"The art dealer? Are you kidding?"

"She was a brainwashed Rado disciple of the highest order, and Mauer worked for her at the gallery. I always suspected she had a thing going with him."

"She treated him like gum on the bottom of her shoe."

"Exactly. Somebody as ice cold as her, that's a sign of love. And the fact that he didn't kill her makes me think the feeling was reciprocal."

Magozzi pressed his temples, hoping to squeeze out a burgeoning headache. Bad idea to drink before noon. Worse idea to listen to Gino's whacked-out hypotheses before noon.

Malcherson sank into the booth, his eyes now their default Antarctic bleak. "Gentlemen, there's something more. Mauer's psychiatrist believes he's coming after you. And anybody who helped you apprehend them, including witnesses at his trial."

"Based on what?" Gino asked.

"Mauer has a hit list of eight people. He didn't give names, but it's easy math—you two, all four members of Monkeewrench, Petra Juric, and Annabelle Sellman."

Magozzi's blood gelled as he thought of his last conversation with that sick fuck.

I will make you pay, Detective. I will make all of you pay.

"Monkeewrench will want to do a forensic examination of the Gustavus hack. That could lead right to him."

Malcherson stood and threw a fifty on the table. "I will get them authorization immediately."

12

IRIS HUNG UP as she pulled into the park's gravel lot, now cluttered with emergency vehicles, cops, and search teams jumbled in groups, confabbing. A BCA van was parked near the trail head, and techs were offloading equipment. She let out a soft, private sigh of relief for the victim. He was in capable hands now, and Wolfgang Mauer couldn't possibly survive this massive response for long. Things just might be okay.

Sampson had been on the phone the entire drive and finally signed off.

"What did St. Bridget's say?"

"There's never been a Sister Lucia there."

Iris stared out the windshield at a robin bathing in a puddle. He didn't seem to mind all the company; maybe he was an exhibitionist robin. "A nun as an accomplice. Brilliant. So how do we find a fake nun?"

"I talked to Drexler too, he's sending old security footage. Maybe something will pop on facial recognition. Monkeewrench could help us out with that."

"Drexler might think he's running a tight ship, but he's not if he doesn't vet the nuns."

"He says he does. Everything checked out on paper."

"He obviously didn't dig deep enough."

"People trust nuns even more than clergy, which makes it a good cover. What did Chief Malcherson say?"

"Magozzi and Gino are in the middle of a meeting; they'll call us back." She leaned forward and flopped her arms over the steering wheel to ease her back. Drexler's chair really was a torture device. "Do you actually believe Mauer is gunning for them? I mean, he's driving a stolen car, he doesn't have any money except what might be in the wallet he lifted, and he's running for his life. It would be crazy to take a detour to the heart of the city and risk that kind of exposure just to get revenge."

Sampson shrugged. "We know he's crazy, so we have to assume he'll try." He opened his window and banked some crisp spring air in his lungs before they visited a corpse that wasn't getting any fresher. He smiled a little as he watched Linus Keating's bloodhounds strain against their leashes, anxious to get back out in the field. Dogs were the hardest-working officers in law enforcement. "Hey, Linus, you catch a scent out there?"

"Hey, Lieutenant, Sheriff. Once I got the girls away from the body, they caught a trail through the woods, but it dead-ended right here in the parking lot." He pointed to a vacant area cordoned off with crime scene tape. "Right where the joggers saw that Nissan. We're regrouping and staking out a new grid, but if he has wheels, the dogs can't help us."

"Thanks, Linus." Sampson leaned back and reached for his travel mug of cold coffee in the console. Caffeine was caffeine, whatever the temperature. "Your car theory was dead-on. Now we just have to find the damn thing."

"We will," she said with confidence that was more than just swagger, which surprised her. *Proud and fighting for the victories to come.*

Sampson sipped and sighed. "Let's start hiking and get this over with."

* * *

Iris was thrilled to see Jimmy Grimm, even though she'd only met him once. He was BCA's senior crime scene tech and the man everybody wanted at their show. He'd also been extremely kind to her on her first day as sheriff when almost nobody else had been. He was quite a large man and in his white coveralls, he reminded her of a jumbo marshmallow. Word was, people called him Michelin Man, the Grimm Reaper, or Janitor Jim, because he cleaned up other people's messes. In her mind, he would always be Marshmallow Man because he was sweet.

"Good morning, Mr. Grimm. It's good to see you again, circumstances notwithstanding. Thank you for coming." Her cheeks flared. *You're not hosting a cocktail party, you moron.*

His rose from his crouch and flipped up his lighted magnifying glasses, lips quirked in a smile. "Sheriff, I only answer to Jimmy, and it's nice to see you again too."

"And I only answer to Iris," she parried, wondering where that sassy, impromptu rejoinder had come from.

"You've earned your title, and then some." He grinned at Sampson. "You're looking fit as a fiddle, so why didn't I see your name on this year's softball roster? Chickening out after BCA handed you your butts last year?"

"Maybe you forgot, old man, but we had to forfeit because our pitcher tore his ACL."

"Oh yeah, that's right. Too bad you didn't have a deeper bullpen, coach."

There was a history here that Iris hadn't been aware of, but of course they knew each other. Sampson had been on the job years before she'd even thought about enrolling in the academy. She'd have to ask him about it and find the real truth behind all the testosterone bluster.

Jimmy got serious and lifted the crime scene tape, granting them entrance into an exclusive club nobody wanted to belong to. "Come on in and take a look. Stay between the markers, please."

Color between the lines, Iris.

Why?

Because you're making a picture for people to enjoy. If you color outside the lines, it won't make sense and they won't enjoy it.

She'd always resented Mrs. Flanders for stifling her creativity in kindergarten, but now she had a little more sympathy for the crotchety old harridan's point of view. Wolfgang Mauer had colored outside the lines, it didn't make sense, and nobody was enjoying it. She didn't want to take a look at what he'd done in his depraved coloring book this time, but once she did, she couldn't pull her eyes away.

The victim was prone in the wet leaves, partially concealed by sticks dressed in fetal leaves that would soon flourish into thick underbrush. There was a lot of blood and mud smeared on his back and matting his dark hair, but the exposed flesh was ghastly pale with death. Without seeing a face, she could almost pretend it wasn't really a person, just a stage prop in the hideous film she was starring in.

"I'd say blunt-force trauma to the back of the head killed him," Jimmy was saying. "He was really pulped, reads rage to me. The coroner will tell us cause of death for sure."

Iris instantly visualized the attack, which popped her movie fantasy bubble and made it real: Mauer ambushing him, pulping him, dragging his dead body off the path. Stripping him, ditching his prison uniform, and putting on his clothes. "He assaulted a guard and stole her baton," she whispered, averting her eyes to the other techs who were scouring the area, snapping photos and shooting video, laying numbered markers, tweezing up possible evidence. The breakfast banana felt like hot lead in her stomach.

"Sounds about right; the head wounds have narrow margins." Jimmy pulled his magnifiers back down again. "I'm going to turn him now."

Iris appreciated the warning and looked at Sampson, whose gaze was impassive and fixed on the body. He didn't appear to be remotely close to vomiting, and she envied him that.

She held her breath as Jimmy rolled the victim over gently. A few rotting leaves clung to his body and beard, which reminded her of the rinky-dink costume she'd had to wear for a play about trees, another of the traumas Mrs. Flanders had inflicted on her. His sightless eyes drilled into hers, as though he was imploring her to bear witness to his truth, everyone's truth: life was suspended by the frailest of threads. One minute you're walking in a park, the next minute you cease to exist.

"Excellent muscle mass, very well built. Early thirties is my guess. Not more than a few hours dead. Some lividity, but not fixed."

"That's what those black blotches are?" Iris asked.

"Yes, pooled blood. But in this case, they'll resolve somewhat."

Sampson crouched down next to him. "Our rough timeline is between 4:30 and 6:30 . . ."

Their voices became distant and distorted, like they were speaking underwater. And then her thoughts suddenly slammed to a halt. "The timeline."

They both looked up at her. "What about it?"

"The sun isn't up until almost seven, so that puts him here in the dark. And it was raining like crazy until sunrise. He wasn't out for a stroll, so why was he here?"

Sampson's brows inched up his forehead. "He was helping Mauer, and Mauer got rid of a loose end. But I don't think this guy could pass as a nun."

"Two accomplices, maybe."

Jimmy gingerly cleared a few leaves from the victim's right arm, exposing a blurry, bluish blob of a faded tattoo. "This is an amateur job, like the kind you'd get in prison with a ballpoint pen. It looks like a tiger."

Iris dared to get closer and didn't faint. Thank God for small miracles. "We ran his prints, no record."

Jimmy shrugged. "It might mean something down the line."

They all jerked their heads toward a squishy, heavy thumping coming their way. Suddenly, two hundred and fifty corn-fed pounds emerged around a bend at a jog. Neville's round face was flushed and shiny with perspiration, even though the temperature was barely above fifty.

"Patrol just found an abandoned Pathfinder with a pancake-flat tire," he wheezed. "Ten miles up Hodgson Road. They ran the plates and it's registered under a Gary Bateman, address in Apple Valley. Pulled the associated driver's license too." He tapped his phone screen and handed it to her. "Hair color's different."

"Which doesn't mean much. But . . . it's hard to tell if it's our victim . . ."

Because his face is all splotchy and black.

Jimmy took the phone. "This man is much thinner, clean shaven, but the bone structure is similar. Impossible to know for sure until they get him cleaned up at the morgue."

It wasn't ironclad, but Iris still felt a thrilling surge of adrenaline as another piece dropped into their murder collage. Her first homicide hadn't belonged to Dundas County, it had been a shard in the mosaic of Magozzi and Gino's case in Minneapolis. But this was all theirs and it was coming together, one clue at a time. Her job was mostly management and oversight, but she'd been plunged headfirst into a detective role, and she liked it. It might even become addictive if she had a proclivity for it.

"Thank you, Deputy. The lieutenant and I will check out the Pathfinder, and I'd like you to head up to Apple Valley and check it out. If there's family at the address, confirm with the driver's license photo, then make the notification."

He nodded solemnly, and Iris noticed his fingers twisting together like he was trying to crochet them. She knew Neville had made notifications before, but never for a homicide, just like she hadn't. It didn't take firsthand experience to know that a reaction to murder was very different from a reaction to accidental death, and questions needed to be asked at the very worst time in a person's life to serve an investigation. She sympathized with his anxiety.

"Deputy, there's a chance Gary Bateman may have been involved with Mauer, so we need to find out as much information about him as possible."

"What if there isn't family?"

"Then keep chasing it down."

"Yes, Sheriff." He saluted and started jogging back the way he came.

Iris looked down at her new, mud-caked Timberlands, wondering if they were ruined. "If Mauer's on foot, he's dead in the water. He can't outrun the dogs."

Sampson nodded in satisfaction. "That's some more good thinking, Sheriff. I'll let Linus know."

Iris narrowed her eyes, strongly suspecting that Sampson was patting her head. "You already thought of that."

"Any cop worth his or her salt would. Of course, he could have stolen another car or caught a ride."

Her lips quivered as she restrained a smile. "Try to stay positive, Lieutenant."

"Yes, ma'am."

13

G INO WAS JOYFULLY swerving through freeway traffic, but Magozzi was too distracted by his call with Grace to care. Until the idiot almost sideswiped a fuel tanker truck.

"Slow down, dammit! Sorry, Grace, Gino is actively trying to kill us. We're headed to the office to pull together our files and send them to Rikker, but we'll come to Harley's right after we're finished." He hung up and glowered at Gino. "You are the worst kind of frat boy at heart."

"All men are, you're just in the honeymoon phase. We all go through it when we finally settle down and have kids. Everything is all serious, no fun or danger, but just wait a couple years—you'll be begging me to take you for joyrides again. What did Grace say?"

"She's on the way to the office. They'll work with Gustavus to get the remote set up. If they can find where the hack originated we have a location to search and they can piggyback on and monitor for activity."

"Assuming there is any activity. If I was Mauer, I would get my ass off the grid and find a nice jungle or primordial forest. Not the lap of luxury he's used to, but either one is a damn sight better than prison."

"Monkeewrench thinks the first thing he'll do is try to access the twenty million he stole from Stankovič. Without funds, he can't execute his escape or try to execute us. That might be how we get him."

"Follow the money, good plan. But they couldn't find it back then and neither could the feds, so what's changed?"

"Mauer is desperate; he's going to be sloppy and use whatever computer setup is in place from the hack. If they can get in, they'll set a trap and he's toast."

Gino nodded as if it actually made sense to him. All the years he'd worked with Monkeewrench, it was still all hocus-pocus to him. There was no point in even trying to understand. "Call Rikker and get a read on the situation down there."

"That's up next," he said, scrolling through his contacts for her number. "And if we end up dealing with her, cut her some slack, Gino."

"I've always cut her slack—"

"You were a total ass to her when she was a newbie."

"Tough love, she didn't know what she was doing. As it turns out, she's a fast learner. And pretty amazing too, getting back on the horse after a gunshot wound that was almost fatal. She has my respect and then some. And frankly, I wouldn't be surprised if she has him in cuffs before suppertime. She's the boots on the ground."

"Let's hope, because this is really screwing up my retirement." Magozzi held up a finger. "Sheriff Rikker, this is Leo Magozzi. Is now a good time?"

"Yes! Thank you for calling back so quickly."

"I'm putting you on speaker so Gino can listen in."

"Of course. Good morning, Detective Rolseth, I hope you're well."

He rolled his eyes at Magozzi. That woman was still the politest damn cop in all of law enforcement. "Back at you, Sheriff. We're on our way to the office to pull our files for you, but I got to warn you, they probably won't be much help."

"Anything new down there?" Magozzi asked.

"A lot, actually."

They listened as she recapped in great detail everything that had occurred in the past several hours, short of what she'd eaten for breakfast, which elicited another few eyerolls from Gino. But it got very interesting when she mentioned two possible accomplices. It got even more interesting when she mentioned Gary Bateman's tiger tattoo.

"There was a real thug connected to our case," Magozzi said. "We never did find out who he really was because he snuck into the country as a refugee during the war like Praljik and Mauer."

"Could he be helpful?"

"No, he's dead. But he had a tiger tattoo, and we came to find out that Praljik had an elite paramilitary force called the Tigers."

"Oh, that's interesting. But the victim isn't nearly old enough to have fought in the war. Mr. Grimm thought early thirties."

Gino snorted at "Mr. Grimm." Magozzi just smiled, thinking Jimmy would be amused by the respectful form of address. "But it's a possible link to Mauer. I assume you have somebody en route to check out Bateman's residence?"

"I have my best deputy on it."

"Tell him or her to seize any computers or electronics. And copy us on everything. If you need extra manpower, we've got you covered."

"I'm grateful for your assistance, detectives, and I'll keep you fully in the loop. Regarding the nun, do you think Monkeewrench would help us with facial recognition? We just received security footage of her from Dr. Drexler."

Gino couldn't help himself. "I don't know, but we'll ask real nice."

Magozzi gave him a warning glance. "Of course they will, send it to them immediately. And tell your deputy to keep a sharp eye out for any references he or she might find to Goran Stanković. He was a friend and associate, and ultimately an enemy of Praljik's. Deep connection there, a lot of animosity."

"Isn't Goran Stanković imprisoned at The Hague?"

Magozzi was impressed that she knew, but she wasn't up to date. "Was. He's being released today into U.S. custody. Mauer stole twenty million in Bitcoin from him, so Bateman could have been playing both sides."

"Goodness, this is complicated!"

"Very."

"Thank you again for your help. I'm sorry to cut this short, but I should go. We've just arrived at the Pathfinder."

"Good luck, Sheriff," Gino chimed in, proving that he was trying hard not to be an ass.

Magozzi hung up as they pulled into the parking garage at city hall. He didn't see any balloons, banners, or half-naked detectives, which he took as a good sign.

"Glad she kept it short," Gino snarked. "She uses a thousand words when ten would do the trick. Drives me nuts."

"Former English teacher."

"She probably got fired for talking too much. Are you ready to give McLaren the bad news that all his plans might be on hold?"

"What plans? What aren't you telling me?"

"Nothing. It's just a party, Leo, no funny business. But this is going to break his big Irish heart—you know how he likes to make a monumental deal out of any occasion. I mean, he threw a kegger when his cat turned four."

"I thought that was for his iguana."

"That was a different party, the one where Freedman fell off the back porch and sprained his ankle. Guy is a human megalith, and he can't hold his liquor. I'll never figure it out."

"The world is full of mysteries."

14

G RACE GAZED OUT the big, mullioned windows of the third-floor Monkeewrench office in Harley's Summit Avenue mansion. He and Annie were making fools of themselves over a child and a dog—two entities that reliably transformed even the most reticent souls into blubbering goofballs. Not that either of them had ever been reticent.

"Uncle Harley is going to take you for a plane ride!"

She chuckled privately at Elizabeth's delighted squeals as Harley swung her in dizzying parabolas accompanied by sound effects more appropriate for a race car. Her little girl would be sorely disappointed when she found out what a real plane ride was like. "Take it easy, Harley, she has a full stomach."

"Elizabeth is far too refined to upchuck on my Aubusson rug. Aren't you, my little Monkee princess? Yes you are!"

Grace had always tried to imagine what it would have been like growing up in a big, doting family instead of a series of orphanages, foster homes, and ultimately the streets, but it was so far beyond her comprehension, she'd simply given up years ago. Experiencing it vicariously through her daughter was an auxiliary gift of motherhood she hadn't expected.

She returned her attention to Harley's expansive gardens coming to life beyond the glass. Tulips, daffodils, bleeding hearts, and peonies were sending exploratory shoots up into the world, and tiny red leaves were appearing on the canes of his roses. In another month, the yard would be awash in fragrance and color. These days she noticed beauty before potential danger. She no longer believed her friendly mailman was actually a serial killer; no longer believed the elderly neighbor with five cats was an assassin. It amazed and befuddled her. Having a precious new life to guard should have inflamed her paranoia, not diminished it. But that might change now that a boogeyman bent on vengeance was out of his cage. Would it be easy to step back into the worn grooves of dread like a barn-sour horse racing for the comfort of its stall?

What befuddled her even more was that she had found love with a man whose job was rife with the threats she'd been running from most of her life. Harley said it was because they both had complicated relationships with death. But sometimes a dark inner voice whispered that fear was such an innate part of her, it had become a twisted normalcy, a dysfunctional comfort zone. She largely ignored it because that voice wasn't giving Magozzi the credit he deserved.

Annie took a seat next to her desk, interrupting her reverie. "Well, I've humiliated myself quite enough for the day. I'm ready to catch a killer, how about you, sugar?"

"More than ready."

"Some nerve he has. He's got to know this won't end well for him."

"He's delusional and a raging narcissist, he probably thinks he's got this in the bag," Harley said as he ended the plane ride and settled in a chair with Elizabeth on his lap. "I'm fantasizing about what I would do to him if he gets within a country mile of us. It's not appropriate to share my visions in front of the princess, but you can use your imaginations."

Annie lifted her chin imperiously. "I can't think of a single time you and I ever saw eye to eye on anything, so this is a providential moment."

"I always knew you had bloodlust. What other types of lust do you entertain?"

"You have always been, and still are, a farm animal, Harley," she huffed. "Although that is truly an insult to all farm animals."

He submitted to a brutal beard-pulling. "Elizabeth clearly has better taste in men than you do. Kind of ironic that the day Magozzi is supposed to turn in his shield, he gets thrown right back into the fire. How do you think he's going to handle retirement, Gracie? He's been living and breathing the job for years, what's he going to do with his spare time?"

"I'm fully confident he'll find something to do."

He shrugged. "He'll need a hobby to keep him busy. I'd be happy to donate a cactus or two. I don't want to see you two start throwing frying pans at each other."

Annie smacked him on the arm. "Oh, for God's sake, Harley, who but you would think a bunch of ugly, spiny plants could fill a void?"

"I'm just saying. I don't really see Magozzi doing macramé, even though it's kind of a thing now."

Grace did wonder occasionally what Magozzi would do with his free time, but she was positive it wouldn't have anything to do with cacti or knotting plant hangers. "He'll adjust, but I have a feeling it won't be as easy as he thinks."

Harley nodded. "You're not worried about Mauer, are you?"

"One insane man versus a bunch of cops and heavily armed computer geeks? I don't think so. But we're all ready if he ever gets this far."

"Then let's get to work and make sure he doesn't."

CHAPTER

15

ROADRUNNER WATCHED IN astonishment as Petra deftly coaxed an alchemy of flour, water, egg, and oil into a gossamer sheet of strudel dough. "This is magic."

"No magic, just patience and practice."

"It's like a piece of silk. Big enough to make you a dress." He was rewarded with a small smile, her obsidian eyes shining brightly in the pale oval of her face. With each passing day they became less haunted, and nothing had ever made him so happy.

"Come, try it, it still needs to be thinner."

He shook his head vehemently. "I can't, I'll ruin it."

"A hole or two is not the end of the world. Besides, this is just a test batch. We'll make it again the day of the party. Now dust the backs of your hands with flour and use them to stretch it like this."

He tried to focus on the demonstration, but his eyes kept wandering to her face. The way she folded her lips together when she concentrated on a task fascinated him.

"See, it's easy," she draped the dough over his hands. "Just bounce and tug gently and it will do the work for you."

Roadrunner was nearly paralyzed with anxiety, but he felt a flush of achievement as the elastic sheet gave a little, behaving as she promised it would—then he gasped in distress when it tore. "Oh no, I'm sorry, Petra. I think I should stick to the filling."

"We'll just patch it up, like I said, not the end of the world. And you've already mastered the filling brilliantly. Your addition of amaretto is inspired."

"It's something Grace taught me when she was making a pie. She said cherries and almonds are best friends. But I'll never be able to do the pastry."

Petra stood on her tiptoes and reached up—nearly as far as her arms could go because she was only five feet, two inches—and patted his cheek with a floury hand. "That's nonsense, Roadrunner never gives up on anything. You'll get the hang of it, I promise, it just takes time, *dušo*."

The word meant "soul." Every time she used the term of endearment, his heart swelled because their souls *were* inextricably linked—by life, by death, and a love that had flourished from the blood-soaked fields of her past and the barren ones of his. "Who taught you how to do this?"

Her eyes grew distant, gazing back to a time before the horrors of war had found her. "Baba and Mama. I was four years old when they brought me into the kitchen with secret smiles. The big beech table was covered in linen, and they told me I would finally learn to make strudel. It's an honored rite of passage for girls, a cherished gift from one generation to the next. 'The finer your strudel, the finer the man you'll marry,' Baba always said. I didn't have an inkling of what she meant by that, but I took my responsibility seriously."

"That's charmingly Old World. And sexist."

"That was Baba, she was ancient and rooted in the old ways. Although the division of power almost always seemed to work out in favor of the women."

"Did she marry a fine man?"

"She did and ruled the household like a benevolent despot."

Over the past year, Roadrunner had learned a lot about her idyllic childhood before the war. But she wouldn't speak about what had happened after her parents and most of her village had been killed and Praljik had taken her. She wouldn't speak about the V-shaped scar on the left side of her face, either.

There are some things you have to keep locked inside forever so they don't destroy you, Roadrunner. If you let them out into the light, they will blacken the sun and kill your hope.

He understood this from his own childhood, but he'd told her his secrets and not only was the sun still shining, he was filled with more hope than he'd thought possible. But he never pushed her. Her nightmares were fewer and farther between these days, and he knew she was getting better. One day, the time would be right to give her the diamond and amber engagement ring he'd commissioned months ago. Diamonds for eternity, amber to represent her connection to a land she still loved in spite of the memories.

Charlie started barking from his phone's speaker—Grace's ringtone—and he shrugged apologetically. "I have to take this, but I think you can do nicely without me."

"You're so afraid of an innocent piece of dough?" she teased, and he silenced her with a kiss.

"I'll be right back."

Petra watched him retreat to the living room to take his call. This tall, shy, awkward man had saved her from freezing to death on a park bench and made her care about life again. He hadn't fully mended her heart—that was impossible—but he'd taken her a long way. The world was still full of good surprises.

She retrieved his cherry filling from the refrigerator and started rolling the strudel, humming a lullaby her mother had sung to her every night at bedtime. For so many years, she'd been terrified to voice it or even remember it, afraid it would call up horrific memories, but now it comforted her. Another gift Roadrunner had given her.

She looked up at him as he walked back into the kitchen and went perfectly still. A pall of darkness surrounded him. "What's wrong?"

He gazed down at the floor as he told her everything because he couldn't bring himself to see the joy drain from her eyes. "I need to get to Harley's and start working on it," he finished miserably.

Petra held her breath, then began rolling the strudel again, furious that one of the happy moments of her life had been snuffed out by the mere mention of a name. "He won't survive long outside those walls."

He walked to her and took her hands, wincing at the sharp pain in his chest as he searched desolate eyes that had so recently sparkled. "He won't, of course he won't, but we can't take any chances. Harley has the best security, I think we should stay there until he's caught.

"No. If he comes for us, I'll kill him, like I should have killed Praljik when I had the chance. And I have to put this strudel to bed before it perishes."

"We'll bake it at Harley's. We'll all be together, we're all in this together, and we'll find him. And eat strudel with a big hole in the middle while we do it. Please, Petra, it's safest for now. And if he shows up there, I'll kill him before you have a chance."

Her face was still, but her eyes were turbulent black waters. "You go now, I'll follow later. I have to see Annabelle first. She's the only one who doesn't know she might have a target on her back."

"Can't you just call her?" He knew immediately it was a stupid thing to say, but Petra, with her infinitely compassionate, patient soul, gave no indication she begrudged him.

"You know I can't, Roadrunner. They killed her sister, then nearly killed us both. We're bonded forever by those monsters as much as you and I are. And her testimony was just as important as mine. If you're worried about me, then you must be worried about her too. She is very strong, very tough, but she's alone. I know you understand."

Roadrunner did understand, knew it was something she had to do, something that was right, but protective instincts were far stronger than reason. "I'm sorry, I'm just panicky about you being out of my sight. Even though I know you can probably take care of yourself better than I can."

She gave him a strange smile that was melancholy, amused, and poignant all at once. "Don't be sorry. You can't fight your nature, you're a born knight in shining armor. Or in your case, shining Lycra. You're kind of like a superhero."

A laugh bubbled from his throat, and he was in awe of this woman who could always find light in shadows; find joy in the recesses of despair. And that quality was wonderfully contagious. "Bike Man?"

"A superhero code name if I ever heard one."

He gathered her in his arms and held tight for a long moment, thinking about the ring in his dresser drawer a few houses down the block. Not the right time, not yet. "Give Annabelle my best and tell her to come to Harley's."

"I will, thank you, *dušo*. Now scurry, scurry, go do your important work." She gently extricated herself and made a shooing motion, but not soon enough to hide the single, betraying tear that slid down her cheek—a single drop of saline that had the power to shatter her iron façade. She loved him even more because he didn't say anything, didn't ask her anything, just stood there patiently. It galvanized her trust in this magnificent, eccentric man and allowed her to voice the thing that broke her heart most.

"Praljik keeps taking things away from me, even from the grave."

He looked down at his mangled hands and thought of his stepfather and the hammer. "That's what evil does."

16

THE TINY RAMBLER in Apple Valley surprised Neville. It was a faded shade of sky blue with pink trim, and the yard was cluttered with bird baths and feeders swarming with a menagerie of different species. There were shabby gnomes wearing chipped coats of paint standing guard by the front door. Spotted ceramic mushrooms sprouted from the scabrous lawn, vying for space among dozens of those plastic, pinwheel thingies that spun when the wind blew. Maybe Gary Bateman had lived in his grandparents' basement.

He imagined a kindly old couple falling to pieces in front of him, and his stomach writhed. There was no way to prepare for a notification and they never got easier. Curmudgeonly Ned Gruber had fainted dead away on his lawn when he'd told him his grandson had gone off the road into a tree. He could still hear Adelaide Curran's unearthly banshee screams for her daughter, like they were coming straight from hell. A single life was encased by stratums of loving, caring people, and a single death caused shockwaves that broke that shell and radiated outward, knocking them all down. Some never got up again.

He mounted the cracked concrete steps with a leaden heart and rapped on a door that had a wooden "Home Is Where the Heart Is" plaque hanging from the tarnished brass knocker. He heard shuffling inside, and a few moments later, an elderly woman with snowy hair, a pruned face, and thick glasses cracked the door as far as the security chain allowed. She was wearing a floral bathrobe over a pink sweater that matched the trim outside.

"Who are you? What do you want? I'm not interested in buying anything and I won't sign any stupid petition."

Apparently, she needed to update her eyeglass prescription. "I'm Deputy Neville from the Dundas County Sheriff's office, ma'am," he said, gesturing to his badge and uniform.

She craned her neck forward and squinted. "So you are." She slid the chain from its bracket and opened the door.

Neville stepped inside a gloomy foyer that smelled strongly of lavender air freshener. The interior of the house reflected the same sensibilities as the yard: old-fashioned, crammed with tchotchkes, and badly in need of maintenance. "Thank you. Your name, ma'am?"

"Louise Bateman. Don't just stand there, come in and sit down anywhere. What can I do for you? Dundas is a fair way south."

Neville selected an armchair upholstered in faded gold velveteen and found it surprisingly comfortable. "I'm here about Gary Bateman."

Her jaw slackened while the rest of her body went stiff as a two-by-four. "If this is a joke, young man, then it's a very cruel one."

"I apologize, but I don't understand."

She clasped her hands to her chest like a praying supplicant. "Gary died four months ago, God rest his soul. Cancer. Almost fifty years together, I still can't believe he's gone."

Neville's mind engaged in some strenuous acrobatics while it caught up with the news. "I'm so sorry for your loss, Mrs. Bateman. There's something very strange . . . we found a man this morning carrying a driver's license with your husband's name and this address. A younger fellow, and his face is a possible match for the photo on the license."

"Possible match? I assume that means he's dead."

"Yes."

"Good. Serves him right for stealing my Gary's identity."

The callous comment set him back on his heels. She looked frail, but spit and vinegar clearly ran through her veins. "Did you and your husband ever own a maroon Nissan Pathfinder?"

"No. We own a white Chevy Malibu, have for eleven years."

A mistake with the DMV? Neville doubted it, but it did happen. "Do you have a son or grandson with the same name? Maybe there's some kind of a mix-up."

"What kind of a question is that? You don't think I would be on my knees wailing if there was a chance kin of mine had died? God never blessed us with children, and if he had, we wouldn't have raised a criminal who victimizes old people. This is just horrible, I have to call my bank."

She was sharp enough to know about identity theft and be worried. "That's a good idea, ma'am, but first, may I show you a picture of him? Perhaps you recognize him. We're looking for any information."

"Why would I recognize a thief?"

"Please, it's important."

Grumbling, she settled onto a matching gold sofa and adjusted her glasses. "So show me already, my bank account could be empty."

She had a personality like coarse-grit sandpaper, but Neville was surprised to find he liked her. Small, smart, and tough, just like the sheriff. He pulled up Bateman's license photo and handed her his phone.

She studied it and put an arthritic finger to her lips. "Never saw him in my life."

"You're sure?"

"Don't get sassy with me, I'm not completely blind."

"I wasn't implying—"

"I've never seen him, sure as you're sitting across from me."

Neville took his phone back and scrolled to another picture. "He has this tattoo of a tiger on his arm, does it look familiar?"

She frowned, deepening the terrain of wrinkles that peaked and valleyed across her face. "You know, I believe I have seen that before. I remember it because it was so poor."

"Where did you see it?"

"On a man who came to fix Gary's computer last summer, but he had dark hair, not blond, and it was longer. Not at all like the picture you just showed me."

"Did you get his name or know what company he worked for?"

"No, I had nothing to do with it. I hate computers. I came home from the grocery store one day, there was a strange man in the office with Gary, then he leaves, that's it. The only reason I noticed the tattoo was because his sleeves were rolled up. It was hot that day and we don't have air conditioning."

"Would your husband have kept a business card or an invoice?"

She scowled at a water stain on the ceiling, one more thing Gary wouldn't be fixing. "I've been through every scrap of paper in this house, and he didn't keep anything after he was diagnosed two years ago. He knew what was coming and he didn't care about keeping records. And I don't blame him. We never had money, and what are a few penny-ante receipts going to do for us when it comes tax time? Nothing. We lived on Social Security and his annuity."

Neville thought of his grandparents, who were in the same boat. "I understand, Mrs. Bateman. Do you happen to have the computer?"

"I recycled it, what would I do with such thing? Gary didn't do anything with it either, except play bridge. I don't play bridge."

17

Petra parked on Summit Avenue and entered the grounds of Mitchell Hamline College of Law. Students and even some faculty were scattered across the campus, on benches in the courtyard or sprawled languorously on blankets beneath budding trees, savoring deliverance from winter confinement. Faces and spirits changed with the seasons, and there was a collective joy here.

She found Annabelle Sellman on a bench near the student center, eyes closed, face to the sun. Her hair was now a fiery red not found on the human palette and much shorter than the last time she'd seen her; the double nose ring was also new. A bit of rebellion after all she'd been through. Good for her.

"Hello, Annabelle."

Her green eyes flew open and her smile was brighter than the sky. She leapt off the bench and hugged Petra tightly. "It's so good to see you."

"And you. I like the new hair and face jewelry."

She blushed. "A little too much for a wallflower?"

"Never. It's exuberant and tells a story of who you are now."

Annabelle shrugged diffidently. "A friend talked me into the hair, but the nose ring was all my idea. Delia had one and I was always so jealous of it, but I was afraid I'd look stupid. I guess it's my weird way of honoring her."

Petra sat down on the bench and took her hand. "You look fierce and I think it's a beautiful way to honor her. Delia would love it. I wish I'd known her." She watched Annabelle's gaze drift, searching for things she would never find. Sisters and innocence didn't come back once they were dead.

"I worshipped her; she was always so brave and fearless. She loved life more than anybody I've ever known. It's so unfair."

"Be brave and fearless and celebrate life for her. That's an even better way to honor her."

Annabelle wiped a tear from her eye, her smile quivering. "Thank you. It's so good to talk about Delia without walking on eggshells. Everybody else is afraid to, like they want to erase her."

"They don't want to erase her, they want to erase their pain. It's not productive, but it's human nature. How are you really, Annabelle?"

"I'm okay. Better. A work in progress."

"Healing always is. It takes time and strength, which you have in abundance. Are you liking law school?"

"I love it. Sometimes it bothers me that hideous things inspired my decision, though. But I suppose nobody chooses their path in a vacuum."

"No. And there should always be something good that comes from suffering to balance the scales. For us, it's passion, purpose. We both need to give a voice to those who can no longer speak for themselves."

"That's *exactly* it. How are you? You've been through so much worse."

"You can't measure tragedy or assign greater import to one over another, Annabelle. It doesn't ease your pain and it diminishes what you've been through."

She lowered her head. "I never thought of it that way. You're right, though. In the back of my mind, I keep thinking that I'll feel better if I remind myself somebody else had it worse. It's irrational."

"And counterproductive, as are many protective mechanisms."

"You're a lot wiser than my psychologist."

"Oh dear. Then you should find a new one."

Annabelle laughed. "You still haven't told me how you are. I guess I distracted you."

"I'm fine. Very good, in fact."

"Does that have something to do with Roadrunner?"

"It has everything to do with Roadrunner."

She clapped her hands together in excitement. "That's wonderful, I'm so happy for you!"

Petra was thrilled to see her let the past go, if even for a moment. Right now, she was just another dreamy-eyed, guileless young woman, anticipating what romances might be in her future. "He came to me when I least expected it. Love is always a surprise, remember that."

"I will." She picked nervously at a loose thread on her sweater, subdued again. "How long did it take you to trust again?"

It had taken decades, but she didn't want to discourage her. "Everybody is different, but you'll get there in your own way, on your own schedule." She took a deep, remorseful breath. "I have something important to tell you."

It shattered her to see the dark succession of emotions play on Annabelle's face—first shock, then fear, then rage, and finally anguish. She was silent for a long time, but when she finally spoke, her voice was even and calm.

"I know you'll find him. You, the detectives, Monkeewrench. I'm not afraid."

"It's okay if you are. We'd like you to come to Harley's."

"Thank you, but I refuse to let that monster control my life anymore. If he comes, I'm ready for him—I finally got my conceal and carry permit."

"I'm glad, and may you never have to use it. Remember, Harley's door is always open to you."

"I will. I moved here to be closer to school, so I'm only ten blocks away in case I change my mind about being afraid."

Petra smiled. "Neighbors help neighbors."

18

MAGOZZI DIDN'T ENTIRELY trust Gino or Johnny McLaren when it came to mischief, so he walked into Homicide with some apprehension. It was a relief but also weirdly disappointing to find things completely normal. A handful of detectives were working the phones, and the usual number of desks sat empty while their occupants were out on calls or following up on leads. None of the furniture had been moved to make room for exotic dancers or a petting zoo, and his own desk wasn't upside down or buried under a mountain of confetti or worse.

"What did I tell you, Leo?" Gino tossed his briefcase on his chair and shucked off his coat. "All's quiet on the midwestern front."

"I'm feeling a little conflicted."

"The blame for your existential crisis sits squarely on your shoulders. You spent the last two weeks telling everybody not to make a big deal, no pranks, so we listened out of respect. Now you're telling me no means yes?"

"Not at all, I truly appreciate the restraint. I don't do well with excessive attention or humiliation."

Gino snuffled. "The day is still young. I'll get those files off to Rikker, then I think we should swing by the Resnick/Feinnes gallery on the way to Monkeewrench. I know you're skeptical, but Madeline Montgomery might have something useful to say."

"It took a while, but I'm sold on your idea. If this asshole really is coming after us, we need to cover every base. Did you call Angela and let her know?"

"Of course I did. I called Helen too."

"She's two thousand miles away in Miami, studying palm trees and beaches."

"And buff, tanned men. She laughed at me like she usually does, and said 'I'm totally safe, Daddy, don't worry.' I told her she should worry a little more about the buff, tanned men."

Magozzi smiled, thinking of the beautiful little girl he'd watched grow into an even more beautiful young woman. "I can't believe she's a freshman in college."

"You and me both. Time is the enemy, Leo." He took a deep breath, glanced around the room, then leaned across their cojoined desks. "How worried are you?"

"I'm terrified, and it's stupid."

"No, it's not. Let's get this fuckhead back in a straitjacket and move on to the partying part."

"Yeah. I look forward to that." He sank into his chair and stared at the dark monitor. He'd spent millions of hours in front of it while drinking bad coffee and trying to function on zero sleep and too much junk food. Now he had no reason to jiggle his mouse and wake up his screen. But he did anyway for old time's sake.

He jumped when an airhorn sounded—actually it almost stopped his heart—then guffawed at the custom screensaver that flashed in huge red block letters: HAPPY RETIREMENT, LEO! MINNEAPOLIS WILL NEVER BE SAFE AGAIN, BUT DON'T FEEL GUILTY. WE STILL LOVE YOU, EVEN THOUGH YOU'RE BAILING ON US.

"Hmm. I wonder how the creative genius behind this got my password."

Gino shrugged innocently. "Probably Espinoza. Or maybe Gloria; that woman is the gestapo of Homicide, she knows everything."

"Uh-huh."

"Goddammit, Leo, I'm going to miss your pretty face!" McLaren shrieked.

Magozzi grinned as McLaren made a beeline toward him, carrot-colored hair standing up in excited spikes. Thankfully, he was fully clothed, but a leopard-print thong might have been more tasteful. He was sporting baggy green and orange plaid pants and jacket, a canary yellow shirt, and a broad pink tie. It was sort of a cross between a zoot suit and a clown costume. He knew Johnny was screwing with him, because even the worst-dressed detective of all time had never looked quite so appalling.

"Miss the bus to the circus?" Gino asked pleasantly.

"Just the kind of comment I expect out of you, Rolseth." He gestured proudly at his ensemble. "You guys are always giving me shit about dumpster-diving for my clothes, so I thought I would give you the thrill of a lifetime on this most significant occasion. It took me forever to put this together." He winked at Magozzi. "Something to remember me by."

"It's definitely a memory that won't fade any time soon."

"Mission accomplished."

"Where's Gloria?" Gino asked. "We haven't had our asses busted all morning, and I feel kind of empty inside."

McLaren uttered a wistful sigh. "I'm hoping she's out shopping for a wedding dress, but I think she mentioned something about a hair appointment."

Gino rolled his eyes. "McLaren, she is never going to marry you, she just likes to torture you. Don't mistake abuse for flirting."

"The course of true love never runs smooth. Shakespeare said so."

"How many times have you proposed to her?"

"Just over two hundred, but I'm a patient man."

"How many times have you gone on a date?"

"I took her to a baseball game."

Gino snorted. "That was two years ago, and she only went because you had seats in Willy Staples's private box."

"I know she's the only woman for me, and one day she'll realize I'm the only man for her. Ebony and ivory will live together in perfect harmony, just wait and see."

"I won't live that long."

McLaren ignored him and pulled a chair to Magozzi's desk. "The chief told us all about Mauer. What can we do to help?"

"There's really not much to do on our end. Iris Rikker has a good handle on the ground search and some leads on accomplices, and Monkeewrench is on cyber. Gino and I are going to talk to Madeline Montgomery, then go to Harley's and get everyone up to speed. Honestly, I don't see him on the run for much longer."

"Super news, but let us know if anything changes. Freedman and I are just doing paperwork today."

"Thanks, Johnny."

He popped up out of his seat like a jack-in-the-box. "Anytime. Your party starts at three, so get your ass back here by then."

"I wouldn't miss it."

"Great, see you later." He paused in mid-step, turned, and cocked his head. "You might want to bring a raincoat."

Gino's raucous laughter got the attention of everyone in the room.

19

THE ILLUSTRIOUS, ELITIST Resnick/Feinnes gallery was draped in banners heralding the exhibition of three wunderkind digital artists instead of Rado's "Syzygy of Art and Technology." On this visit, there were no protesters railing against the glorification of brutality against women, and Magozzi fervently hoped this new generation had some positive, peaceful messaging. But he knew too much about the darkest corners of the human psyche to be overly optimistic. Controversy attracted crowds and crowds padded bank accounts, morality be damned. Rado had been a master of the formula.

Gino badged the young security guard at the front desk whose name was Homer, according to the tag on his shirt. A distinguished name forever tainted by *The Simpsons*. "Detectives Rolseth and Magozzi. Is Madeline Montgomery in?"

Homer looked at them curiously, wondering what their business was. Heist? Art forgery? Fraud? He'd probably never know unless it ended up in the papers, but the speculation would keep him entertained until the end of his long, tedious shift. "Yes, but I haven't seen her on the floor in a while. It's been pretty slow this morning. I'll ring her."

"Thanks." Gino looked around the gallery. He would never understand modern art—it seemed like the whole point of it was to annoy the hell out of you, and he got enough of that on the job. What was so wrong with a bucolic landscape?

"She'll be out shortly, detectives."

"Great. Does Mike Vierling still work here?"

"No, he decided to take retirement seriously and move to his cabin up north. Did you work with him?"

"Nah, he was St. Paul, but we didn't hold that against him." The guard grinned. "Man, he had some great stories."

"But mostly about fishing, am I right?" Magozzi asked.

"Oh yeah. The forty-pound muskie that got away."

"When he told us the story, it was thirty pounds."

"Sounds like Mike. The next time he tells it, it'll be sixty pounds." Gino nodded. "At least."

*   *   *

Madeline Montgomery was still as anorexic and imperious as she had been on their last trip here, but she was visibly shaken to see them, which watered down her attitude a little. Their presence had dredged up a nightmare she'd been trying hard to forget, just like everyone else involved.

"I was hoping I would never see you two again," she said in a pinched voice.

"Thanks for the warm welcome," Gino said. "By the way, the feeling is mutual."

She pursed her bright red lips. With her black hair, black clothing, and geisha-white skin, Magozzi thought she looked like a vampire who'd just fed.

"I don't imagine you're here to buy art."

"No, we're still deplorable cretins. Cretins who need your help, Ms. Montgomery. Can we speak somewhere privately?"

She nodded stiffly, and they followed her back to her stark office, now bereft of the resin blob chairs that had been designed by her sociopathic former idol.

Gino took a seat without invitation in one of the new chairs that resembled a scorpion *en flagrante* with a giraffe. "Wolfgang Mauer busted out of Gustavus," he said without preamble.

Her stone-gray eyes widened in alarm, and she reflexively covered her mouth. "*He's* the one who escaped?"

"Yeah."

"I don't understand how I could possibly help."

"You probably spent more time with him than anybody other than Praljik. You may have some ideas about where he might go to seek shelter. He's already killed again, and he has a hit list of all the people he perceives wronged him, which might include you."

She shrank a little, her condescension all but evaporated. "I know absolutely nothing about him. I was dumbstruck when I found out he was a monster."

"You didn't chitchat around the watercooler?"

"Hardly, Detective Rolseth. I never spoke to him about anything except work. He was an employee, not a friend."

"He never mentioned anybody in passing?" Magozzi asked.

"He never mentioned anything that wasn't related to his job. He was always in his own world, his digital world. His *sick* world as it turns out." She shivered and tugged her cashmere wrap more tightly around her shoulders. "God, I still can't believe I worked with a . . ." Her voice broke and she looked away.

Gino shifted in his bizarre chair, which was more ergonomically pleasing that it looked. "I'm wondering about avid collectors or anybody who might have exhibited an unnaturally keen interest in Rado, somebody who might be willing to help him."

"You can't be serious! When the whole grotesquerie was revealed, most buyers either destroyed their pieces or junked them, at great personal cost I might add. I know because I heard from them. They most certainly would not help that *beast*!"

"Glad to hear there's a collective conscience in the art world, but I'm not talking about people who were duped by his whole art-technology schtick or jumped on the investment bandwagon. I'm talking about people who maybe identified with his point of view once they found out what it was."

She gaped at them. "Massacres? Rape camps? Torture camps? That is inconceivable."

"It's not to a couple of cops. You can't think of a client like that, maybe someone who pinged your creep radar or was just a little too enthusiastic about his art? For lack of a better term."

"My clients are not deranged."

Gino folded his arms across his chest. "How would you know? I mean, Mauer fooled you big time, and he's about as deranged as they come."

Magozzi watched her face transform into a white mask of rage. He stepped in before Gino could further alienate her. "You haven't had any enquiries about his sculptures?"

She regained her composure. "Not a single one. There have been rumors of a black market, but I can't attest to the veracity. True or not, I wouldn't know where to begin looking."

Magozzi thought of the cesspool known as the dark web, the biggest emporium in the world for illicit goods and services, and completely anonymous. That was a dead end, and so was Madeline Montgomery. No way she'd been Mauer's lover; her revulsion was too authentic.

Gino tossed a card on her desk. "I'm sure you threw out the last one I gave you, so here's a replacement. Call us if you think of anything. And be vigilant, Ms. Montgomery. I don't have to tell you he's dangerous and hates women."

* * *

"No easy answers there," Gino moped as they climbed into the car.

"You were expecting a slam dunk?"

"No, but I was hoping for one."

"There are never easy answers in this job. We have to work for it."

"Unlike the rest of the lazy populus that takes the first hit on a Google search as gospel. Whatever happened to the great philosophers who actually thought about stuff? Now everybody just regurgitates somebody else's bad ideas from a hundred and fifty years ago. We're the last of the truth seekers, Leo."

"You're cheery this morning."

"It pisses me off."

Magozzi clipped his seat belt, praying that Gino had gotten philosophy and the *Grand Theft Auto* School of Driving out of his system. "I felt sorry for Montgomery."

"I didn't."

"That was obvious. You know what I've always admired about you most?"

"My charm and good looks, of course."

"Your compassion, especially when it comes to women. But you were a dick to Rikker for no reason, and you were a dick to Montgomery—"

"Because she's a horrible person."

"She's snotty, but you don't know she's a horrible person, and it's obvious she's hurting. You're the farthest thing from a misogynist, so what's going on with you?"

Gino rolled his head back and closed his eyes. "You want the real answer?"

"I don't want a fake one."

"I think I'm burning out. The shiny nugget of gold at the end of every case started looking like a dried-up dog turd when you told me you were retiring. All these years we kept each other sane, and I don't know if I can do this without you, Leo. I don't know if I want to."

Magozzi had a lightning-bolt flash of lucidity. He'd spent a lot of mental energy repressing his inner devil's advocate so he wouldn't question the wisdom of his choice, which was wholly justified in so many ways. But truth always found a way through any maze of psychological mines, no matter how cleverly you placed the ordinance. "Honestly, I'm not so sure I want to retire anymore, either."

Gino opened his eyes and looked at him. "Don't go flying off the handle. When we get to Harley's, you're going to see Grace and Elizabeth and forget you ever said that. And think about it— would it be so bad if we retired together? Hell, we could go to the lake anytime we wanted, throw in a couple lines and drink all day. Reminisce about our triumphs. Maybe catch a sixty-pound muskie."

"Do they really get that big?"

"I don't even know what a muskie is."

20

S AMPSON WAS GRIPPING the edges of his seat as Iris sped down the dirt road. Beneath the mud was nasty washboard, and the car was skittering like a drop of water in a hot skillet. "Are you trying to put us in the ditch?"

"My ex was a back seat driver."

"Well, I'm sitting in the front seat, so I guess you can't really draw a parallel."

She suppressed her amusement and eased up a bit. "Don't worry, I aced the driver's course."

"Which is on pavement. You're still a city girl, but believe me, I've seen bad things happen when you don't respect washboard."

"High speed chase on a gravel road?" she teased.

"After the senior class party out at Sunrise Dam. The night was pretty fuzzy, but I do remember clods of grass and dirt smacking the windshield."

"Seriously?"

"Seriously. Man, I got my ass chewed when I brought the car home after I'd sobered up."

"You were *driving*?"

"I think so. Can't really say for sure, though."

Iris's stomach quivered with restrained laughter. "Oh my God, you're a criminal."

"You're only a criminal if you get caught."

"That's pretty specious logic for a sworn lawman." She tried to imagine him as a wild, drunk kid flying down a country road, hell-bent-for-leather in his parents' Buick, and couldn't.

"I'm fully reformed, of course."

"Good thing. Otherwise I'd have to fire you." She slowed to a crawl when she saw flashing lights up ahead. A deputy was standing near a grove of aspen trees, waving to them. "Is that Byron Willis?"

"Yep. You've met him?"

"A couple times. He seemed genuinely nice."

"He is. Has a great wife and four of the cutest kids you've ever seen. He lives around here and knows this part of the county and its people better than anyone. If there are hidey-holes in all this empty space, he can lead us right to them, which could come in handy if the dogs don't catch a good scent."

Iris got out of the car and greeted Willis warmly, then he and Sampson shared a brief moment of bonhomie before they all focused on the SUV. It was pulled well off the road onto a trac-tor trail, but the leafless aspens did little to conceal it if you were coming down Hodgson from the north. This broad swath of the county was open farmland and there wasn't much cover anywhere—advantageous for them and the State Patrol airship that was trolling the skies.

Willis pointed at the ground. "As you can see, it's pretty much a mess after the storm. There are probably prints in all that muck, but no way of knowing which way he went, and there's enough grass in the field that he wouldn't leave a trail. Linus and his hounds are your best bet."

"He's on his way."

"Good. I checked the hood, and it was cool, so it's been here a while."

"Did you take a look inside?" Iris asked. "Perhaps find a map with an X marking his final destination?"

Willis's face froze for a moment, then he chuckled heartily. "No, ma'am, I didn't touch anything but the hood. Didn't want to mess things up for you."

Sampson smiled, surprised she'd shown her light side. Little things like that built good will and loyalty fast. "I'll send our coordinates to the State Patrol and get some teams out here, Sheriff."

"Thank you."

While he made his call, Iris slipped on a pair of gloves and opened the passenger door. The keys were still in the ignition and there was a little blood on the driver's seat upholstery. Nothing in the console or glove compartment. The rest of the vehicle was clean too. Crime scene would take care of the details. "Is there anywhere around here he could take shelter or steal a car? Residents who might have seen something?"

"Nearest house is the Dunbar farm, about a mile north, and they have a big barn."

"Seems like a good place to start. We'll check it out."

Willis shifted his feet anxiously, his leather service belt squeaking with the movement. "I'll come with you, Sheriff, if you don't mind. The Dunbars are both the worst kind of drunks, mean as badgers when they're on a jag, which is pretty much always. I've had to deal with them too many times, so they know me. I could be helpful."

She'd always known there were rotten apples in Dundas County, just like anywhere else, but she'd never taken that thought beyond abstraction until now. In very few words, he'd just painted a vivid and frightening picture of a *real* cop's job, where rotten apples sometimes went ballistic just because the police showed up at the front door, where a good man like Byron Willis filled his mind with images of his wife and kids before he knocked, just in case that was the last time he would ever see them. Bulardo had been a fluke, nobody had seen it coming, but living with mortal danger on a daily basis was something different.

"By all means, I appreciate that."

He gave her an earnest look. "I've been meaning to say something for a while, Sheriff. I hope you'll indulge me."

Was he going to complain about the broken vending machine in the breakroom? Discuss her leadership style? Call her out as an imposter? "Go ahead, Deputy."

"You went through hell and back the very first week of the job, and you lived through the thing all of us fear most. And here you are. You have my respect, and I have your back."

Iris was dumbstruck. "That's the nicest thing anyone has ever said to me. Thank you."

His cheeks colored. "Everybody feels the same way, just wanted you to know."

She changed the subject to lighten the poignant, awkward moment. "Just how dangerous are the Dunbars?"

"Probably more dangerous to their son than anybody else. It's a sad situation; he's ten and a good kid. I hate to say it, but he probably won't be that way much longer if he stays there."

"What about child protection?"

"They've been there a few times before but could never find anything that would stick. It's a shame."

Sampson pocketed his phone and trudged back through the mud. "Airship is on the way. And Neville called. Gary Bateman isn't Gary Bateman."

"What do you mean?"

"Doctored up license, fake vehicle registration. The real Gary Bateman was an old man, been dead for a while. His widow didn't recognize the photo of our vic on the license."

Iris started chewing her lower lip as she wrangled with the new information. "So we have no idea who's in the morgue?"

"No, but Louise Bateman said a computer repairman did some work for her husband last summer and he had a bad tiger tattoo. It has to be the same guy."

"Mauer's techie on the outside?"

"Fits one hundred percent, but she didn't know what company he worked for. Neville is calling around to repair shops, but so far nobody's heard of a Gary Bateman."

"That's probably a dead end. Our victim was already working as a tech before he stole that identity, so he was using a different name. Or he could have been a freelancer." Iris squinted into the pale spring sun. It felt hot on her face, but the breeze had a chill that permeated her padded jacket. It would be a few weeks before the air temperature moderated. Then again, it might snow tomorrow. "Do you think Jimmy could get a rush on the autopsy? Not the full autopsy, I just want his face cleaned up—that's the one thing you can't steal or fake. Maybe Monkeewrench can get a match."

"I think Jimmy can get a rush on anything." Sampson got back on the phone just as a big, black truck approached, followed by two more. Linus and some search teams. Between the hounds and the helicopter, maybe they could cinch this up soon without facial recognition or repair shops. It never hurt to be optimistic. Even if you were ultimately disappointed, it was better than being pessimistic from the get-go, because in that frame of mind, you started out depressed.

CHAPTER

21

THE HOUNDS CAUGHT a scent the minute they jumped from the truck. They pulled Linus north across the field while search teams fanned out in their wake. The State Patrol helicopter circled at low altitude, spiraling farther outward with each pass.

Willis tracked their progress with interest. "If the dogs keep in that direction, they'll run smack into the Dunbar place."

"We'll follow you there." Iris glanced at Sampson. "Would you like to drive, Lieutenant?"

He shrugged affably. "I believe I'm in good hands. You aced the driver's course, after all."

"You might pay for that," she taunted, getting behind the wheel. "Willis told me the Dunbars are bad news."

"They are. But Mauer's a million times worse, and if he's cornered, we don't know what he'll do. We also don't know if the man he killed had a gun, so stay sharp."

That was a sobering thought, one that hadn't crossed her mind. But three of them against two drunks or one psychopath seemed like decent odds. "Have you ever been called out to their place?"

"Back when I was still on patrol. They've always been trouble, and having a kid didn't change anything."

"Willis told me child protection has been there a few times, but nothing ever stuck. I was a mandated reporter as a teacher, and nothing ever stuck in the cities either."

"It's damn hard to take a child away from their parents."

"For good reason, but it's gut-wrenching to see kids you know are abused or neglected and you can't do anything to help them. You need a license to do just about anything except raise children."

"You sound like you're on the precipice of a very dangerous slippery slope."

"I'm not advocating it, it's just frustration and maternal instinct. You don't have to be a mother to feel the pain."

"For what it's worth, I think you'd be a great mother, if that's on your agenda."

"I have goals, not an agenda. They're totally different."

"I agree with you there."

Willis put on his right blinker, and she followed him down a long, rutted driveway that terminated at a dilapidated farmhouse. It sagged on its foundation, looking very much like it had let out a deep breath and given up on life. Large gaps in the siding exposed the tar paper beneath, and portions of the roof had been patched with plywood. The old barn was in worse shape, on the verge of total collapse. Iris thought of the ten-year-old boy who lived here and felt very sad.

The garage door was open, revealing a hoarder's cache of junk but no vehicle. She got out and looked around the bare yard. The only ornamentation was a heap of broken pallets, scattered pieces of scrap metal, and a rusty swing set that canted dangerously to one side. "Do they own a car, Deputy Willis?"

"An old Ford truck held together with dental floss and bubble-gum." He pointed to the fresh tire tracks. "Dick probably took it back to the shop this morning. It spends more time there than anywhere else but the Tipsy Swede."

The Tipsy Swede was a notorious drunk tank, a place where people went to forget or fight. Iris had never crossed the threshold and had no plans to do so in the future. "Let's find out."

They mounted punky wooden steps up to the front door, hands on their holsters. Her heart was beating double-time as Willis knocked on the door.

"Mr. and Mrs. Dunbar? This is Deputy Willis. If you're home, please answer the door, it's important."

No sound, no movement, just dogs baying in the near distance. "They're getting closer," Iris whispered. "I think he was here."

"He might still be." Sampson unholstered his gun and Iris followed suit.

Willis knocked with greater urgency. "Dick? Alice? Answer the door."

"Maybe they're at work," Iris suggested hopefully.

"As far as I know, they've never held down jobs. If they are home, my guess is they're stone-cold out. Which means Mauer could have stolen the truck right out from under their noses. Travis, are you in there, son?"

A snake of dread slithered down Iris's spine. *Travis.* The name suddenly made the child real, and he might be in there with a killer. Bound and gagged. Or worse. All nervous thoughts about tangling with drunks fled from her mind, and without a single thought as to what might happen next, she tried the knob and the door swung open. "Police, we're coming in!"

She sounded so sure and decisive as she stepped inside, but her body felt like an overcooked noodle. How could her gun be so steady when her arms were useless, limp strands of linguine? Her heart was so loud in her ears, she barely registered "Clear!" as they went from room to frigid, depressing room, worse than anything she'd seen outside.

Willis opened a door that led to the basement and flipped on the light switch. "Travis? Are you down there?"

They covered him as he clambered down wooden treads hollowed by a century of traffic. She watched the corona of his flashlight bobble and sweep over cobwebs and fire hazards.

"Clear down here."

"Upstairs," Sampson said.

Iris flinched with every aching creak and groan of the staircase, praying it wouldn't give out. Her muscles were screaming—not from strenuous effort, but from tension and the constant influx of adrenaline. She'd read that your body produced a finite amount before it had to restock the coffers. What happened if you ran out when you really needed it?

Sampson went through the open door of the first bedroom, gun raised, then froze like he'd run into a wall. "Jesus," he whispered.

Iris didn't want to look, because she *knew* something bad was in there. And there most certainly was, but it was her job to look at the bloodied heads of the man and the woman sprawled on the floor, to bear witness to another senseless killing. And how stupid that "senseless killing" was part of the modern argot—weren't all killings senseless?

"Travis!" Willis shouted, thumping down the short hallway to the second bedroom.

Before she and Sampson managed to duck out of the horrible place to follow him, he was back, his face bleached and stricken, his body shaking. She wanted to run, run, run, fast and far, she *couldn't* look at—

"He's not here. He's either hiding or that bastard took him. Or . . ." His voice fizzled away.

Iris didn't know where the calm came from, but her thoughts were bizarrely cogent as she ticked off a checklist as if she'd been doing this her whole life. "We need to get out an Amber Alert and a BOLO on the truck immediately and search every inch of the property. Warrants on any phones, Mauer could be using them right now. Does Travis have a friend he might be staying with? It's spring break, so maybe he wasn't even here."

The stiff agony on Willis's face smoothed a little. "Yeah. Yeah, maybe. Malcolm Schelling."

"Anybody else?"

"My oldest daughter goes to school with Travis and says that's his only friend in the world. I'll call right now."

Iris took a deep breath and held it as she entered Travis's room, fearing it might hold something terrible that Willis had overlooked. But the small space was too barren to hide any secrets. There wasn't even a closet, just a single Metallica poster taped to the wall and a bare mattress on the floor covered with a brown comforter. The fabric was so thin and faded, she could barely make out the pattern of dinosaurs. A dingy gray pouf protruded from a tear in a brontosaurus, and that, of all the things she'd seen today, made her want to cry.

There was a framed family photo on an overturned plastic milk crate next to the bed. Travis was front and center with a big, gap-toothed smile, white-blonde hair, and eyes as blue as a summer sky. She passed it to Sampson. "For the Amber Alert."

"We'll see that smile again in person, Iris. Believe it."

"I have to." Her eyes wandered around the room, absorbing more sad details: a sizeable collection of dust bunnies in a corner; black mold climbing up a peeling wall; a pile of rank clothing and towels. Everything that was here and wasn't here gutted her completely. She felt like a ragdoll without any stuffing. Not even any dingy, gray poufs.

Sampson touched her arm. "Are you okay, Iris?"

She opened her eyes, not realizing they'd been closed. "No, are you?"

"Hell no."

22

Magozzi and Gino let themselves into Harley's mansion and took the stairs instead of the elevator to the third floor Monkeewrench office. No one registered their presence initially; all the faces were focused and intense as four pairs of hands flew over keyboards in silence. The fifth pair of hands and the woman they belonged to were notably absent.

Harley was the first to snap out of his digital fugue state. "Leo!" he bellowed, jumping out of his chair. He clapped him on the back, almost toppling him. "This bullshit's a hell of a farewell. But don't worry, my friend, this asshole will be strung up by the gonads faster than . . ." He frowned. "Have you two been drinking or is that my imagination? Not that I'm judging."

"We had a beer with the chief this morning. He insisted," Magozzi said.

"No shit? Guess miracles happen every day."

"Where are Grace and Elizabeth?"

Annie sashayed over in stilettoes that matched her dress and the streaks of pink in her platinum bob. "She's putting the wee one down for a nap, and Charlie's helping. You and Gino plumb wore the both of them out at breakfast." She patted his cheek. "I'm going to miss seeing you in a suit. You look mighty fine in one."

Gino puffed out his chest and straightened his tie. "What about me?"

She batted her jeweled eyelashes. "You too, sugar. As a matter of fact, you're more my type—I do like a man with a little flesh on his bones."

He gave her a full-beam smile. "I'll take that as a compliment, Miss Annie."

"Oh, it was definitely meant to be one. If you weren't so happily married, I'd snatch you right up for myself."

Magozzi watched with immense amusement as Gino blushed, something only Annie could elicit. He was an unwavering hard ass, but her dexterous enchantments always disassembled him.

Roadrunner waved his bashful greeting. "Hi, guys. I just secured the link with Gustavus. Hopefully, whoever pulled off this attack for Mauer isn't as talented as he is, but regardless, finding the source of a hack takes time."

Magozzi gave him a fond smile. "We've got good, old-fashioned shoe leather going for us too. Lots of folks working it on the ground. Did Sheriff Rikker send you the footage of the nun?"

Roadrunner nodded. "Yeah, and facial recognition is running. But it's pretty poor quality, bad angles, so I can't promise anything."

"She'll be sending another photo for facial rec, the man Mauer killed in the park. His prints didn't pull a criminal record, but he was using a fake identity he stole from somebody he was doing computer repair for last summer."

"Great, that could really speed things up. I hope the photo is better quality."

"It will be. It's a morgue shot."

Roadrunner's face went pale. "Oh."

Gino's nose lifted like Charlie's did whenever he caught a whiff of sausage. "I smelled something amazing when we walked in. What's cooking?"

Petra looked up from her computer with a coy smile. "Cherry strudel."

"Oh my God. I might faint. But . . . I suppose it's for Leo's party."

"It's just a test batch. I'd love your opinion, as you're such a devoted gourmand."

His grin was bigger than the Cheshire Cat's. "Always happy to offer any assistance I can, Petra. Are you going to make those dumplings too?"

Magozzi snorted at Gino's shamelessness, then turned when he heard the clack of Grace's English riding boots on the maple floor. Boots she still wore even though nobody was out to slash her Achilles tendons anymore. Her black hair was pulled into a tight ponytail and it made her look like a very stern cheerleader. He wanted to reach out and touch her, hug her, kiss her passionately, but public displays of affection were strongly discouraged. "How's the cherub?"

"Sound asleep. Charlie too."

Harley resettled his muscular bulk in his chair. "What's the news from the frontier?"

"We just talked to Rikker again on the way over; it's a mad-house down there. Mauer killed two more and he has a new vehicle. They also think he may have kidnapped a ten-year-old boy."

Magozzi watched Grace's long, dark lashes settle over her eyes. She was thinking about Elizabeth, just like he was.

Annie, on the other hand, was outraged. "Why on God's green earth would he take a child when he's running for his life?"

Magozzi shrugged. "Leverage? He has a hostage to bargain with if he needs it."

"Or he formed some sick bond with him. Knowing his psychopathology, I can see how that might happen," Petra said bitterly. "At least they have a car and a phone to track now. And with a child abduction, they can bring in the feds."

"With all the federal charges against Mauer, I guarantee the FBI is already on this. His escape was a premeditated act of genius, so insanity is going to be a tough sell after this. They wanted him in a supermax penitentiary from the get-go, and they were right. It's where he belongs."

Grace startled him by touching his arm. It wasn't exactly a PDA, but it was nice. "Is there anything else we can do, Magozzi?"

"Thanks, but we already dumped a load on you. You've got your hands full."

"Hardly," Roadrunner piped up. "We're not even using a quarter of our processing power."

"And I'm not using ninety-nine percent of my brain power," Harley added. "Roadrunner can't help you in that department, but I am at your service."

Magozzi smiled when a pen came sailing across the room and connected with its target. "Well, we did visit Madeline Montgomery—"

"Is she still as charming as an ice pick?" Harley interrupted, rubbing his head as he glowered at Roadrunner.

"Pretty much, but she's also scared."

"You think she knows anything?"

"No, but she said there are rumors about a black market for Rado's work. The dark web's another place to look if nothing else turns up, even though that's probably hopeless."

"We got you, and never say never."

Petra let out a strange sound and all eyes turned to her. Roadrunner was out of his chair and by her side before any of them could blink.

"What is it, *dušo*?"

Magozzi didn't know what the term meant, but it was clearly an adoring one. You could almost see threads of electricity dancing between them, and it was a beautiful thing. What wasn't so beautiful was the desolation in her eyes. She hunted war criminals for a living and knew more about the dark side than anybody else in the room. Considering the present company, that was a very grim distinction. She addressed him and Gino specifically.

"As you know, Monkeewrench designed a beautiful program for me, and among many other things, it monitors the status of all the demons we've captured so I can keep an eye on them. Mauer's has been updated, but he's not the only one. Goran Stanković is at large now too."

"What the hell is going on?" Harley blustered. "How do you escape from a prison in The Hague?"

"The same way you escape from any prison—you have help," Gino muttered. "They're mortal enemies; they can't possibly be working together. But this is a pretty damn big coincidence."

Magozzi felt like a two-year-old trying to put together a ten-thousand-piece puzzle of a blank wall. "It may be just that; coincidences do exist."

"They've been twisted together for decades," Petra said. "Stanković wants his money back so maybe he's planning to come after him. Or they struck some kind of a deal through the accomplice to help each other out. An enemy is better than nothing if you don't have any friends."

Gino snuffled skeptically. "Better chance of getting killed by a meteor."

"Meteorite," Roadrunner corrected politely.

"Tomato, tomahto, whatever. If they did strike a deal, there's only one reason, and that's to put the other guy in the dirt and take all the money. Best case scenario, in my mind."

"It doesn't matter if it's connected," Grace pointed out. "They're on the run and they'll both make mistakes. That's how we catch them."

23

G ORAN CELEBRATED HIS liberation with a fourth lowball of Polish vodka. The plan had been exquisitely executed— much more like a military exfiltration than a prison escape—and it had gone off without a bobble. Of course, there had been some tense moments, moments of doubt, particularly in the confusion and chaos after the diversionary bomb had detonated in Scheveningen. But there was no point in revisiting past events—all that mattered was his freedom. He'd been reborn for the second time in his life, and colors seemed brighter, the air smelled sweeter, like night-blooming jasmine.

He gazed down at the patchwork of fields and forests and thought it quite beautiful. They'd entered American airspace two hours ago, but as far as the FAA and the regional airport in southern Minnesota knew, theirs was a domestic flight originating in Vermont. Novak and his team had done the near-impossible, neutralizing U.S. Marshals and making a flight disappear, and for this, they would be rewarded richly.

He raised his glass to the former Serbian spy chief, who was currently one of the world's largest arms dealers. There was no place safer than with a man whose criminal activities surpassed your own. By comparison, Goran was nothing more than a petty thief. "Well, done, friend. You gave me new life, something I've been anxious for."

Novak let out a ragged laugh and downed his tequila, something he'd learned to appreciate during his time in Mexico. "And you've made me a wealthier man for it. We make a very good team, you and I, and I'd like to continue the relationship. You have many talents, talents I could use, but you're a wanted man with limited opportunities. I can ensure your safety and anonymity in certain parts of the world where I do business."

Goran bristled. The prospect of owing fealty to anyone, especially Novak, sickened him. But what he said was true. He couldn't very well start over here or anywhere without solid allies and unbreachable cover. "I think we might be able to come to an understanding."

"Good." Novak rubbed his stubbled jaw or at least what was left of it after the ambush in Tehran. "I've procured a new identity for you and a nice Minnesota farm in the middle of nowhere. My team will assist you with security until you can make your arrangements with Mauer as per our agreement. I hope this won't take long."

"It won't. I have plans. I've been working on them for two years."

"They'd better be flexible ones, because I've recently been informed that the little bastard escaped his insane asylum and is still on the run. With a kidnapped child no less. Of course, he's always had daddy issues."

Goran jerked in his seat like a man in an electric chair. "What?! That wasn't supposed to happen yet!" he screeched. "Why didn't you tell me this before?!"

Novak gestured expansively around the private jet. "You were enjoying yourself, as you deserve to. There was nothing you could do about it at 30,000 feet in the air anyhow."

"When did he escape?"

Novak tipped his head in manufactured sympathy. "This morning, local time. I'm sure he's too busy running to cash out the account. Although he is a resourceful son of a bitch. I certainly hope you didn't pay for the information up front, because if you did, Aleksandar may have swindled you in favor of Mauer. Or he's double-dipping. After all, he has two very interested parties in a single alphanumeric sequence."

Blood pounded in his ears, deafening him. "I'll handle this."

Novak burped and refilled his glass from the bottle between his knees. "Make sure you do—a portion of the funds you hope to repatriate belongs to me as part of my premium."

Novak was, and always had been, a rapacious, condescending asshole, and it took all of Goran's strength to keep his fury in check. "There is nowhere in the world Wolfgang Mauer is safe, you can count on that."

"I *am* counting on it, but how do you find . . . what is the saying? A needle in a haystack? Perhaps you know at a certain juncture in my life I was highly valued as a bounty hunter. And my quarry was truly challenging, not some soft, spoiled, Americanized brat."

"Your point being?" he snapped.

"I could be helpful. For a price. Say, another million dollars?"

Goran was again blinded by rage. He was going to kill this odious prick very slowly and creatively, but his gratification would have to be delayed. "The tequila has made you delusional."

"It's just business, Goran, and good business is symbiosis. You need me, and I would like some more of your money, it's really very simple. Enjoy the farm life, let me handle this, and everyone will be happy. And what's a million dollars among friends?"

"Absolutely not—this is *my* business to finish. I want to look Mauer in the eye, and I want to hurt him until he gives me back what is mine before I kill him."

"I understand, and I would never deprive you of your pleasures. But in your situation, with every cop in the state looking for him, you're at quite a disadvantage. I could deliver him with no risk to you."

"I *will* find him."

"Do you even know where to start looking?"

Goran didn't have a goddamned clue, and his slight hesitation didn't go unnoticed.

"I take that as a no. Fortunately, I happen to know where he might be going. You see, it's so important to keep your enemies close, and Peter Praljik and I kept in touch. If you'd done the same, you might not be in this quandary right now."

"Tell me where he is."

Novak's lips curled into an oily smile. "If I do that . . . well, there's no honor among thieves as they say. What's to stop you from taking all the money and disappearing?"

"If you're such a good bounty hunter, why would you worry about that?"

"Oh, I would find you, but it would be a waste of my time. And things wouldn't end well for you."

"And what's to stop you from doing the same thing? No, we work together. For five hundred."

Novak gazed pensively into his glass of Herradura, pretending to consider the counteroffer. "I think a million is just about right, old friend. And I'll let you do all the wet work as a bonus. That seems like a bargain to me."

Goran felt the comforting pressure of the Russian combat knife sheathed at his hip. What was a million dollars when Novak wouldn't live long enough to see it? "It's a deal."

CHAPTER

24

THE AFTERMATH AT the Dunbar farm was bedlam as law enforcement teams of all stripes descended on the scene. An escaped killer was bad enough, but a missing child was a tragedy that amplified the urgency a thousandfold. Every new face reflected Iris's own panic as they spread across the property, praying they would find a terrified hiding boy instead of a body.

Ultimately, the exhaustive search had yielded neither, but Iris had found small sneaker prints she hadn't noticed before next to the fresh tire tracks near the garage. It wasn't conclusive, but the moment she saw them, she knew Mauer had taken the orphan he'd created, and God only knew what he was planning to do with him. Or what he already had.

She was pacing by the car, trying to keep hope alive and frustration at bay. The logistics of managing so many moving parts in the field weren't just impractical, they were overwhelming. She needed to be at her desk coordinating, not tromping circles in the mud, relying on sketchy cell coverage while Travis was in the wind with a stone killer.

She found Sampson by the barn waving his phone around, trying to pick up a signal. "We're done here; let's do the notification and get back to the shop."

"Willis is taking care of that. He knows Dick's mother and Alice Dunbar's parents too."

"Bless his heart."

Sampson looked around the forlorn farmyard. "He said all three of them are solid, hard-working folks who could never figure out what happened to their kids."

"All of this is so sad." She wasn't in the mood to drive, so she tossed him the keys. "Do your worst."

Sampson kept his silence on the drive back to give Iris some time to decompress. They'd all be running on adrenaline and nothing else since this morning, and the brain and body were useless under that much strain if you didn't let it recover, even if it was just for a twenty-minute car ride. But she was intense, almost obsessive, and part of him had been expecting a nonstop monologue about the case and what their next steps should be. The woman could talk the spots off a leopard, but to his surprise, she didn't say a word. When he heard her let out a cute little grunt, he knew why. She'd fallen asleep.

Iris jerked in her seat, disoriented for a moment before she realized she'd actually lost consciousness. How mortifying. What kind of sheriff napped when their county was in the middle of the biggest shitshow in its history? "I could use some coffee," she tried for her perkiest voice, but it still sounded sleep garbled. There were some things you just couldn't fake. It was like answering the phone in the middle of the night and assuring the caller they hadn't roused you from a deep sleep. What was so embarrassing about sleep?

"I think I dozed off," she confessed.

"Me too. But somehow I managed to stay on the road."

"Must be all that experience driving drunk."

Sampson glanced at her and saw her fighting a smile. "I shouldn't have told you, you're never going to let me forget it."

"The joke will get old in a few years and we can move on to something else embarrassing from your past."

"Only fair I get some dirt from your youth to hold over your head. It's good for team building."

"That's never going to happen, Sampson. I was in the church choir, honored my parents, never did anything too fun or too dangerous. I didn't even have a drink until I was a junior in college."

"I'm sorry to hear that."

"In a way, I am too, but it's never too late to rebel. Maybe I'll try running with scissors."

"You're a daredevil at heart."

"I got married, didn't I?" She looked out her window and was shocked to see they were already within spitting distance of the county courthouse, home to the sheriff's office and jail. How long had she been out?

"You're funny when you first wake up."

"I wasn't sleeping, just resting." She gasped when he pulled into the parking lot. The media was firmly entrenched around the courthouse en masse, anxiously waiting to ambush anybody driving an official car. Before she could tell Sampson to turn around and get the hell out of here, the horde spotted them and descended on their car like a phalanx of overly coiffed zombies. She'd never had to deal with this level of media presence before, and it made her already queasy stomach churn violently. For the first time in her life, the spotlight was on her, and if she screwed up this case, the whole country would hear about it.

"Ready to 'no comment' your way through the gauntlet?" Sampson asked.

Her eyes jittered over the crowd of eager Barbies and Kens, the cameras and microphones, the satellite vans. "If these jerks had seen what we saw today, they wouldn't be so bouncy and bright."

"Think of it this way—they're doing us a favor, plastering Mauer's photo, the Amber Alert, and our tipline number all over the airwaves. You'll have to make a statement. Just a little snack before the multiagency press conference to soothe the savage beasts."

"If I'm talking to them, I'm not doing my job."

"You're the big boss, it's part of the territory. Dundas can't afford an information officer or press liaison or whatever they're calling them these days."

"I have stage fright."

"Pretend you're in front of a classroom."

"Yeah, right. These people aren't students, they're sharks on a chum trail."

"Okay, then picture them all in their underwear."

"I wish you hadn't said that. I have a very active imagination."

"Come on, let's get it over with." He nudged her supportively. "You'll be fine, Iris."

She puffed out an anxious sigh, wondering if a sheriff vomiting on camera would score big ratings. "What am I supposed to say?"

"The investigation is active and at a critical juncture. You're not taking questions at this time and thank all the agencies that are working with us. Promise a press conference later. Mention the tipline. Like that."

"That was good. I especially liked the 'critical juncture' part. Why don't you give the statement?"

"Because I'm not the sheriff."

The moment she stepped out of the car, she was bombarded by shouted questions.

"Sheriff Rikker! Can you confirm three murder victims have been discovered in Dundas County?"

". . . is Wolfgang Mauer responsible?"

". . . do you have any leads on his whereabouts?"

". . . is the Amber Alert on Travis Dunbar related to the escape, and if so, is there a connection between him and Mauer?"

". . . will the FBI be brought in for the child abduction?"

". . . are people safe?"

Iris wanted to clamp her hands over her ears and scream. She might have if not for Sampson's steady presence beside her as he shooed away the crowd to give her space. "This is an active investigation in the early stages and requires our complete focus," she said in a calm, confident voice she was absolutely certain belonged to someone else. "I'm afraid I can't comment at this time or answer any questions at this critical juncture, but I assure you progress is being made. This is a statewide effort and I'd like to thank the Bureau of Criminal Apprehension, the State Patrol, and all the local departments who are assisting us. There will be a press conference once we are able to share details without compromising—"

"When?" a shrill chorus of voices demanded.

She tried to keep her irritation from showing. Were they even listening to her? "As I just said, when we have information we can share. In the meantime, your help keeping this at the forefront of the news is appreciated, and I have no doubt it will aid in a swift conclusion to the situation. Please, anyone with any information, call our tipline. Thank you for your patience."

The questions didn't stop. The crush of perfumed, clamoring bodies was suffocating, but Sampson cleared a swath with gentle authority. "Please give the sheriff room."

"Thank you," she whispered as the doors of the courthouse closed on the sharks.

"You did good, Iris."

"So did you. You're a great bodyguard."

"I live to serve and protect, ma'am."

"You're also a smartass."

"I've never been accused of that before."

"Uh-huh." Iris looked around the lobby and froze. The melee outside was nothing compared to the buzzing hive of industry inside.

Rachel, the sheriff's department bulldog and Jewish mother, caught sight of them and changed trajectory midstep. Her face was scarlet, her hair uncoiling from the bun she always wore like gray electrified wires.

"The tipline is on fire, Sheriff. I've got every assistant with a spare minute helping out, but it's a bursting dam and the only things spilling out are schmucks calling about UFOs and barking dogs. These people, they make me furious. 'What don't you understand about a tipline dedicated to a missing child and an escaped killer?' I ask them. 'You're wasting our time and resources, where is your heart, your soul, your brain?'"

Iris knew she wasn't being hyperbolic. "Do they answer you?"

Rachel flapped her hand in disgust. "Of course they don't answer me, they're all meshuga. I just talked to tech, Dunbar's phone is off so they can't ping it. But the phone records came in. Last call was this morning, to a burner phone. Untraceable." She scowled in disapproval. "You both look like roadkill. You need to eat something, you can't run on fumes on a day like today. I'm ordering pizza and I won't hear an argument from either one of you."

Sampson bowed slightly and tipped his hat. "You won't get one, ma'am."

25

TRAVIS PRESSED HIS nose against the window and watched the scenery flash by. He'd only been on the freeway twice, but never this far before, and it was scary and exciting all at the same time. The empty farmland was behind them now, and the landscape was filling up with houses and businesses and malls. And traffic, the traffic was crazy! There were so many cars, it was like the Walmart parking lot on Saturday, except these cars were moving so fast, they melted into a blur of colors and chrome. Far ahead, he could see taller buildings floating on the horizon like a mirage.

"Is that Minneapolis?" he asked Peter George.

"It is. You've never been there?"

"No. I've only been to Burnsville to see a movie with my friend Malcolm."

"Which one?"

"*Dune: Part Two*. Have you seen it?"

"I haven't had much time for films lately, sorry to say."

Travis couldn't believe there was a person alive who hadn't seen it. "You have to, it's *so* good!"

"Maybe we can see it together."

"That would be amazing! Hey, that's pretty cool how you fixed the truck. I suppose you have to know about all kinds of cars in your job."

"You're right about that, Travis. You have to be an amateur mechanic, just in case." He glanced at his passenger. The poor kid's stomach was growling so loudly, he could hear it over the roar of this piece of shit truck that didn't have a radio, heat, or a muffler. The muffler situation could get him pulled over, but he didn't have any other options at the moment.

Wolfie felt a simmering rage building. What kind of monsters starved and abused their child and couldn't bother to take care of their vehicle? The goddamn thing probably wasn't even registered. Travis's parents had been disgusting, worthless parasites, and he'd done the boy and the world a favor. "You know, it's good to have company on a long drive. Are you enjoying our road trip?"

Travis bobbed his head enthusiastically.

"I'm pretty hungry, how about you?"

The mention of food made Travis's stomach twist painfully. "Me too. I didn't eat breakfast." Or supper the night before, but he kept that shameful fact to himself.

"There's a McDonald's just ahead. Do you like McDonald's?"

"I love McDonald's!"

"Two Egg McMuffins coming up." He took the next exit ramp.

"But . . . I don't have any money."

"That's okay, I've got plenty."

"Can we get hashbrown cakes too?"

"You can get a hundred hashbrown cakes if you want."

Travis didn't have any siblings, but Peter George was like the big brother he'd always fantasized about. He asked questions and listened to his answers like he was a grown-up. He laughed easily and made him feel safe, like nothing could hurt him when he was in his presence. He didn't want this day to end, so he was increasingly worried about what would happen once they got to the city. Peter George had a job, and he was pretty sure hanging out with a kid wasn't a top priority. What if he just left him in Minneapolis and told him to figure it out? How would he get back home?

He broached the subject reluctantly. "What are we going to do today?"

"First, I have to stop at a colleague's apartment to pick up something. Then we'll go to a very beautiful house where I'm staying. It belongs to a family friend."

"Don't you have your own house?"

"I'm in between lodgings at the moment."

"Oh. What about the truck? Your boss must want it back right away."

Wolfie was again impressed by the boy's swift, linear way of thinking. He didn't miss much, and with a proper education, he had real potential to do something with his life now that his parents were out of the way. "He'll pick it up there. Then we can go swimming. She has a pool."

Travis decided to add a pool to his mansion plans, even though it was already right on the beach. "But it's way too cold to go swimming now."

"It's an indoor pool. You can swim all year, and the water is always warm."

"Whoa! I didn't know you could have pools inside your house! Is she rich like your dad?"

"Yes. She's famous too."

"For what?"

"She's an artist. My dad helped her get started. I've known her since I was a child, so we're very close."

Travis was momentarily speechless with excitement, his body squirming with nervous energy. "I've never met anyone rich or famous before."

"You'll love her, and she'll love you. I have a lot of work to do once we get there, but we can stream *Dune: Part Two* later, once I'm finished."

It was a dream come true, and he didn't want to ruin it, but there was still the matter of what would happen after they swam and watched *Dune*. "That's so awesome, but my folks will start to worry if I'm not back by tonight. Will you give me a ride home?"

"We'll call them later and tell them not to worry. You know, Travis, I was thinking you could spend a couple days with me, like a vacation. How often do you get to stay at a famous person's house?"

"I've never even been on vacation!" Reality suddenly smacked him down hard, and he shrank in his seat. "But . . . they'll be mad."

Wolfie's rage was cresting. Travis didn't care what they thought, he was just afraid of getting beaten. "I bet your parents make you mad sometimes too. And sad. Mostly sad, am I right?"

Travis lowered his head and felt prickles behind his eyes. "Yeah."

"So, don't you think it's about time you give it right back to them? They deserve it."

"Yeah, but I'll get whipped something fierce for it."

Wolfie reached across the seat and patted his shoulder. "That's never, ever going to happen again. I promise you that."

Travis turned away and wiped his eyes with his sleeve, and like earlier, he spoke before he registered the words coming out of his mouth. "There's this old gun in the barn. Sometimes I think about . . . I feel so bad . . ."

"I understand, and it's nothing to be ashamed of, son." Wolfie was surprised he'd used the word "son," but it felt good, *right*, on his tongue. He wasn't alone anymore, and neither was Travis. "Everybody thinks about killing, they just don't like to admit it. It's perfectly normal."

Travis dared a glance across the seat to see if he was teasing him, but Peter George looked very serious. "Really?"

"It's the truth."

"But . . . isn't killing a sin?"

"Thinking about it isn't."

"But if you actually *do* it, it's a sin, right?"

"Not if you do it for the right reasons."

"What are the right reasons?"

"It varies from person to person." Wolfie pulled into the McDonald's drive-through and ordered two of everything on the breakfast menu. He enjoyed watching Travis inhale more food than a grown man could eat in two days. He even seemed to like the yogurt-granola cups. Hopefully he wouldn't vomit, but as a precaution, he decided to stay in this empty area of the parking lot until he was sure the boy's shrunken stomach could handle the onslaught. A kid puking out a window at freeway speed would draw unwanted attention.

26

MAGOZZI SLIPPED INTO the extravagant nursery Harley had modeled after Versailles or the Winter Palace or someplace equally over-the-top ridiculous. He spared no expense when it came to the people he loved, but Elizabeth had been the recipient of his greatest excesses. She slept in a gilded, eighteenth-century crib that had bedded generations of royal children. A curtained canopy of silk and gold thread shimmered down in a protective veil from the twenty-foot ceiling. The furniture he hadn't been able to source from premiere auction houses had been custom made from ebony and rosewood in the style of the rest of the castle plunder. Real fairytale stuff, as breathtaking as it was outrageous. She was too young to understand she was being spoiled rotten, but boundaries would have to be established once she had situational awareness.

She was sound asleep and Charlie was snoring beneath the crib. Charlie's ears twitched when Magozzi parted the curtains, but he didn't wake up. The old boy was showing his age, and Magozzi couldn't bear to think of a world without him.

Elizabeth didn't stir either, even as he stroked her petal-soft cheek. He would never be able to explain what happened to him whenever he saw or touched her. It was all-encompassing, other-worldly love so powerful it was almost suffocating, and it seemed impossible that the source was this tiny human. Yet his most recent meditations on retirement persisted, shifting, breaking apart, and reforming like clouds on a windy day. He felt confused and guilty, like he was betraying his girls by even thinking about postponing his life plan, but he'd get it sorted once Mauer was either locked up or dead.

He heard soft footsteps behind him and smiled back at Grace. "I never get tired of looking at her."

"I don't either."

"We did good."

"Agreed. But you'll be sorry if you wake her up. Go to your party, Magozzi. People are waiting for you."

"That's what I'm afraid of."

"I've never known you to be a coward."

"You have no idea what McLaren is capable of."

"Stop being melodramatic. Come on." She took his hand and led him back to the office, where Roadrunner was doing yoga contortions in the corner.

"No hits on the nun," he said as he transitioned into a stretch that made him look like a grasshopper. "But we're about to jump into Gustavus hard."

"I'm already jumping in hard," Harley groused. "When you're finished with your human pretzel routine, I could use your help."

"I'm centering myself in preparation. You should try it."

"I don't even know what that means, and I don't care, because I was born ready."

Magozzi was relieved to see the customary sniping between best friends. He hadn't witnessed Harley's mysterious depression, but Grace had told him about it. "Thanks, everybody. I'll see you all later." He noticed Gino and Petra were missing, and he knew exactly where to find them.

A few minutes later, Magozzi was in the kitchen, wolfing down the most sublime piece of pastry he'd even eaten. Petra was looking on with a serene, satisfied smile until Gino blindsided her with a bear hug.

"Marry me, Petra," he implored.

Her smile escalated into delighted laughter. "I think Angela would have something to say about that. And Roadrunner."

Gino released her and shrugged affably. "Can't blame me for trying. Think I could have one more piece?"

Magozzi had to drag him out to the car. Gino spent half the ride to the office effusing about his strudel-inspired awakening. Magozzi had never heard him wax so eloquently about any food, not even his wife's magnificent cooking.

"You have cherry filling on the corner of your mouth, Gino."

"I'm never washing it off, that would be sacrilegious, like taking the shroud of Turin to the dry cleaners."

"You better dial it back when you tell Angela about it or she'll get jealous."

"I'm going to tell her it sucked and she shouldn't even try it."

"Good luck trying to convince her with that besotted look on your face." Magozzi dug in his pocket for his ringing phone. "Great, it's Rikker. Maybe they caught a break. Hi, Sheriff, you're on speaker."

"Hello, detectives."

Her voice wasn't so chipper anymore. In fact, she sounded downright despondent. Magozzi understood. She'd had to look at three dead bodies before noon, and Mauer's escape and a missing child sat squarely on her shoulders. It was a heavy burden for any cop, but especially one who hadn't even worked the field before wearing a star. "What can we do for you?"

"I wanted to let you know our tipline finally received a promising call."

"Lots of cranks, am I right?" Gino asked.

"Lots."

"That's the problem with tiplines, but it only takes one good call to turn things around. We've been there plenty of times. What did they say?"

"An over-the-road trucker saw an old Ford matching the Amber Alert description at a McDonald's in Lakeville, just off 35W. He also said there were two people in the vehicle, and one looked like a child."

"When did he see them?"

"About half an hour ago."

Magozzi felt a nascent panic unfurl in his gut. "He's heading north right toward us."

"If he stays on the freeway. Lakeville and surrounding departments are blanketing the area and scrubbing traffic footage, but since he might be in your vicinity by now—"

"We're on it," Gino interrupted. "Any word on when Monkeewrench can expect the morgue shot? It could really help us."

"I just spoke with the coroner's office and they'll be sending it momentarily. I'll pass it on the minute I receive it. Did Monkeewrench have time to run facial recognition on the nun?"

"Nothing popped," Magozzi said. "But they're into the Gustavus system now."

"That's wonderful news, thank you for letting me know. Also, the phone Mauer stole from the Dunbars' home isn't on, but we're monitoring it in case he tries to use it again. The last call made was this morning to a burner. A dead end, unfortunately."

"Thanks for keeping us in the loop, Sheriff. We'll do the same. And take care of yourself," he said, meaning it. After he signed off, he looked at Gino. "You were relatively nice to her. Almost supportive."

"She's doing a good job under the circumstances, I wouldn't want to be her. Still too polite, though. Call Anderson and get him on the local traffic footage. New guy gets the scut work while we party."

"He's been detective for a year."

"So? He's still the new guy. And his first name is Anders. People with the same first and last name are automatically docked."

"Anders isn't the same as Anderson."

"Close enough."

Magozzi rolled his eyes and made the call while Gino pulled into the parking garage and their reserved slot by the door. A single red balloon emblazoned with a skull and crossbones was tethered to the door handle.

"I told McLaren to get black balloons," Gino carped.

"What's with the skull and crossbones? I'm retiring, not dying."

"It represents our grief."

"I'm flattered. Are counselors going to be present?"

"That depends. Do you consider adult entertainment therapeutic?"

"You're insane if you think I'm falling for that."

Gino smirked at him. "It was worth a try."

27

Z ELDA HAD BEEN in her studio when the special phone she always carried startled her. She'd been hoping for the call, praying for it, but hadn't dared believe it would actually come; so many things could have gone wrong. How foolish to doubt her ability to make things happen, to doubt Wolfie's genius and Aleksandar's skill and devotion.

She'd immediately abandoned her work and dashed to the big house to dismiss all the staff—she trusted all of them, but no chances could be taken—then called her most devoted compatriot Silas, who would take care of the truck without questions. He was very good at getting rid of things quietly and forever.

There were many preparations to make for Wolfie's arrival, and solo, the work had taken some time. But now everything was perfect—the caviar and champagne were on ice, sterling bowls of tulips and ranunculus rioted in every room, and the heated bathtub in Wolfie's suite was filled with sandalwood-scented water, set to a perfect one hundred degrees. The cleverly concealed safe room with the computers and other provisions he'd asked for was ready. It was a day of great celebration. But she was having misgivings about the second part of their plan. Vengeance was the noblest of human acts, and there was no question that Wolfie should kill the Eight. They deserved to die. She'd spent two years researching and compiling dossiers on all of them in order to make it possible. But now that the time had arrived, revenge seemed an outlandish course to pursue. He was free to start over in any number of places, places where he would never have to look over his shoulder. Money certainly wasn't an issue, Peter had made certain of that.

But Wolfie was as pigheaded as any man, and she had to convince him that his mission was too dangerous, at least now, and the risks of proceeding as planned were not just untenable but illogical. Perhaps with this new taste of liberty, he would come around to her way of thinking, but she had her doubts. He was as reckless and intransigent as his father had been.

Zelda finally retreated to her study with a cup of raspberry tea and switched on the TV. She fully expected the coverage of his escape to dominate the news, but her heart turned cold when she saw not only Wolfie's face on every channel but that of an angelic-looking young boy. She turned up the volume.

"Law enforcement has just confirmed the murders of three individuals in Dundas County. Names have not been released at this time, and no word on whether the murders or the abduction of Travis Dunbar are related to the escape—"

"Of course they are, you idiot!" she screamed at the TV, throwing the remote across the room before lowering her head in her hands. "Dear Jesus, what have you done now, Wolfgang?"

28

H ARLEY'S FOCUS WAS intense and singular as he pored over the Gustavus computer logs, looking for anomalies in connections, users, system behavior, or any other glitches the prison's intrusion detection had missed. They had a solid security protocol and the most advanced software, so whoever breached it was skilled and would keep their IP cloaked by Tor and a virtual private network. And without an IP, they didn't have a location to give to Magozzi and Gino.

But plenty of hackers had been tracked through an unencrypted exit node or because they'd failed to update their VPN. Human error was as predictable as the sun rising every morning, and there were clues and mistakes somewhere in the millions of lines of code. They just had to find them. Even if they'd had a platoon of geniuses working on it, it would be a Goliathan task, which is why he and Roadrunner had created the Beast—a wicked parallel processor that could parse and analyze massive amounts of data in a matter of hours or days, not months. And with AI now integrated into the program, it was even more efficient. But the Beast's alert hadn't sounded yet, and until it did, it was eyes-on detective work.

When he started seeing in triplicate, he pushed away from his desk and rummaged in his drawer for a bottle of liquid tears. "What's the progress on the Beast, Roadrunner?"

"It's scanned twenty-one percent so far. Not bad considering the volume of data it's crunching."

"Did you find anything on the dark web?"

"I poked around a little, and there are loads of sketchy art purveyors who deal in pieces of questionable provenance, but no Rado sculptures. They aren't illegal, just undesirable."

"They're desirable to the right buyer."

"Who would be totally anonymous and pay in crypto. That's a double negative for tracking anything down. It's a last resort."

Harley looked around the empty office. He'd been so consumed, he hadn't even registered everyone else's absence. "Where did the ladies go?"

"Petra is on a Zoom with D.C., and Annie and Grace are taking Charlie for a walk before they leave for Annie's appointment."

"What appointment?"

"To pick up her dress for the party."

"That woman has more clothes than New York, Paris, and Milan Fashion Week combined and she needs a new dress?"

He shrugged. "It's Annie, what can I say?"

Harley decided to broach a delicate subject that had been troubling his heart ever since they'd gotten the news about Mauer. "How is Petra really doing? I mean, this dredges up a lot of bad, bad history."

"It does, but she's so strong, Harley. I marvel at it every day."

"I'm glad you two found each other, buddy. We all are."

Roadrunner looked up and smiled. "Thanks, man. I am too."

Harley's recent angst suddenly seemed so unforgivably selfish. When Roadrunner suddenly wasn't at his beck and call every hour of every day, he'd turned into a pissy baby, moping over his own loss instead of celebrating his best friend's gain. Annie had actually gone easy on him. "I'm starving. Is there any strudel left?"

"You're seriously asking that after Gino was here?"

"You're right, stupid question. I'm going to order something to eat. Want a Carnivore Special with anchovies?"

"Very funny. I'll eat pizza, but I'm ordering. I don't trust you."

"When haven't I been respectful of your stupid dietary restrictions?"

"Pretty much never. And they're not stupid."

"Hell if they're not—you live on bananas and lawn clippings, which is a crime when you have a cook like Petra in your life. If you were any skinnier, you'd be invisible. I'm just trying to keep you alive by sneaking in some amino acids and common sense every now and then."

Roadrunner folded his arms across his concave chest. "It's actually good to have you back in asshole form. What was wrong with you anyhow? Midlife crisis?"

"I am *not* in midlife, and I *don't* have crises. What I am is a highly complex man who is occasionally taken by profound philosophical introspection. But you're a computer with legs, I wouldn't expect you to understand the torments of my towering intellect."

"You are so full of shit—"

A loud alert interrupted, but it wasn't coming from the Beast. "What's that for?"

Roadrunner started hammering on his keyboard. "That's face rec. I plugged in the morgue shot . . . hot damn, we got a ninety-eight percent match."

Harley clomped over. "Fantastic! So who was this guy?"

"Aleksandar Nichols." He scrolled through dozens of Instagram posts featuring a young, muscular man with sun-bleached hair and dimples. There were beach volleyball scenes, some surfing photos, panoramas of the ocean, and night shots of Santa Monica Pier. "These are all from a few years ago. There's nothing recent."

"He looks like a harmless beach bum. Not at all like he would be in Minnesota cavorting with a killer."

"It's confirmed he was doing computer repair and stealing identities last summer. He had to live somewhere, so maybe we can find him in public records or through a driver's license."

"What about his online bio?"

"He loves cats, malicious hacking, and quality time with psychopaths."

Harley reared back on his worn boot heels. "Oh my God, did you just crack a joke?"

"I hope you don't think I was serious."

"You never crack jokes. You really are happy, aren't you?"

Roadrunner ignored him. "It says here he graduated from Caltech with a master's in computer science five years ago. He might have been a black hat for hire."

Harley smacked his hands together so hard it sounded like a gunshot, and Roadrunner jerked in his chair. "I don't think so. Mauer got his degree at Caltech, remember? And they're about the same age. A thousand bucks says they knew each other. I'll start cranking on public records and find his phone. If Mauer used it, we might get somewhere."

Roadrunner waved him away distractedly and kept scrolling through photos. From what he could tell from the landmarks, they'd all been taken in California, so he started a records search there, which pulled up a valid driver's license.

"D.L. is California."

"Got it. Keep looking through his Instagram account, a picture is worth a thousand words."

A few minutes later, Roadrunner did a double-take and enlarged a shot of Nichols in a swimming pool with another man, locked in an intimate embrace against a backdrop of fuchsia bougainvillea. Both of them were mugging for the camera, and the post had heart emojis cascading across it. "Harley, come here."

He rolled his chair over and looked at the screen, then his jaw slid open. "Holy shit, that's Mauer. They were lovers . . ." He saw all the blood leach out of Roadrunner's face. "What? What's wrong?"

He stabbed the monitor viciously. "They both have tiger tattoos."

"Yeah, so? Lovers get matching tattoos all the time . . . oh shit. Praljik's Tigers."

"Petra told me he branded his *special* orphans in the camps with a rusty fountain pen. Some died from sepsis. *That's* how he knew Nichols first."

Harley was almost flattened by nausea. He didn't know if Petra had escaped before she'd been branded too, and he really didn't want to know. "Eyes on the prize, buddy. Mauer had his lover bust him out, then killed a loose end, and that's where he's holed up, I guarantee it. He's got no place else to go. Let's find this fuckstick."

29

MAGOZZI WAS EVEN more reluctant to step into Homicide this time around, because he heard a lot of boisterous noise coming at him from the end of the hall. It was the same kind of trepidation he'd felt as an eight-year-old, walking down a St. Paul street with his grandpa on their first solo outing together.

Hear all that noise coming from down the block? That's Grundy's, and that's where I'm taking you. Best burgers in the world, you'll see. Don't tell your parents I took you to a bar.

I won't. How come it's so loud? Is there a party?

It's pretty much always a party at Grundy's. It's a place where folks go to blow off steam.

Magozzi didn't consider his retirement party an opportunity to blow off steam, but apparently the guests did.

Gino sighed happily. "Sounds like the bacchanalia is in full swing, Leo. Everybody's probably already drunk as skunks and ready to push your face into the punchbowl."

"I'll shoot anybody who tries."

"That would be one way to go out with a bang."

"Pun intended, I'm sure. I should probably check in with Grace before—"

"That's the lamest attempt at evasion I ever heard."

Magozzi had never been so happy for the distraction of the formidable Gloria stalking toward them in a blue caftan and sparkly platform heels, beaded cornrows chattering with each purposeful, heavy step. She was a whip-smart, gorgeous steamroller fueled by sass and attitude, the unrivaled queen of Homicide who ruled the throne of the front office. There was no one else on earth, not even Malcherson, who could smack down their unruly bunch with a look. McLaren didn't stand a chance.

She stopped short of getting in their faces, but jabbed a long, pointy fingernail at them both in quick succession. "You're late. Get in there before the natives start tearing down the cubicles."

"You look even more ravishing than usual," Magozzi vamped.

She flipped a noisy sheaf of hair dramatically. "Of course I do; I just got my hair done."

"Have you seen McLaren's new suit?"

"That pasty little twerp has finally lost his damn mind. Not that he had much of a tether on it to begin with."

Gino chuckled. "Methinks the lady doth protest too much."

Her eyes narrowed into kohl-lined slits. "What's that supposed to mean?"

"It means the way you hurl insults at him makes me think you're deflecting your true feelings—"

Magozzi coughed to cover a guffaw.

"You like your bits and bobs, Rolseth?"

"Love them."

"Then you'd be very wise to keep your trap shut." She grabbed Magozzi's arm and bullied him into the room. "Good luck. I had nothing to do with this except plan everything."

Magozzi tried for stoic when he walked into the cheering crowd, but he couldn't control his smile. And why should he? This was absolutely fantastic. The room was wall-to-wall detectives from every division, cops from every precinct, and even a few retirees had shown up for the festivities. He was barraged with backslaps and plastic cups filled with green stuff that smelled like jet fuel, most of which ended up on his new suit jacket. There was plenty of bluster and smack talk and more than a few misty eyes. He convinced himself the punch was responsible for the emotion so he didn't get misty-eyed himself.

Tommy Espinoza, MPD's resident computer geek, shoved his way through the crowd, his shocking blue eyes twinkling in his broad face. Eyes from his Swedish mom, skin and hair from his Mexican dad, body from his diet of junk food, he was the jolliest of all souls in the MPD. His skill set made him even more beloved. He proffered a huge gift bag draped in curly ribbon. "You're always harping on me for cleaning the good stuff out of the vending machines, so here's a month's supply of Cheezy Puffs. Well, it's a month's supply for me, maybe a year for you." He warned Gino with a look. "These are for *Leo*."

"Hey, I wouldn't think of pilfering from my partner."

"Yeah, right." Tommy turned back to Magozzi and put a hand on his shoulder. "You're breaking my heart. I'm going to miss you and all that sketchy stuff you had me do over the years. It's not going to be the same without you."

"I'm quite certain I didn't hear that," Malcherson said, approaching from the flank and surprising them all.

Espinoza's cheeks flushed. "Cheezy Puffs, sir?"

Malcherson actually smiled, then clapped his hands loudly. The room went dead quiet. "I'd like to say a few words, but I understand we have a special guest, so I'll let them take the floor first. Please, everyone, clear a path."

The chief raised his hands and the crowd parted like the Red Sea. Moses couldn't have done any better. Magozzi tried to make himself smaller when the room suddenly erupted with whoops, shouts, and wolf whistles as someone cued up EMF's "Unbelievable," a perennial favorite of strip clubs even after twenty-five years. Not that he knew from personal experience.

Everybody had their phones raised, and, like a vision straight out of hell, Johnny McLaren appeared, strutting toward him in the fabled leopard print thong. Magozzi elbowed Gino so hard he almost doubled over; it was his laughter that finished the job.

"Hey, I warned you, didn't I?" Gino gasped, wiping tears from his eyes.

"You did just the opposite, you son of a bitch."

"Am I unbelievable or what?!" McLaren crowed as he executed an awkward pirouette and nearly toppled.

Magozzi's face was burning, but then he took in Johnny's ribby white torso, his stick arms and legs, the flashing green of his mischievous eyes, and started laughing too. As preposterous and truly distasteful as it was, McLaren had given him a gift that he would remember and laugh about as long as he lived, and that was a very rare gift indeed.

Gloria rolled in a huge cake with black and red frosting and wielded a chef's knife threateningly. "This cake is *not* free, people, so don't even think about touching it until I finish taking collections. Magozzi's a kept man now, and he needs his own pin money."

There were plenty of chortles as she shook out a brown paper grocery bag and worked the crowd. "Pony up—gifts are good, cash is better."

In a supremely ballsy move, McLaren sidled up to her and spread his arms wide. In most work environments, the move would be decried as sexual harassment, but in this situation, he was essentially throwing himself on a pike. "I would contribute, Gloria, but I don't have room for my wallet."

She raised her chin in haughty appraisal. "Looks to me like you could put a semitrailer in that thing and still have room for a wallet."

Ty Overgaard from Narc started shrieking with laughter, and the whole room blew up. But McLaren was utterly unfazed as he swished away. "Told you I'd get the girl," he called over his shoulder.

Gino leaned over and whispered in Magozzi's ear. "The thong was Gloria's idea."

"You can stop yanking my chain now."

"For real, I'm serious. I think the whole thing was a setup, and man, did she stick the landing."

"Actually, I think McLaren aced her at the end. Look at her, she's mad as a wet hornet." It was a miracle Magozzi heard his phone above the clamor, and he seized the opportunity to duck into a conference room where he could almost hear himself think. "Grace!"

"It sounds like you have an impressive turnout."

"You don't know the half of it." Or maybe she did. He wouldn't put it past Gino to loop her in, and she'd been awfully cagey this morning when the topic had come up. But he wouldn't hold it against her. "Any news?"

"Harley and Roadrunner ID'd the dead man. His name is Aleksandar Nichols. Mauer's lover."

"*What?* I thought his sexual proclivity was violence against women."

"His only proclivity is using and hurting people, gender has nothing to do with it. We did a records search and found an address in Chanhassen. Harley just texted it to you and Sheriff Rikker. Hopefully Mauer's there and you can end this."

"How about a phone—"

"It's off or gone. Mauer's too smart to carry around a beacon."

Stupid question. "We're on our way." He heard a soft, anxious sigh on the other end of the line, which was very unlike Grace.

"Be careful, Magozzi."

"Always."

"I know this is personal, but don't let it be. See you later."

He listened to the dead air of a disconnected call, wondering if there would ever come a time when "Love you" replaced "See you later." The sentiment had been there for a long time, but he still wanted to hear it. The day Grace could finally verbalize it, his life would be complete.

Gino popped his head in the door. "What's up?"

"Vest up. We have an address."

30

IRIS SLID HER plate of discarded pizza crusts in the trash as she ended her second call. They'd come in fast and furious, one right on the heels of another. The stubborn engine of this case was finally gathering steam. Tumblers were falling into place. The stars were aligning. She pressed her temples, trying to squelch the clichés her semi-delirious mind was churning out. A hot stone massage and a glass of wine would be good right about now. Or electroshock. Maybe Dr. Drexler could help her out . . .

"Magozzi again?"

She jerked her head. She'd almost forgotten Sampson was there. "That was Hopkins PD. They just grabbed traffic cam footage of the Dunbar truck on 212 westbound. Time stamp was forty minutes ago. That's a straight shot to highway 101, which goes right into Chanhassen."

"Take a break from the phone, I'll give Magozzi and Gino a heads-up."

"Do it from the car—let's go."

"Why? They're already en route. By the time we arrive, it will be over one way or the other."

"If I'm driving, we might beat them."

"And if Mauer's not there it'll be a waste of gas and time. If he stays on 212, he's already out in the weeds, which would be the smart thing to do. Western Minnesota is one giant field with a million little roads going in every direction. Or he could be taking a circuitous route to the cities. Better to stay here and keep scrubbing footage in case he has other plans."

Iris crunched on two tropical fruit–flavored antacids that should have been marketed as chalk-flavored. Dammit, she was micromanaging again. Magozzi and Gino had this, and Sampson was right; their time would be better spent in the office in case Chanhassen didn't pan out. She had absolutely no interest in optics or personal glory. But in spite of the preponderance of logic that told her to stay put, it felt *wrong* not to be there. "This started in Dundas County and one way or another, it's going to end here."

Sampson shrugged. "True enough, but it doesn't make sense for us to haul ass up there when it's already covered."

Had he always been such a resolute pragmatist? "Some things don't have to make sense to be right. You can't honestly tell me you don't want a piece of this, even if it's a piece of nothing."

Sampson's mouth didn't move, but his eyes did the smiling for him. "No, I can't tell you that."

She thumped her hand on her desk. "Alright, then, we're going. That's an order."

"I was hoping you'd say that."

"If it makes you feel more productive, you can get in touch with California while we're on the road so they can so they can handle Aleksandar Nichols's notification."

*   *   *

Wolfie pulled the truck into the empty lot behind an office park that had gone belly up last year. It was an ideal hiding spot: no surrounding buildings or homes, and it was set back from any main traffic arteries. It was a mile from Aleksandar's apartment, but he'd always been a runner, so the round trip would be effortless, especially in his dead lover's Nike Alphaflys. Hell, he'd crawl a thousand miles over broken glass to get the flash drive—extra insurance in case Zelda tried to control him just like Aleksandar had tried to control him by withholding it. That had made his killing even more pleasurable. He'd always planned to get rid of that greedy piece of shit once he'd served his purpose, but pretty Aleksandar had accelerated his own execution. Stupid prick.

He shut off the truck and glanced at his little passenger. He was gazing out the windshield at the boarded-up building apprehensively, and Wolfie knew he'd have to improvise a convincing story for this astute boy.

"I'm going to go meet my colleague, but I want you to wait here, okay?"

"He lives here?" Travis asked doubtfully.

"No, I just parked here because his street's all torn up. Why don't you lie down and take a nap in the sun? I wish I could take one. All that food made me sleepy, you must be too."

"I'm not tired at all."

Of course he wasn't. He was a kid on the adventure of his life.

"Can't I come with you? I wouldn't be any trouble and I could stay back so your colleague doesn't even know I'm there."

Wolfie understood the separation anxiety Travis was feeling because he'd experienced it himself. He'd received a dose of human kindness and now he was clinging to it like a starved leech. But there was no time for assuaging insecurities. "I need you to stay here and keep an eye on the truck, it's very important. We don't want anybody to steal it, because I would get in a lot of trouble."

"But what if someone does try to steal it? What do I do?"

"Nobody will as long as you're in here. That's why I need you to stay, okay?"

He sighed dispiritedly. "O-kay. But it's going to be boring without you."

Wolfie hedged. He would be gone at least half an hour, and boredom was torture, especially at Travis's age. No matter how eager he was to please, no matter how obedient he was, the temptation to venture out and explore would be irresistible. And if anybody recognized him . . .

"I wish the radio worked."

He hadn't even thought of Aleksandar's Mp3 player until now. He reached into the knapsack at Travis's feet and pulled out the Astell&Kern and a pair of earbuds. "This is better than a radio."

Travis perked up instantly. "What is it?"

"It's a digital audio player with so many songs on it, you couldn't hear them all in a month. Who do you like to listen to?" He watched the boy's eyes grow into two huge saucers.

"I-I love Metallica," he stuttered excitedly.

"So do I. I told you we think alike. Which album?"

"Um . . . I don't know any albums, just some songs."

Not knowing the complete Metallica discography was another tragedy piled on top of the many the boy had suffered. He'd lived a life of complete ignorance and deprivation in every sphere of life, but that was going to change. He cued up *Kill 'em All*—an early effort, but brilliant and still his favorite—placed the buds in Travis's ears and cranked the opening cut. When Travis closed his eyes and started head-banging, he knew it would be his favorite album too. The boy's evolution was appropriately starting with "Hit the Lights." The idiom referenced darkness, the end, but Wolfie had always seen lights turning *on* whenever he heard it. To him, it represented a new dawn with limitless possibilities.

CHAPTER

31

C HANHASSEN WAS A charming southwestern suburb with an
abundance of lakes, parks, nature preserves, and tree-lined
streets. Magozzi hadn't been here since his ex-wife dragged him to
the arboretum years ago. Unenthused about looking at a bunch of
plants, his expectations had been low, but it turned out the place
was captivating. Unfortunately, the good memories vaporized
when he discovered the ulterior motive behind the visit: her third
extramarital affair had been with a landscape architect. Like all
lawyers, Heather was diligent about research.

The address Harley had texted landed them at a sprawling
Dutch colonial on a corner lot near Paisley Park. According to
property records, it was owned and occupied by Dean Helgen and
converted to an up-and-down duplex in 2020. Magozzi pulled up
next to a Chanhassen squad parked down the block. A beefy officer with a buzzcut and a nameplate that said KAUL got out, looking uncomfortable in his constrictive ballistic vest. It was probably
rare that this peaceful community got a call more serious than
kids egging a house on Halloween, and he figured it was his first
time wearing one. They sucked, but the alternative sucked worse.

"Afternoon, detectives. We've been here about ten minutes, no
action except the owner just got back from the grocery store. He
lives downstairs."

"Thanks, Officer Kaul. How many are you?"

"Four. My partner is on foot around the back, and the other squad is trolling the area. We have more backup hanging in the Grab 'n Go lot a few minutes away, we didn't want to spook anybody with a heavy presence."

"Good thinking."

Kaul glanced up the street with a grim expression. "Do you really think Mauer's in there?"

"We're hoping. Anything you can tell us about Dean Helgen or the property in general?"

"He's a retired dentist. I grew up a few blocks away and he's lived here as long as I can remember. When his wife died, he converted the top floor and started renting it out. Never had a call or any problems. How do you want us positioned?"

"Front and back yard while we approach, cover all possible exits and assume Mauer is armed. Also, Sheriff Rikker and Lieutenant Sampson from Dundas County are on their way."

Kaul nodded. "We've got you."

Magozzi looked up at the shuttered, second-floor windows as they approached and felt the sizzle of adrenaline in his veins. If Mauer was here, whether he ran or fought, the encounter was going to end a lot differently than it had the last time, because Magozzi was ready and he was pissed. His eyes and ears were honed to catch the slightest movement or sound that wasn't birdsong or the distant hum of traffic on Prince Rogers Nelson Memorial Highway, but he didn't sense anything out of the ordinary in the sleepy neighborhood.

Gino rapped on the door, and they waited on either side, just in case there was a nasty surprise waiting for them instead of a retired dentist. A few moments later, a darkly tanned, older gentleman in a grass-green polo shirt and chinos answered.

"Dean Helgen?" Magozzi asked.

"That's me. How can I help you?" His eyes slid to their holsters and the police in his yard, and he took a few alarmed steps back. "What's wrong? What's happening?"

"We're Minneapolis detectives, is anyone else here or in the apartment upstairs?"

"N-n-no. I'm here alone. Are you sure you have the right address?"

Magozzi assessed his demeanor for red flags or any indication that he was under duress and saw none. His eyes only revealed befuddlement that his quiet life in a quiet town was suddenly embroiled in a drama he didn't comprehend. "Are you absolutely certain nobody is upstairs?"

"Positive, I would have heard them. It's an old house, it creaks and groans with the lightest step as I found out when I started renting."

"But you were just grocery shopping, correct? So you wouldn't necessarily know if someone had slipped in when you were gone."

Helgen blinked, bewildered. "How did you know I was grocery shopping?"

"Gone what, an hour?"

"About that. I don't understand, I haven't done anything—"

Gino gave Magozzi a sharp look and interjected. "We know that, sir, we're only interested in your tenant, Aleksandar Nichols."

Helgen relaxed a little, but his eyes were still wary and fixed on Magozzi. "He doesn't live here anymore. He moved out recently." He opened the door wider. "Would you like to come in?"

Magozzi relaxed a little too. A hostage never invited cops in because a hostage always had a gun to their head or a loved one's out of sight. "Thank you."

They stepped in, eyes wide open, but there was nothing sinister or off-kilter, just a lovely home filled with history, love, and memories. The woodwork and flooring were original and beautifully restored, and the spacious living room was crammed with antiques polished to a mellow gleam. Family photos were ubiquitous, filling walls and covering most horizontal surfaces. "When did Mr. Nichols move out?"

"I'm not entirely sure. I spent a month in Arizona and just got back two days ago. He was gone, everything cleaned out. He left the place as neat as a pin, and there was a stack of cash to cover two months' rent and a note to hold it for him in case he needed to come back. I found that odd, but he was a bit odd too."

"How so?"

"He was a shut-in. Very quiet, never had people over, and I only saw him on the first of the month, when he paid his rent. I think he worked a lot; the lights were always on. He moved in quite a bit of computer equipment, and I know from my grandson that tech folks work all hours."

"Any idea where he went?"

"Not a clue. I knew nothing about him. He's in trouble, isn't he?"

"He was murdered."

Helgen covered his mouth. "Oh . . . oh no."

"We need to search the apartment."

He groped in his pocket and withdrew a keychain with shaky hands. "Of course, follow me. There's a private entrance out back."

"Mr. Helgen, please stay here and lock your door."

*   *   *

Magozzi could hear his heart thudding in his ears as he and Gino mounted the wooden stairs to the second floor, guns drawn. Kaul was right behind them.

"Police, open up!" Magozzi shouted. He repeated the command and hammered on the door. They both jumped to the side and raised their weapons when it creaked open onto an empty room.

"Helgen wouldn't leave this door unlocked," Gino whispered.

Magozzi didn't think so either, and his heart wasn't thudding anymore, it was galloping. "Let's do it."

Clearing a building produced a very special kind of terror because every corner, every shadow, every doorway could conceal a mortal threat. The terror was amplified by the tales of eleventh-hour tragedies that had been haunting Magozzi all week. He was raining flop sweat by the time they finished the search. It had only taken minutes, but it felt like centuries. "We're clear. Officer Kaul, go ask Helgen if this door was locked."

Kaul let out a deep breath, like he'd been holding it for a long time. "Be right back."

Gino looked around the apartment, which boasted the same oak floors and original woodwork. The air was stuffy, tinged with the smell of cleaning products. The only furniture in the living room was a leather sofa and an old rolltop desk. It was nicer than any place he'd ever rented in his years before Angela and the kids. He turned when he heard Kaul on the stairs.

"Mr. Helgen says the door was definitely locked; he checked it this morning."

"Thanks, Officer. We're done here, you can be on your way but keep some patrols around here just in case and canvass local businesses, especially gas stations."

He gave them a salute. "Done. Call if you need us for anything else."

Magozzi let out a frustrated sigh. "Goddammit, we missed him, Gino."

"Yeah. Let's toss this place, see if he left anything behind."

They searched every nook, cranny and crevice, but the place was neat as a pin, just as Helgen had said. Not a scrap of paper or dust mote, not a hair in the bathroom sink, not even loose change between the sofa cushions.

They stepped out just as Rikker and Sampson arrived. Magozzi had forgotten just how petite she was. And how cute. Her short blonde hair framed a heart-shaped face, and her eyes were a remarkable shade of aquamarine, but not so innocent anymore. He'd also forgotten how tall and imposing Sampson was. Standing together, they looked like they belonged to different species. "Sheriff, Lieutenant, good to see you."

"You too, detectives," Iris said.

Gino made nice and jumped in to shake their hands first. "Glad you came up, even though this is a wash. Nichols moved out and we're pretty sure we just missed Mauer." He gave them a quick briefing, then gestured them inside. "Take a look for yourselves."

The rolltop desk immediately caught Iris's attention because she had one very much like it, but this was in far better shape. The oak had been refinished in a warm honey tone, and the brass knobs and lock plate gleamed. "Why would he show up here at all if he wasn't planning to use it as a hideout?"

Magozzi shrugged. "Maybe he was, then saw the cops and bolted. Or else he was looking for something."

Sampson was in the kitchen, going through cupboards. "Can't see how he went unnoticed in that dilapidated truck this long with all the eyes on him. Think he found another vehicle?"

"Either that or he found a place to go to ground," Iris said, still focused intently on the desk. "You said it, Sampson—it's not hard to disappear in this neck of the woods. He could be hiding in a barn in Lester Prairie by now."

"The net's spread wide," Gino said. "We might not get him today or tomorrow, but we will get him."

She nodded absently and rolled up the cover of the desk. Empty cubbyholes and empty drawers. Then she noticed the brass medallion on the back panel. "My God, this *is* a Ridgemont."

Gino bit down a nasty comment about antique shopping at a possible crime scene. "Are we supposed to know what you're talking about?"

"Dale Ridgemont was a small furniture maker. He was famous for rolltops, but he only made thirty-two before he died of the Spanish flu. I have one just like this, it was my great-grandmother's. Probably the most valuable thing I own."

"Well, that's absolutely fascinating."

Iris shot him a wry smile. "Only if you're into antiques, Detective Rolseth, and somehow, I don't think you are. But *this* is fascinating." She opened a side drawer, rooted around, and withdrew a board covered in threadbare red velvet. "All Ridgemonts have a false-bottomed drawer."

The men swarmed the desk like scavengers on roadkill. "Is there anything in there?"

Iris clicked on her mini-Mag and shone it into the deep drawer. At the very back was a flash drive, taped to the side wall.

Gino rocked back on his heels and grinned at her. "Well, done, Sheriff, my apologies. I'll never think uncharitable thoughts about old crap again."

"Or me, I hope. But I don't take it personally. It's an honor to work with a detective of your skill and stature, and I take all criticism, spoken or implied, as an opportunity to improve."

Magozzi clamped his hand over his mouth so he didn't dissolve into hysterics. Talk about an ace. Game, set, and match, Iris Rikker.

32

TRAVIS COULD TELL that Peter George's meeting hadn't gone well. His face was stormy when he returned, and he hadn't said more than a few words since. When his dad got like this, he knew to keep his mouth shut and disappear. But he couldn't disappear, so he sat perfectly still and didn't ask any questions. He didn't even listen to music in case Peter George would feel better and talk to him.

"I'm not mad at you, I'm mad at my colleague," he finally said.

Travis let out a relieved sigh.

"I just needed a little time to cool off and think. You're a good boy, giving me space."

"It's okay, I do the same thing when I'm mad. Your colleague must be a real asshole."

He blurted out a surprised laugh. "A *real* asshole. He stole something very valuable from me. But I'm not thinking about him now, I'm thinking about how much fun we're going to have as soon as we get to my friend's house."

"Will we be there soon?"

"Pretty soon."

Travis contentedly watched the countryside roll by, and finally the truck slowed and stopped in front of a colossal gate that eased open slowly. They drove into a park that was a whole lot fancier than the one in Dundas County, which didn't have any gates at all, just a chain across the entrance when it was closed. This road wasn't dirt either; it was smooth and paved and wound up through a forest of towering trees that arched gracefully over the drive. It was like a secret tunnel. "I didn't know we were going to a park."

"This isn't a park, Travis. This is my friend's place."

He was stunned speechless for a moment. "I . . . don't believe it."

"You'll see."

Travis's eyes stretched wide as he took in sloping expanses of lawn and woods, stone terraces jammed with tulips and daffodils, and rows of lilacs interspersed with funny trees that had no leaves, just big white flowers that looked like they were made of tissue. He gasped when they rounded a bend and a massive, stone house with columns holding up a second-floor balcony came into view. There was even a pond with real live swans. "This is really somebody's house?" he whispered in disbelief.

"It's pretty amazing, right?" Wolfie parked the offensive truck beneath a weeping willow and shut it off. His ears were ringing from the prolonged noise pollution, and he hoped his hearing wasn't permanently damaged. The only redeeming thing about it was it had gotten them here. "You stay in the truck while I greet our hostess and tell her she has another guest."

"She won't be mad, will she?"

She's going to be furious. "No, she loves kids. Just sit tight."

"Okay." Travis opened his window and breathed in the scent of lilacs as the double front doors of the house opened. A tiny older woman stepped out with a big smile that looked frozen in place. She was wearing a long green and yellow dress that reminded him of Malcolm's mom's parakeets. Her hair was dark and she had a lot of it, piled high on top of her head and fastened with gold clips that glinted in the sun.

But what entranced him most was her jewelry. He'd never seen a person wear so much, not even on TV or in movies about rich people. He wondered how somebody so small could carry all that weight without tipping over. She was mesmerizing and also a little frightening, like some exotic creature in a zoo.

He watched Peter George and the woman hug each other for a long time. Their voices were carried away by the breeze, but he could see she was crying and wondered why. Suddenly, she pulled away from him and her smile burned out. Then her mouth started moving really fast, just like his mom's had last week when his parents were fighting on the porch. He'd spied on them from the safety of the barn, but he hadn't been able to hear their conversation either. He cowered, fearing this would end in the same way, but Peter George didn't hit her, he just listened, so maybe they weren't fighting at all.

Still, it made him fearful, especially when she glanced at him, then started walking toward the truck. Her smile was back, bigger than before, and she opened her arms in a welcoming gesture, but maybe she was really planning to eat him like the witch in *Hansel and Gretel* because he was an intruder. He tried to scramble backward, but the seat belt kept him fast in place. When she was close enough to touch, he noticed she wore a lot of makeup and her face was strangely smooth and tight. He'd figured her to be much older than his mom, but maybe she wasn't.

"You really are a pretty little pet," she cooed, offering her jeweled hand through the window. "You need some work, but we'll take care of that. Welcome to my home, Travis. I'm Miss Zelda."

He shook it warily, marveling at all the jewels flashing rainbows in the sun. "Uh . . . hi."

She opened the squeaky truck door and gestured toward the house. "Out with you, it's time to go inside and celebrate."

Travis balked. Nobody but Malcolm wanted him in their house, so why would somebody as important as her? "What are we celebrating?"

"I haven't seen Wolfie in the longest time."

"You mean Peter George?"

Her brows peaked in surprise. "So that's what he calls himself? How delightful!"

"Peter George isn't his real name?"

"All his friends call him Wolfie and so should you. It's a nickname. We all have them, don't we? What's yours?"

Travis blushed and looked away, thinking of the playground taunts of "Stinky" and "Pigpen," his father calling him every bad word he'd ever heard and some he didn't know. "I don't have one."

Her smile faded. "Well, then, I'll think of something wonderful for you because I can tell you're special."

He didn't want to tell her he wasn't special at all, because she might not want him here anymore. "Do you think I could go see the swans?"

"Of course, we'll feed them later after we get you both settled in." She extended her hand and wiggled her fingers. "Come, come."

Travis was still afraid of her, but Peter George—Wolfie—was beaming from the porch, waving him forward, so he plucked up his bravery and took her offered hand. The gold rings felt cool and clicked like marbles. "If he's staying with you, how come you haven't seen him in a long time?"

"That's just a boring adult story; it doesn't matter."

He supposed it didn't. "You have an accent. Where are you from?"

"I'm from Europe. So is Wolfie."

"But he doesn't have an accent."

"No. He came here as a young boy."

"Was his dad from Europe too?"

"Yes. We all came here together. Like a family." She chuckled and squeezed his hand. "Wolfie told me you were a very bright, inquisitive boy. Perhaps your nickname should be Rado. It's short for *radoznao*. It means 'curious' in my language. And the irony is brilliant, he'll absolutely love it!"

Travis didn't know what irony was, but it was cool to have a foreign nickname, and even cooler that his new big brother would love it. He wasn't so scared of her anymore and felt bad about thinking of the *Hansel and Gretel* witch. "Can I really go swimming?"

"Ah, he told you about my swimming pool! You're most welcome to, just as soon as you bathe. Everyone must before getting into the pool."

That didn't make any sense—wasn't a swimming pool just a big bathtub?

"And I'll get you something decent to wear. You'll be positively handsome once we get you styled properly."

Travis blushed and followed her up the stone steps where Wolfie was waiting. He knelt down and ruffled his hair. Nobody had done that since Grandpa Dunbar had gone to heaven, and it made him feel warm and safe inside, like Grandpa was still watching out for him. He could almost smell cherry tobacco.

"I told you my friend was nice, didn't I?"

Travis nodded emphatically. "We're going to feed the swans later."

Zelda glowered at Wolfie over the boy's head. "Put the truck in the garage, Silas is waiting for it. Then we'll all have champagne before you two urchins get yourselves cleaned up."

33

TRAVIS WOULD NEVER be able to describe Miss Zelda's house to Malcolm because he had no point of reference that enabled him to process what he was seeing. As his hungry eyes roamed the vast, fantastical interior landscape of colors, textures, and shapes, his sense of reality distorted until he was certain he was dreaming. But how could he dream about something so far beyond his imagination?

What caught his eye most was a long second-floor hallway visible from the main foyer, because it bristled with tall, black things that looked like the alien artifacts in his *Monsters From Space* comic book. Each one was twisted into different shapes, but all of them had holes like Swiss cheese. He couldn't imagine what they were or what possible use they could have. "What are those?" he whispered, afraid they might come to life if he spoke too loudly.

"They're sculptures," Wolfie said. "They're my father's work. He was an artist too, just like Miss Zelda. And the holes are actually secret messages."

Travis was mesmerized. "Is there a code to decipher them?"

"You want to know what they mean?"

"No, he doesn't," Zelda interrupted brusquely. "Let him use his imagination. What do you think you think of them, Travis?"

"I . . . I think they're really cool. It's like a magic forest."

"I never thought of it that way, but you're right!" Zelda claimed his arm. "Escort me to the dining room, we'll have a sip and a bite, then you can take your bath while the adults catch up. Wolfie, I've decided to call this charming boy Rado."

He threw his head back and roared. "Brilliant! It's perfect. This was all meant to be!"

Travis smiled and tried to muster a laugh as loud as his, even though he didn't know what was so funny. Zelda steered him to another dreamscape where there were big chairs around a table that seemed a million miles longer than his house. It was laden with silver trays and bowls of food he didn't recognize. He watched her take a tiny pancake and heap a spoonful of shiny black-gray beads on top of it. "Taste this and tell me what you think."

It didn't look like anything a person should eat, but he couldn't refuse. He was a guest, lucky to be here. "It's not baby rabbit turds, is it?"

Her laughter echoed in the immense space. "Oh, you're going to kill me! Would I feed rabbit turds to a boy as lovely as you?"

She was leaning in close to him, face animated, dark eyes flashing. He thought of the *Hansel and Gretel* witch again and took a tiny bite.

"Well?"

It wasn't as horrible as he thought it would be, but it wasn't good either. "I like McDonald's hashbrown cakes better." There was another startling squall of laughter, and then Wolfie placed a strange, skinny glass in front of him. It was filled with straw-colored liquid that sparkled with little bubbles. He didn't like the taste right away, but after he'd taken a few sips, it tasted better, and so did the black-gray stuff. Then his mind got soft and fuzzy. It was a strange feeling, but it was a good one.

* * *

Wolfie carried a boneless, semi-conscious Travis to the bedroom in the towel he'd dried him with after his bath. The chip of Xanax in his champagne had worked its wonders—a necessary measure to ensure uninterrupted time to do his work. And really, the poor thing deserved a peaceful rest for once in his life. If everybody had access to tranquilizers, the world would be a much better place.

He dressed him in the tiny cashmere pajamas he'd pulled from Zelda's extensive children's wardrobe. All of her clients were wealthy and privileged, and many were parents who required their spoiled, undeserving offspring to be equally well-dressed, even at bedtime. Now Travis would enjoy such a life, free of cruelty and misery, and would always worship him as a savior.

He smiled when the boy stirred slightly, then turned over, his small hands tucked against his cheek. So sweet, so innocent. "Life is going to be perfect from now on, Travis." Wolfie closed the bedroom door quietly, then took the stairs two at a time, relishing his freedom and sense of purpose. It was time to honor his father by killing the people who needed to die, get the funds for his new life abroad, then find the perfect place to settle. He liked Travis's idea of a tropical island, but the small population and the isolation might grow tiresome. When the Eight were in hell where they belonged, he would discuss it with the boy.

He walked through the empty dining room and scooped the last of the caviar into his mouth. Zelda had an artist's temperament and was likely brooding somewhere. Normally, he wouldn't care, but she had things he needed. He eventually found her pacing furiously in her study.

"Calm down, Zelda. I have things under control."

She spun and leveled a malignant gaze. "You leave a trail of bodies, kidnap a boy, and there's nonstop coverage on national news when it could have been a footnote. And you think things are under control."

Her flair for drama was exhausting. "They were spur-of-the-moment, strategic decisions, all necessary."

"No, you do what you want, you always have, just like your father. What were you thinking, dragging that poor child along?"

"I already told you, it bought me the time I needed to get here. My only other option was to kill him and I wouldn't do that. I couldn't. It would have been an abomination against my father and God." His lips curled into a smile. "You should know that, as a nun."

"You think this is so funny? I devoted all my time and energy to your escape and making arrangements for your future. I even cultivated Annie Belinsky as a loyal client. Do you know how hard it's been to look her in the eye for two years and pretend I didn't want to kill her?"

"I'm grateful for all of that."

"Why did you kill Aleksandar? He loved you, he never would have betrayed you."

Wolfie scoffed. "Aleksandar has always been an avaricious pig and a liar. Once he executed the hack, he was not only useless, he was a threat. And the snake *did* betray me." And betrayed you, he thought, although he could never tell Zelda that Aleksandar had hacked her computer to get the account information at his request. "My only regret is I didn't have time to make him suffer."

Zelda sank into the chair at her desk. "You can't keep the boy, Wolfgang. It's too dangerous. And you can't stay here much longer or you won't survive. I've already spoken with my connections in Morocco and Hong Kong. You could be on a plane in hours and a free man when you land. Golden passports for your taking. Accept that gift and disappear."

"Travis stays with me—"

"Are you really planning to sacrifice yourself for him? Because he'll find out who you are and what you did and he'll turn on you. And me. Now he knows where I live because you brought him to my sanctuary, goddamn you. He's a liability."

"Travis is going to help me with my unfinished business.

Zelda shook her head briskly. "No, your unfinished business has to wait. Don't be an idiot and risk your freedom for valor. Even thinking about it now is insanity. There will be plenty of time for reparations at a later date."

"Avenging my father is a solemn duty."

She scowled. "I *know* that, Wolfie, I'm just asking you to wait and salvage your life."

"Justice is my only purpose now, and there is nothing more important. Waiting would be treason, the ultimate betrayal."

"Then you'd better dig a grave for yourself."

Wolfie glared at her. "Maybe you can live with being a coward and a traitor, but I can't. I won't."

She slammed her hand on the desk. "Shut your foul mouth. Your father wanted you to have the best life, not throw it away. You have a fortune in Bitcoin that he entrusted with me. Take it and leave immediately. Without the boy. I will arrange to have him returned to wherever he came from."

Wolfie felt the dark and ugly thing rise up inside him, a thing he couldn't always control. But he owed her everything, so he knew he had to calm down and end this conversation before he did something he would regret. Or would he regret it? "That's not going to happen, Zelda, and you know it. Did Aleksandar set up the computer in the safe room?"

She looked away briefly and nodded in resignation.

"Do you have everything else I asked for?"

"Yes."

"And a car?"

"Take Aleksandar's."

He studied her face. It had been very beautiful once, but now it was old, strained. No amount of surgery could hide the march of time. "When will Annie Belinsky be arriving?"

"You will *not* touch her here! You will not touch anyone on my property and bring the police to my door!" she hissed.

"My dearest Zelda, I think you've known me long enough to understand I'll do what needs to be done."

"Is that so? Perhaps you forgot that I'm the only person who has *all* the account information. Your father designed it that way to protect you. I have an obligation to him too, and that's to keep you from destroying your life. And mine."

Wolfie could almost feel his skin stretching as the ugly thing inside rose closer to the surface. Fucking Alex, fucking Zelda. "How do you expect me to start a new life without any money? You'll give it to me *now*."

Her eyes flashed in defiance. "I have an appointment to keep. You'll get it when Annie Belinsky is safely on her way home, then

I want you gone." She scrabbled in her desk drawer and tossed him a plaited leather fob with a single key. "The guest house I recently acquired in St. Paul. The Monkeewrench mansion is only a few blocks away."

"You're kicking me out?" he asked incredulously.

"You refuse to listen to logic, so, yes, I'm kicking you out. I love you with all my heart, but I won't pay for your mistakes."

Wolfie felt the last connection to his restraint snap, and he pulled the guard's baton from his waistband. "Then I'm sorry for you."

The last thing he anticipated was a lightning streak of movement as she chopped down on his wrist, disarming him with ruthless, martial arts precision. The pain was blindingly intense, and he bent over in his chair as a wave of nausea swamped him. He was a fool to forget what Zelda had once been and was still capable of.

"You should be ashamed. I know your father would be. You broke his heart so many times, but he never turned his back on you. *You're* the traitor, Wolfgang. And now I'm not so sure I'll give you the money. I don't think you deserve it."

She'd always been a manipulative, controlling *bitch*. She couldn't help herself. "That's not your choice, it was my father's."

Zelda ignored him. "You'll be safe at the St. Paul house, it's under one of the LLCs. Did I tell you Detective Magozzi is retiring?"

"No. So fucking what?"

"There's a party there tomorrow night. Everyone you hate will be there. And that's my parting gift to you. If you do regain your senses, I welcome you back. If you don't, I'll pray for you."

CHAPTER

34

ON THE WAY back to Dundas County, Iris tasked Sampson with ferreting out a decent coffee shop with a drive-through. She didn't want to walk into any public space in clothes that were certainly permeated with the smell of death. How could they not be? She'd been within kissing distance of three dead bodies in the space of a few hours. Even if she didn't stink of the grave, the experience must be branded across her forehead. G for ghoul, patron saint of corpses. She checked the rearview mirror. Nope, nothing there, but maybe it was something only other people could see.

Sampson excelled at his mission, finding not only a Benji's Java Hut right off the freeway but one with a Randy's Donuts across the street, also with a drive-through. A cop cliché paradise.

They sat in a CVS parking lot under the bare arms of a gingko tree, eating raspberry bismarks and slurping large blacks in companionable silence. They were both processing the case in their own ways, but she had no idea how Sampson arranged things in his mind.

To her, a mystery was like a children's game of blocks, each representing a clue or piece of evidence. You placed one on top of the other until you had a finished structure. Unfortunately, they'd run out of blocks before it was complete.

"I want to talk to Rieger. And to Drexler again."

"And all this time, I figured you were just gloating over how you took the bark off Gino," he teased.

"I wasn't and I didn't."

Sampson snuffled. "Are you kidding—did you see Magozzi? I thought he was going to suffocate, he was trying so hard not to laugh his ass off."

"Boys. All of you," she huffed, secretly pleased her little act of defiance had been noticed.

"But I know you're way too evolved for that kind of pettiness, so I honestly thought you were driving yourself crazy over what's on that flash drive like I am. I was wrong."

"Whatever's on that piece of plastic doesn't help us now, and it might not help us later. But that nun is the second accomplice and nobody's been able to find her, not even Monkeewrench. Drexler coordinates with security, but the buck stops with him when it comes to visitors, and he doesn't strike me as sloppy, so how did she get in more than once?"

"Am I catching the scent of conspiracy?"

"No, but it's weird. We've been sprinting so fast trying to reach the finish line, we never went back to the beginning. The guard, Danielle Rieger, worked with him for eight years, she knows him, the procedures, and has access to computers and cameras. She may have noticed something she didn't realize was important."

Sampson wiped powdered sugar from his lips with a flimsy brown napkin, musing on the difference between the way he and Iris saw things. He thought like a cop—a good one—but she thought like a detective. "I'll call Mercy."

* * *

Iris had always hated hospitals, just like everybody else in the world, but after her extended stay in one, they triggered an almost irrepressible panic. Seeing Danielle Rieger made it worse because she didn't see a stranger, she saw herself two years ago.

Her head was wrapped in gauze, and there were ugly black and yellow bruises cupping her bloodshot eyes from the impact of the blow to her head. Her face was screwed up, and she was very still—Iris knew all about that. When the pain was so bad, you didn't dare move.

"We're very sorry to disturb you, Ms. Rieger."

"I'm happy to have a distraction. Once the visitors go home, the pain and boredom settle in."

Judging by the floral arrangements on the window ledge, she'd had a lot of them. "We're very glad you're alright. Will you be going home soon?"

"I hope so, but the concussion is serious enough that they might keep me overnight for observation. Frankly, I'd rather have needles shoved under my fingernails. I hate hospitals."

A woman after her own heart. "I completely understand."

"I know you do. I'm very glad you're alright too, Sheriff. I voted for you and I'll vote for you again."

No, you won't, because I'm not running again. "That's so kind of you to say. We won't keep you long, just a few questions."

She nodded gingerly.

"Did you know Wolfgang Mauer?"

"I knew about him, knew he was dangerous, but I've never been in contact with him." She touched the side of her face and winced. "Except for this. I just don't understand how he could have gotten out. The security protocol at Gustavus is first-rate."

"The system was hacked. We believe Mauer was responsible through proxies on the outside."

Her jaw dropped in disbelief. "How? He never had visitors, no contact with anybody except Dr. Drexler or the medical staff."

"It's also possible he had inside help."

"Oh, no, that's not possible. It's not like a regular prison; our patients have no unsupervised time either with other patients or the staff, even in the open ward. And none of us would help a murderer."

"Dr. Drexler said as much, but apparently Mauer had one regular visitor, a nun from St. Bridget's named Sister Lucia. Does that sound familiar?"

"There are a lot of nuns who visit from St. Bridget's, but I don't know names or who they see. We just do a headcount from the approved visitors' list when they arrive, then check them out as they leave."

"Dr. Drexler approves all visitors?"

"Yes."

"Sister Lucia isn't from St. Bridget's; they'd never heard of her. We were surprised that slipped through."

Danielle Rieger was stunned. "That's not like Dr. Drexler, he's very meticulous. I suppose she could have come from another diocese. I really wouldn't know, you'd have to talk to him."

"We will. It seems odd that someone so meticulous would make that kind of mistake."

Clarity widened her eyes. "You think the *nun* is an accomplice and Dr. Drexler is somehow complicit?"

"We have to look at everything, even if it sounds unlikely."

She shook her head vehemently, regretting it when the pain in her head flared. "Dr. Drexler would never . . . it must have been an oversight . . . or maybe a typo."

And there it was, hesitation, uncertainty, and the flush that accompanied a secret about to see the light of day. "Ms. Rieger, if something is on your mind, please tell us. It could be very important to the investigation. Don't forget, we're trying to find a monster who's already killed three people since he escaped. By all accounts, you're lucky to be alive."

Her face went whiter than the sheet covering her, and she crossed herself. "Dr. Drexler hasn't been himself. I hear he's going through an ugly divorce. He's been distracted, sometimes short with us, which isn't like him at all. And . . . well, on a few occasions I've smelled alcohol on his breath. Hard times are no excuse for dereliction of duty, but he's always been a good man and an excellent administrator."

"Thank you for being honest, Ms. Rieger."

"Please don't tell him I said so. I don't want to lose my job."

Iris didn't mention that he probably wouldn't be around long enough to fire anybody. "You have our promise."

CHAPTER

35

WHEN GINO AND Magozzi arrived at Harley's sprawling red stone mansion, they found him crouched in the front flowerbeds, an Amstel Light in hand. Magozzi loved this fantasy kingdom replete with treasures and surprises, but knowing that Grace, Elizabeth, and Charlie weren't here left him with a hollow feeling. This place just wasn't the same without the full coterie in residence, and he suspected Harley felt the same way, otherwise he wouldn't have been aimlessly rooting around in gardens that had barely begun to show life.

Harley rose and lifted his bottle. "You two want a beer, wash off the road dust?"

"I'm too pissed off to drink," Gino seethed. "I can't believe that sack of shit slimed right out from under us."

"Ah, but you have a secret cloak-and-dagger flash drive, that's bound to be good. Come on, let's go see what's on it."

They followed him to the elevator, and Magozzi obsessed over the glossy, burled walnut panels as he always did. For some reason, this luxurious but relatively simple feature enchanted him—in his opinion, it was one of the most beautiful things in a house filled with them. Which made the cacti all the more mysterious. He didn't understand their place in Harley's myriad collections, but he suspected they were the source of fond memories from the past of an abandoned child who didn't have many. The man was an unabashed sentimentalist. "Still no luck with the IP?"

"Not yet, but we'll get there."

"I suppose it doesn't matter much anymore. It'll probably lead us right back to where we just were."

Harley gestured with his beer, sloshing a little on the rich green carpet of the elevator floor. "*Au contraire*, my friend. Aleksandar Nichols wasn't living there anymore, so he launched the attack from somewhere else. My guess is that's where you'll find Mauer, maybe shacking up with his fake nun."

Gino sighed in frustration. "Or maybe his fake nun gave him a different car and he's long gone."

"I would be. Unless he really is sticking around to kill us all, which makes him not only insane but a fucking idiot. You sure you don't want a beer? It'll cheer you right up."

"No offense, Harley, but if he's planning to kill us all, somebody should stay sharp."

He studied his bottle pensively, then took another swig. "There is that. But he's not going to last long enough to try."

Roadrunner was pacing the floor of the office when they walked in. Magozzi figured he could cover the considerable real estate in less than ten strides, where it would take a person of normal stature thirty.

"It took you guys forever to get here."

Magozzi smiled and turned over the flash drive. "That's because I was driving. Gino has been trying to get rid of me all day via vehicular manslaughter."

"I could get rid of you a lot easier than that without risking my own hide, Leo."

Roadrunner ignored them and rushed back to his desk with the enthusiasm of a kid at his first carnival. He plugged it in and started attacking his keyboard. "It's encrypted."

Harley rolled his chair over. "No shit. How deep?"

"Don't know yet, I'm working on it."

Harley glanced over his shoulder. "This could be a while, guys. Take a load off, or better yet, go see the new upholstery in the dining room. You're gonna love it, Leo, it's even better than your tie."

"It's supposed to be a surprise," Roadrunner scolded.

"Uh . . . yeah, eighty-six that, don't go anywhere near the dining room. Go back to the party. It's probably still in full swing."

"It is, I called on the way here." Gino pulled out his phone, scrolled, then passed it over with a wicked smile. "A video of Part One."

"That crazy fucker!" Harley roared, tears spurting out of his eyes. Even taciturn Roadrunner was shaking with restrained laughter.

"It wasn't *that* funny," Magozzi muttered, sinking into a marshmallow-soft sofa that offered a view of all the computer stations.

"Are you kidding me, you were busting a gut just like everybody else." Gino winced as he rubbed his side. "By the way, I think you bruised some of my ribs."

"I was laughing because I was in shock. I still am. In fact, I may need therapy."

"Bullshit!" Harley bellowed. "This is the funniest thing any of us will see in our lifetimes."

Roadrunner nodded his agreement. "Even I look better half-naked. McLaren must really love you."

Magozzi tried hard to remain stoic, to check the betraying smile that was yanking at his lips, but the effort was hopeless. "I do like the part where Gloria smacks him down."

Harley wiped the tears from his eyes as he tried to catch his breath. "Yeah, that was epic. Hell, if you don't go back to the fun, I will."

"Yeah, come on, Leo. We're not done with you yet, saddle up."

It was inevitable. And Magozzi was actually looking forward to getting his ego stroked some more. But his warm, fuzzy feelings were dampened by his recent ambivalence about his next step. A lot of people had gone to a lot of trouble to celebrate his retirement and what if he changed his mind? All the planning and parties,

McLaren's sacrificial humiliation, the new upholstery and Annie's dress . . .

Gino sat down next to him and nudged him hard in the ribs—fair play. "Hello?"

"Yeah, sorry, just let me check in with Grace first, give her an update." Her phone rang once, then went to voicemail. He tried two more times with the same result, which bothered him. Grace never shut off her phone and never let it go dead. The last time that had happened, she'd been trapped in the north woods of Wisconsin, hiding from an army of maniacs with automatic weapons. He knew he was overreacting, but he asked Harley about it anyhow.

"Probably a temporary glitch with the provider. Or maybe they're temporarily out of range."

"Out of range? Just where exactly is Annie's appointment?"

"I don't know. Do you, Roadrunner?"

"No clue, but she was complaining about the drive. Check her schedule; she's the only one of us who writes down everything."

"Because she's the only one who has manicures, facials, or massages every other day." Harley clomped back to his station and scanned the office calendar. "Says here Zelda, 938 Holliday Lane in Covina. That's kind of out in the sticks, forty minutes away at least. Probably spotty cell coverage there. Don't worry about it."

"Yeah, leave her a message and let's hit it, Leo."

They were on their way to the elevator when Roadrunner's voice stopped them. "Hang on, guys, I just got through the encryption."

"That's pretty weak encryption if you got in already," Harley needled.

"It was three-layer, 256, asshole. I'm just that good. But there's only one document and it's small."

"Whatever, open it, for God's sake."

Harley, Gino, and Magozzi gathered around him like warlocks conjuring a magic potion and waited breathlessly as he clicked his mouse. A single page appeared on the screen. Harley and Roadrunner scanned it, then both whooped in unison, but all

Magozzi saw were a bunch of numbers, letters, and symbols. "Looks like gobbledygook to me."

Harley was practically jigging in his clunky jackboots. "It's not gobbledygook, you're looking at money."

"Yeah, but what does it *mean*?"

Roadrunner looked up at them with the kind of tolerant smile reserved for the very weak of mind. "He means it's money, literally. The keys to Mauer's remaining kingdom: his crypto wallet, the exchange name, and the Bitcoin key."

Gino leaned over and squinted at the monitor. "How can you tell?"

"Isn't it obvious?"

"You're hilarious. Is there a username or password in that mess?"

"No, but it doesn't matter. Getting in is kindergarten-level stuff."

Harley was nearly salivating as he rubbed his hands together. "Gentlemen, we are going to clean him out just for fun and set up a honey trap. Once he accesses his account, we'll reel him in. Told you he wouldn't last long. Now move along, we've got work to do, and you, Leo, have loyal subjects waiting."

36

Dr. Drexler looked like he'd been savaged in a rugby scrum. His silver hair was sticking out from his head, his suit looked like it had been balled up in a closet for a year, and his face shone with perspiration even though his office was cold.

"I'm hoping you're here with good news, Sheriff, Lieutenant," he said glumly.

"Not yet, but things are moving very swiftly. I believe this might be the largest callout of manpower in the state's history, and we just heard the FBI is going to be assisting in the hunt. Mauer is living on borrowed time. Is there any progress on your end with the hack?"

Drexler shook his head. "IT is still working on it, as is Monkeewrench, I understand. Our maintenance staff is examining the generator and locking mechanisms in case there was also a physical failure, and my team and I are scouring footage from last night and this morning. I'm very concerned Mauer has either slipped away or found a place to go to ground."

"We'll find him wherever his is."

"I hope it's soon. How can I help you?"

"We have some follow-up questions about the nun imposter, then we'll let you get back to it."

"Go ahead."

"We'd like to know how she got through your security on multiple occasions."

Drexler scowled and tapped his computer monitor. "I've been looking through the St. Bridget files and I can't understand how it happened. Prior to visits, they send us a full list of nuns who will be attending, and a Sister Lucia was approved by them each time."

"But she obviously wasn't approved by them."

"I understand that. Something is wrong on their end, and I'm sure Mauer is responsible. If whoever was working for him found a way to hack our security, then he could easily do the same to St. Bridget's and add the name to the list."

It was a good point. "You don't conduct your own vetting process?"

He lowered his eyes. "Not as thoroughly with St. Bridget's, given our long-standing relationship, which is my fault. I'm sure you understand that I won't be here much longer, but I'll make certain my successor doesn't make the same mistake." He shook his head sadly. "In this world, you can't trust anything to be what it seems. Nothing is sacred anymore."

"You said Mauer requested the visits. Did he specifically ask for Sister Lucia?"

"I don't recall. I see dozens of patients in the course of a week."

"Which is why you keep records of your interactions with patients. Have you looked through them?" Iris watched a droplet of sweat run down the slope of his nose and plop on his desk blotter.

"All of Mauer's records, including audio of our sessions, were scrubbed in the hack."

"You must have them backed up to an off-site server or on the cloud."

"Both, but they're not there either."

She sagged in the same torturous chair she'd sat in earlier. Most leads in a case turned out to be dead ends. This was one of them.

"I grew up Catholic," Sampson offered, apropos of nothing. "Our nuns did a lot of community outreach. Nursing homes, hospitals, homeless shelters in the cities. They always went by bus. Is it the same with St. Bridget's?"

"Yes, of course."

"Then Sister Lucia had her own transportation. Do you have cameras that cover the parking lot?"

His weary face lifted hopefully. "We do."

Twenty minutes later, they had a screen capture of Sister Lucia getting out of a black Hyundai sedan, the rear California license plate clearly visible. Iris and Sampson fled Drexler's office like Satan himself was on their heels, without so much as a thank you or goodbye.

In the Gustavus lot, very near the spot where Sister Lucia had made the mistake of parking, Sampson plugged the plate number into the national registry. They were both shaky with adrenaline, caffeine, and sugar as they watched the spinning ball on the computer screen.

"I didn't know you were Catholic."

"Only on Christmas Eve and Easter Sunday."

"I was a lapsed Lutheran, but after Bulardo, I've been reconsidering my relationship with God."

"In this job, you either lose your religion or find it."

The spinning ball finally disappeared and the screen settled on a page. The Hyundai was registered to Aleksandar Nichols, Westwood, California.

Iris let out a dejected sigh. "This doesn't get us anywhere, it just confirms that the nun and Nichols were working together, which we already knew."

"It gives us more than that. Nichols drove the Nissan to pick up Mauer, so this car is still out there somewhere. And it might be Mauer's current getaway vehicle."

37

GORAN STARED BALEFULLY at the imposing iron gate and fencing that stretched as far as he could see. His blood was so hot with fury, he expected his flesh to blister any moment. First, Novak had insisted on camouflage, which brought back very bad memories, then refused to tell him where they were going or what to expect. They'd been driving forever, and now they were parked in front of an ornate gate in the middle of nowhere without explanation. Goran's temper was frayed to the last filament and it was torment to keep it intact, but he had to for now. "What the fuck is this place, Novak?"

"Zelda's house. She was my deputy chief—do you remember her? A very formidable woman of many skills."

"How would I remember who worked for you? So help me God, if you dragged me here so you could moon over an ex-lover's house, I'll shoot you where you sit."

"Don't be stupid. Zelda was an intimate of Peter's going back to the war and practically a mother to Wolfgang. He's here; I can feel him like crabs on my balls."

He scoffed in disgust. "And what's your plan? Storm the house based on your balls?"

"There you are, being stupid again. This is just recon. We confirm he's here, then we strategize."

Goran ground his molars and felt something give painfully. "How the fuck are we supposed to get in without setting off
security?"

"We find a suitable entry point with good cover and scramble
the Wi-Fi, which will disable the system. Then we walk in through
the woods and assess the situation. I have infrared sensors and nice
little things that drop a man without a sound in case there are
guards."

"And what if the security is hardwired?"

"Well, I guess we run like hell and reconnoiter."

"You are insane."

"And you have absolutely no sense of humor. You never did.
Contingencies are my specialty, trust me."

Goran felt a hard ball form in his stomach. Trust Novak.
Right. The only consolation was that he was an international fugitive too and had just as much to lose.

*   *   *

Travis held his breath as he swam up through murky water, desperately trying to reach the surface so he could breathe again. But
the water was an evil, living thing, a monster, pulling him down
deeper the more he flailed. His arms and legs were growing weaker,
weighted and useless from the long, bitter fight, and he felt himself
sinking down, down, down . . .

He jerked up in a strange bed and gasped for air when he
finally gained consciousness, blinked at a dim room he had no
memory of. His body ached worse than it ever had even after the
hardest beating, and there was a burning, throbbing pain in his
head that splintered his thoughts before they could fully form.
This couldn't be real.

But then he slowly became aware of something soft and very
real on his skin, the weight of a comforter, the fluff of pillows
beneath his head. A light breeze sifted in through an open window,
carrying the scent of lilacs. This wasn't a dream or a nightmare.

But how had he gotten here? Into these soft pajamas? Why was
his hair wet—did he go swimming? Fragments of the day began

to knit together, but there were a lot of blank spots. The last thing he could remember was sitting at a table with Wolfie and Zelda and drinking fizzy liquid that made him feel foggy and funny.

Travis crawled slowly and carefully out of the big bed, and his feet landed on plush carpet the color of plums. A wave of dizziness made the room tip crazily, and he had to steady himself against the wall as he looked around. Heavy cream curtains were partially drawn over floor-to-ceiling windows, and a vase of flowers sat on a cabinet that looked like it was made out of mirrors. At the foot of the bed was a bench with gold legs, its seat covered in some kind of curly, silky fur. He wondered if the legs were real gold. Probably. Someone like Zelda would only have real gold furniture.

He walked unsteadily to the door and peered down the hallway with the magic forest sculptures.

"Wolfie?" he called out tentatively. It felt weird to call him that, but he liked the nickname a lot. And Zelda had said that's what his friends called him. He smiled. They were for sure friends.

"Wolfie?" Still no answer. But the house was so big, they wouldn't be able to hear him unless they were nearby. He walked up and down the hall, calling out, checking rooms, then crept down the broad staircase, feeling like a thief even though he would never steal anything, not even gold. "Wolfie? Zelda?"

He got lost a dozen times winding through a great maze of rooms, and eventually circled back to the front door. Maybe they were outside; it was a nice day. And if he couldn't find them, he'd explore a little and go visit the swans on his own. He was sure Zelda wouldn't mind.

*   *   *

Goran was crawling through the sodden loam of the forest floor like a goddamned mudpuppy, fantasizing about killing Novak for many reasons. His primary grievance at the moment was being subjected to this indignity when it was clearly unnecessary. They'd breached easily enough, they hadn't seen another soul, and the infrared hadn't picked up any heat signatures, outside or inside. He was familiar with the workings of Novak's sadistic, damaged mind and was becoming increasingly convinced that he was being fucked with for the sheer sport of it.

"Mauer's not here. Nobody is here," he whisper-hissed.

"Be patient. Wait."

"For what, Mauer to suddenly materialize out of thin air?"

Novak suddenly tensed beside him and handed him his binoculars. "This is why patience is so important."

Goran snatched the binoculars and focused on a pathetic waif in black pajamas, ankle-deep in water as he tried to commune with two agitated swans. "This is so important? Some idiot kid talking to birds who probably have brains bigger than his?"

"He's not just a kid, he's *the* kid, the one Mauer kidnapped. I knew that bastard was here."

"When Mauer abducts somebody they get tortured and killed."

"Not little boys. I guarantee this is Mauer's new pet, like father, like son. We'll take him."

Goran almost lost it. "What the fuck are we supposed to do with him?"

Novak's jaundiced eyes flashed in the shadows of the trees. "He's bait. Mauer will do anything to get him back. You should know this—you're the one who gifted little Wolfgang to Peter in the first place. And you know what happened when you tried to take him back. It's full circle."

Goran did remember that unpleasantness. And the more he thought about it, the more brilliant Novak's impromptu plan seemed. People imagined full circles as lovely and poetic, but they were really just snakes biting their own tails. Now *that* was poetic.

CHAPTER

38

IT WAS GRACE'S understanding that most urban dwellers felt a
sense of tranquility when they ventured out of the city and into
the countryside—it satisfied an instinctive need to commune with
the natural world. But she always felt a frisson of panic instead of
peace. It was antithetical to logic—cities were filled with people
and people were dangerous—and yet most of the times she'd been
in mortal danger, it was out in the middle of nowhere where calls
for help went unanswered.

In the back seat of the Range Rover, Elizabeth was scribbling
in a coloring book with a pink crayon, chattering to herself or
Charlie, it was impossible to know for certain. In the shotgun seat,
Annie was applying a fresh coat of lipstick in the same shade as the
crayon.

"In my opinion, it's one part midlife crisis, one part separation
anxiety," she continued her running analysis of Harley. "I get it,
but it's purely pathetic for a grown man."

"Magozzi says men never grow up."

"No truer words have ever been spoken. I'm just relieved Harley saw the light without a lobotomy, something I've been considering for the past week."

Grace thought of the big man with an even bigger heart. When
he loved, he loved deeply and forever, but lives and relationships

were constantly shifting sands. Adapting to change was something they all shunned after chaotic childhoods bouncing between foster homes, group homes, and sometimes no homes at all. Permanence had become a holy grail, an unhealthy ideal impossible to attain. "I'm glad he talked to you. You weren't too hard on him, were you?"

"An iron fist in a velvet glove, it's the only way to get through to someone as mulish as he is. But there's no question in my mind that he'll find a new distraction, hopefully nothing as senseless as his cactus collection." She capped her lipstick and gazed out the window. "As much as I dearly hate the country, this is about as pretty as it gets. Such a shame it's chockful of dirt and bugs. Take the next exit, sugar."

*   *   *

Grace wasn't moved by luxury or displays of wealth, but she couldn't help but admire Zelda's estate. And it *was* an estate in the truest sense of the word, an idyllic country property with acreage, guest cottages, ponds, and a small lake nestled among undulating hills and woods. At the peak of a sharp rise, the view opened up, revealing a silvery ribbon of creek below, twisting through a standing audience of budding trees. The remoteness of this place predictably tweaked her nerves, but she was carrying both her guns, and nobody had tried to kill her in a while, so she tried to stuff down the paranoia. As she approached the enormous main residence, Elizabeth chirped in the back seat and pointed out the window.

"Pretty birds!"

"They're called swans, sweetie."

"Swams!"

"Swans. With a N."

Elizabeth took that under consideration. "Swamns."

Annie turned in her seat. "Swa-n."

"Swa-neh."

"You're a genius, little girl."

Grace stopped at the front walk. "Drop you here?"

"No, her studio's down that little road up ahead."

Grace piloted the truck down a charming, cobbled drive that led to a stone cottage tucked in a copse of mature trees. "Zelda's done well for herself."

"Because she's brilliant, and doll, she could work miracles with that old duster of yours. Zhuzh it up a little, maybe add some grommets and spikes. Or marabou feathers, that might work."

"I'll leave the drama to you, you wear it so well."

"Why, yes, I do, don't I?"

Grace had no use for fashion and knew nothing about it, but she was fairly certain it couldn't thrive in the vacuum of the rural midwestern countryside. She told Annie as much.

"Oh, Gracie, you're positively brilliant, but a fashion fetus. I'm getting you a subscription to *Women's Wear Daily*."

"I'm supposed to know who she is?"

Annie gaped in disbelief. "Zelda came out of nowhere and stormed onto the scene in Europe in the aughts, then moved her atelier to New York and became all the rage here. This is just where she comes for inspiration. Come meet her, she's a hoot, and she loves children and animals."

Grace couldn't think of a single thing less appealing, but there was no reason to be rude. "No thanks. I want to see if Harley and Roadrunner cracked the flash drive or traced the IP. And I should check in with Magozzi."

"Just come on in if you change your mind." Annie flounced out of the truck and blew her a kiss. "This shouldn't take long."

Grace smiled at the Monkeewrench diva mincing up the cobblestones, then unlocked her phone. No signal. Not particularly alarming considering where they were, but the paranoia she tried so hard to suppress started banging against the cage where she kept it imprisoned.

* * *

Goran pressed himself flat against the wet ground and held his breath while the Range Rover rolled by slowly, mere feet away, only risking a glance upward when he heard the sound of tires on pavement fade away. He jumped when Novak placed a heavy hand on his shoulder.

"Don't panic, they're gone."

"Don't panic? We have no idea who they are, what they want, or when they'll come back, goddammit. We need to get out of here."

"After we get the boy. Or Mauer. He has to show himself eventually."

Goran snatched the binoculars and focused on the swan pond. "The kid is gone, and I'm sure as hell not going to look for him or Mauer. We have to leave *now*."

"You're welcome to, but I'm not going anywhere without my money."

His money? Goran felt the knife he'd taken off the body of a Spetsnaz officer come to life, burning against his hip. It had a soul, a killing soul, he believed that. One that needed to be fed regularly, and right now it was very hungry. Novak had shown his hand, and by doing that, had rendered himself obsolete.

It was dinnertime.

39

WOLFIE HAD LOCKED himself in the safe room to ice his temper and his throbbing wrist so he didn't kill Zelda. Now that he'd crossed the mental Rubicon and come close, he realized he *would* regret it. In spite of their occasional philosophical disagreements, she had always been fiercely loyal. She'd engineered his escape and given him a future of his choosing. You didn't murder friends just because they annoyed you.

He couldn't understand why she was being so unreasonable, though. But then, she always had been a control freak, and the last thing he wanted was a dysfunctional relationship complicating his life, especially now that he had a son. Once he was far away from here—Morocco seemed like a better option than a tropical island—he would be far out of the sphere of her influence and he could start fresh with Travis.

His residual anger drained away as he checked the weapons, the boxes of electronic equipment, and the explosives. Beautiful, beautiful explosives, all prewired. As promised, she'd acquired everything he'd asked for, including smaller practicalities, like a nice cache of burner phones, signal jammers, and a new identity. Phone numbers for discreet private jet services and contacts in Morocco and Hong Kong. She'd even filled a box with makeup, prosthetics, clothing, and a wide selection of wigs. He was particularly fond of the long, gray dreadlocks. This was all he needed once he left the property, which would be sooner than planned, but he was convinced that fate was intervening, directing him down a different, better path. It wouldn't be the first time it had happened.

It made him nervous to wait until tomorrow night for his grand finale, and maybe he wouldn't have to; this was a fluid situation. But regardless, the guest house was in a perfect location. Zelda had promised it would be safe, and he believed her. She was many things but never a liar. However, autonomy was crucial because she was unpredictable, and he'd learned long ago you couldn't rely on anybody but yourself. He would get the account information on his own and then he would be totally free.

Child's play, he thought as he sat down at the computer. Aleksandar had hacked the information from Zelda as a failsafe, so of course it would be on this very machine. And Peter had given him the username and password a week before he'd died, as if he'd presaged his own imminent demise.

He started poring through files and logs, but after an assiduous search, a horrifying conclusion slowly began to unfurl in his mind like a poisonous flower. Everything was intact except one very important file, the only one in the log that was empty, wiped clean. That was virtually impossible to do, so he *knew* Aleksandar, that FUCK, had bleached it. Or possibly swapped out the motherboard because he'd been trying to control him. To fuck him. But he wouldn't have scrubbed Zelda's computer, it was too risky, and she was out of the house by now, in her studio with Annie Belinsky. At this very moment, Annie was probably being fitted for a beautiful new dress she would never have the opportunity to wear, at least not for long. It was an uplifting thought.

Buoyed by positivity, he locked the safe room, slid the concealing wooden panel back into place, and sprinted to Zelda's office. It was a clean, modern space in an otherwise overstuffed house. Not that her taste in décor wasn't as exquisite as her taste in clothing, but he'd always found it a little antiquated and stifling.

Wolfie was very pleased to see some of his father's photography on the walls and his favorite sculpture. He'd been too young to remember the massacre it referenced with any clarity, but he knew it was the greatest triumph of the war, killing hundreds of traitors, the same people who'd killed his parents.

He sat down at the birchwood desk and jiggled the mouse to wake up the screen, which was unlocked. Zelda had never been particularly security-minded when it came to electronics, something he'd been lecturing her about for years.

The monitor flickered and showed a page that informed him there was no Wi-Fi connection. No matter, he'd switch it over to ethernet when he was ready. All he had to do now was find the file. He kept his eye on the wall clock and his ears pricked for any sounds that would indicate she had returned.

After fifteen minutes, he hadn't found a single file that wasn't business related, and the rest were CAD design files, Adobe, or Excel, which soured his mood. It was possible she'd concealed the information in one of those programs as a feint. But he didn't have time to look at every goddamned one of them.

Wolfie scrambled in the only desk drawer, knowing she had a proclivity for all things analog. She even kept her passwords in a notebook. He groped through scissors and pens, lipstick, paper clips, a calendar, and several small journals that contained nothing but sketches and fabric swatches.

She was fucking with him, just like Alex, making sure she was the alpha and omega, the only person who could guarantee his success. He would have to apologize to her, and it refueled his irritation—*she* was the one who'd thrown the tantrum. *She* was the one being irrational. But once he had the final, most critical pieces of information—and he *would* get it, either voluntarily or by gunpoint—he could leave with Travis. Get settled in the guest house. Access his account. Plan for tomorrow or maybe tonight.

Travis. Jesus, he'd been so consumed, so plagued by obstacles, he hadn't even thought to check on him. He'd never heard of anyone having an adverse reaction to tranquilizers, but he was a child.

It would be tragic if he didn't survive long enough to enjoy the amazing new life awaiting him.

He rushed down the hall, pushed the door open quietly, and his heart stuttered when he saw the empty bed. "Travis?" he called, checking the bathroom, under the bed, the closet, and even the armoire.

He bolted out of the bedroom in panic, shouting Travis's name as he careened down the hallway and checked every second-floor room before bounding down the stairs. He envisioned him floating face down in the pool. The clever boy could have found it easily if he'd ventured far enough into the house to smell the chlorine on the lower level.

He wasn't there, or anywhere else in the house, which meant he'd wandered outside, probably to look at the stupid swans. He pushed open the front door and froze as it suddenly occurred to him that Monkeewrench would be helping the cops now just as they had before. If Annie Belinsky was here and saw Travis wandering around, or him wandering around looking for the boy, his plans would be destroyed. Unless he killed her, but that would cascade into a whole new set of problems. Zelda had been right about that.

He took deep breaths, trying to quell his panic. Every minute that passed, Travis was out in the open somewhere and he couldn't do a damn thing about it.

Serenity. Focus. Think.

And just like that pivotal moment at the Dunbar slum when Peter's words inspired him, he came up with a solution. It was waiting for him in a box in the safe room.

40

G RACE WALKED UP and down the cottage's driveway, trying unsuccessfully to capture a signal. This is why smart people who lived in the country still had landlines, but landlines were also susceptible to outages. Did they even think about what they'd do in an emergency if neither worked? Magozzi's lake house was remote, but it had perfectly reliable cell service and two landlines with different providers. She'd made certain of that before he bought it, although she still kept a satellite phone there too.

She climbed back in the Rover, where Elizabeth was conversing with Charlie in the special nonsensical language that always made her smile. The spring sun had heated the black interior, so she cracked the windows to let in the crisp, lilac-scented breeze.

"Mama, Chawry wants a swan-neh."

They would have to work on diction. "I think Charlie is silly. What would he do with a swan?"

Elizabeth consulted him, and Grace leaned back in her seat, enjoying the one-sided banter until she caught movement out of the corner of her eye. Adrenaline seared through her veins as she reflexively reached for the SIG Sauer under her arm. The reaction was instantaneous and exhausting, and the one thing in her life she couldn't control. She was working on it, but she had to work harder because Elizabeth would soon be old enough to notice, and that would teach her fear.

Her reaction had been a waste of adrenaline, as it often was—the offending party was a stooped old man with gray dreadlocks, wearing a broad-brimmed hat and coveralls. He was pushing a wheelbarrow full of mulch and his only weapon was a garden rake. Not the stuff of terror. Still, she didn't like how this place put her on edge, and she considered dragging Annie and her dress to the car and getting the hell out of here. But fleeing an elderly gardener would be a major setback. She would give Annie five more minutes before she went in.

*   *   *

When Wolfie spotted the Range Rover and none other than Grace MacBride, he was temporarily blinded by an explosion of emotions—mostly rage but also exhilaration. *Both* Monkeewrench women were here. And MacBride was oblivious to his presence and clearly feeling secure in her surroundings. He could take the two of them now so easily, consequences be damned. It would be Zelda's problem anyhow, and there was absolutely nothing to connect him to her.

The temptation was almost uncontrollable as his hand twitched on the Beretta in the pocket of his coveralls. He imagined the smell and taste of their fear when he confronted them. The euphoria of hurting them and watching them die. He would lose the opportunity to complete his entire mission before he disappeared, but maybe two was enough for now. A warning shot across the bow, a show of power. Go to Morocco, regroup and reenergize, then take the rest of them at a later date. He was certain his father would approve of this compromise.

*   *   *

Grace let out a gusty sigh of relief when Annie exited the cottage with a garment bag and the beatific smile of a woman who had just experienced religious transfiguration.

"Gorgeous?"

"Simply breathtaking. There are no words for the tambour beading on the yoke. Open the back gate, will you, sugar? This is a museum piece and requires its own passenger compartment. Preferably one without children or pets, no offense."

She complied. "None taken."

"Any word from the boys?"

"No service."

Annie slammed the gate, then climbed in, chucking Elizabeth's chin and patting Charlie's head before turning front and buckling up. "Well, then, let's get back to civilization before we get eaten by bears or lions or jackalopes."

*   *   *

When the Rover started to move, Wolfie slipped out of view behind the house and held the gun with a steady, two-handed grip. The Italians did a few things right: clothes, cars, and Berettas.

When he peered around the corner and saw the SUV draw closer, a smile curled his lips. Like shooting fish in a barrel . . .

A shrill cry pierced the air as a flash of black burst through the woods, heading straight for the driveway. Wolfie sprang across the lawn like a methed-out gazelle and intercepted Travis just as he was about to round the corner, knocking him down and pushing his face into the ground. "Don't make a sound. Don't even move."

The boy's body trembled and hitched with sobs beneath him. Wolfie was angry, very angry, but pity and remorse supplanted it. Travis was terrified, unquestionably revisiting ugly episodes from his past and probably thinking he might die this time. He was also feral and had no idea how to behave, especially since he hadn't been given any direction. Dammit, he should have laid down some ground rules.

"It's okay, just be quiet until I tell you it's safe." Wolfie eased off him, but the little shit flailed and screamed again. He had no choice but to smash his hand over Travis's mouth and drag him into the house through the garage. This was definitely going to erode some trust.

*   *   *

Grace braked suddenly.

"What's wrong, sugar?"

"Did you hear that?"

Annie listened and looked around. "I hear birds and frogs. What did you hear?"

"It sounded like a scream."

"Peacocks," she said decisively. "Zelda must have a dozen of them roaming around the property. Beautiful creatures, but they caterwaul something awful."

Grace loosened her death grip on the steering wheel, but she wasn't entirely convinced. "Maybe, but it sounded human to me."

"Have you ever heard a peacock before?"

"No."

"Trust me, they sound more human than humans, and they're not the only critters that do, especially around mating season, and we're smack in the middle of it. If you'd grown up in the Mississippi sticks like I did, you'd know this."

Grace nodded and took her foot off the brake. "I'm sure you're right." She wasn't sure at all, but she trusted her instincts, and they were telling her to leave this place.

CHAPTER

41

W HILE HARLEY WORKED on cracking into the Bitcoin account, Roadrunner retreated to the cold room that housed the Beast. When the array of processors was computing, it kicked out enough heat to self-cannibalize and melt the fragile circuitry. Hell, it kicked out enough heat to roast a hog, so he always kept the room at 65 degrees, lower if it was operating full-bore.

He sank into a plush sofa in front of a wall of monitors, each dedicated to a particular task. Harley had a penchant for hyperbole and had dubbed it mission control, but in truth, it really was like a miniature version of NASA's, just posher. He focused on the screen that detailed the current progress log, but there was nothing that needed eyes-on, so he relaxed and watched the green bar creep up until it was almost tickling sixty percent. Its incremental movement and the persistent background hum of the rigs was soothing, almost hypnotic. This room was his sanctuary, and he often retreated here for solitude, even if there was no work to be done.

A tap on the glass door startled him out of his contemplation, and he smiled at Petra and waved her in.

"I'm not interrupting any black magic, am I?"

"Even if I was entering nuclear codes to blow up the world, you wouldn't be interrupting."

"Since I know that will never happen, you're not scaring me."

He patted the sofa. "Tell me about your Zoom."

She kissed him on the cheek and sat down next to him. "It was Washington boring, although I did learn something interesting: a small bomb went off in Scheveningen. That's how Stanković was able to escape."

"He had high-level help."

Petra nodded. "He was once a very powerful man and apparently he still has important friends from those days. And whoever they might be, they're all evil."

"Does Interpol have any leads?"

"They wouldn't tell us if they did, not at this stage. But they requested our files on him, so I'm guessing not yet."

"They'll get him, Petra, just like we'll get Mauer." Roadrunner found himself staring at her bare ring finger, imagining what the amber and diamonds would look like there, then examined his own. How would he ever get a wedding band to fit over the mangled joint?

Petra was watching him curiously. "I don't know what's got you so fascinated, but your Beast is talking to you."

A soft chime filtered into his awareness. How hadn't he heard it? Sheepish, he returned his attention to the bank of monitors. Rows of information were populating one screen so fast, it was dizzying to watch. Finally, it stopped when it reached a set of numbers, flashing red against the black background. Roadrunner beamed at her like a proud parent.

"My baby got through, Petra! Get Harley, tell him we have an IP address." He barely registered her departure as his fingers flew across the keyboard, looking for the physical address that matched the IP.

Moments later, Harley crashed through the door like a tsunami, Petra right behind him. "Where did the hack come from? Is it Chanhassen?" His enthusiasm wilted when he got a good look at Roadrunner, who was startlingly unresponsive. "Shit, you look green, buddy, are you okay?"

Petra felt something fearful uncoil in her stomach, just as it had earlier, when Roadrunner had walked into her kitchen with a dark pall surrounding him. "*Dušo*, what's wrong?"

Roadrunner looked up at his best friend and hopefully future wife with panicked eyes. "The Beast traced it to 938 Holliday Lane. Where Grace and Annie are right now."

*　*　*

Magozzi's brain was on fire, and his guts felt like something savage had tried to rip them out. It wasn't the first time he'd been seized with heart attack–level terror when it came to Grace MacBride. And it was *his* fault for bringing Monkeewrench into law enforcement in the first place and putting them all in danger over and over again. But Grace didn't see it that way.

Have your ever heard of free will, Magozzi? We want—no, we need to help, because nobody was there to help us. Look at how many lives we've saved across the country with our software. It's a duty and a privilege, not a death sentence.

But what if it *was* a death sentence this time, for Grace, Annie, and Elizabeth? He slammed his hands against the dashboard. "Bloody hell, Gino, you pick now to drive like my fucking grandpa?"

Gino was calm as a rock, not because his heart wasn't ready to blow up, but somebody had to keep their head on straight. "I guarantee your grandpa never drove like this. I'm pushing one-twenty and Covina PD is on their way. Just keep calling Grace."

Magozzi lowered his head and squeezed his temples, trying to silence all the bad thoughts colliding in his head. "What if he's there, Gino?"

"Don't even think about it." He listened to Grace's phone ring through the speaker, then roll to voicemail again. "Are Harley and Roadrunner positive about this? I mean, what does a famous designer have to do with Nichols and Mauer?"

"Not a single connection they can find so far. That's the weird thing."

"So maybe it's a mistake, computers aren't perfect. Or a misdirection. We know Aleksandar Nichols was working from Chanhassen—"

"Nichols wasn't in Chanhassen when the hack went down," Magozzi said impatiently.

"But it doesn't mean he was at this Zelda person's house. He could have set it up to look like it was coming from some random address when he was someplace else. Isn't that what Tor is for, to hide where you are?"

Magozzi held his breath for a minute so he didn't hyperventilate. "I appreciate what you're trying to do, but it isn't helping."

"I'm not done. Why would Nichols execute the hack from Covina, which is at least an hour away from Gustavus? He wouldn't, he was the pick-up guy. If everything went according to plan, he had to be down there to scoop up Mauer at a moment's notice. After all the planning, he's not going to leave him roaming around in the woods, waiting for a ride. I'm telling you, Covina is a ruse."

"That is really lame, Gino, and you know it."

"Come on, I have a point."

Magozzi was so far into the red zone that there was zero solace in conjecture. "I just have one question."

"Ask away."

"Does this piece of shit go any faster?"

CHAPTER

42

WOLFIE SET TRAVIS down on a bench in the mudroom and crouched in front of him, sickened by the fear and shock in his eyes and the tears staining his cheeks. "I'm taking my hand off your mouth now, but don't scream. You're safe."

Travis recoiled and curled into a shivering, fetal ball. "Who . . . who are you?"

He tore off the hat and dreadlocks. "It's me, Wolfie."

"It's really you?"

He patted the boy's head and his heart squeezed when he flinched. "It's okay, it's really me."

"But . . . why were you wearing a disguise? Why did you scare me and throw me on the ground?"

"I'm sorry, but I couldn't help it. Travis, there are some very bad people who want to hurt me. I had to keep you safe so they didn't hurt you too, and it was the only way."

Travis sniffled and wiped his nose on the sleeve of his cashmere pajamas, which horrified Wolfie but would have enraged Zelda. Thank God she wasn't here to see it; she'd probably take off his head.

"Are they the same people who hurt the man?"

Wolfie sank back on his heels as acid flooded his stomach. "What man?"

"In the woods. I think he might be . . ." A fresh spate of tears spurted from his eyes.

No, that was impossible. He'd been making up stories and spooked himself. "It was probably just a trick of the light—"

"I'm not lying!" Travis shouted.

Zelda burst into the mudroom and froze when she saw Wolfie in coveralls, the discarded wig, and Travis in full meltdown. "What the hell is going on?"

Wolfie stood with a conciliatory expression that pained him deeply. "Travis woke up and went exploring. I had to get him inside before . . ."

She nodded brusquely and knelt by the bench. "Why are you so upset, Travis?"

"Tell Zelda about what you thought you saw in the woods."

"I . . . did see it. A man. He wasn't moving, and there was . . . there was blood."

She rose unsteadily. "Where?"

"B-behind . . . the . . . shed. B-by the pond."

Zelda went to a closet and retrieved a pistol from the gun cabinet she kept there. "You two go upstairs to the safe room and stay there, do you understand?"

"I'm going with you," Wolfie said.

"NO. We don't know who he is or if there's somebody else out there. Upstairs now, I'll handle this." She slipped off her python stilettoes, prototypes of the flagship shoe for her next line, ironically themed "Snakes in the Garden." How very appropriate.

"Why aren't you on your way upstairs?" she snapped, pulling on a pair of mud-brown rubber boots.

Wolfie glared at her as he tried to pry Travis's hands from the bench. "I'm working on that."

"Travis, go upstairs now!"

He looked up at her with liquid, fearful eyes that went dead at the same time his body went limp. Wolfie had to carry him upstairs again.

43

Zelda found the body only a few yards into the woods; the killer hadn't even bothered to conceal him. His neck was bloody carnage, but his face was intact, and she almost dropped to her knees when she recognized it. How was it possible that Novak was *here*? How was it possible that someone had killed this devil who she thought would outlive them all?

The shock wore off quickly—once a soldier, always a soldier—and she moved in to examine his body. His throat had been cleanly slashed; he'd been betrayed by an equally skilled comrade, but she couldn't begin to imagine who that might be or where they were now. The only thing she was certain of is that they would be back. If they'd ever left.

The shadows of the past are very long. Always remember that, Zelda.

Peter in his infinite wisdom.

She spun around when she heard the schuss of tires on the drive and screamed inside when she saw a police cruiser through the tree trunks. She'd forgotten to close the gate after Annie had left and now there were *cops* here? This was a monumental disaster. Everything was starting to implode and she had no idea why or how it had happened.

She tossed the gun into the woods, kicked some leaf litter over Novak, then emerged calmly, willing her heart to slow. Two young officers got out, looking around in their suspicious, wary way. But they were also jittery, like they were expecting an ambush. Another bad sign.

"Good afternoon, officers." She forced brightness into her voice. "How can I help you?"

The slender, brown-haired one appraised her fine dress and mud-covered boots. God, she hated cops. They always saw something in nothing. Of course, this time there *was* something.

"Is everything alright here, ma'am?" the plump blond partner asked.

"Just fine, except I haven't been able to find any morels. They should be popping up everywhere after all the rain." She glanced down at her boots, praying to God she hadn't stepped in any blood.

He smiled in surprise. "I was hunting myself this morning. I found a few small ones, but we need some heat to really get them going."

"You're exactly right, I should have thought of that. What brings you here?"

"We have reason to believe there's a dangerous fugitive in the area. We're checking around to make sure everybody is okay."

Acid crept up her throat. "How terrifying. I'll be sure to keep my security armed at all times."

Skinny brown looked at her skeptically. "Have you seen anything or anyone suspicious?"

"I rarely leave the property, so I haven't seen a single soul in days, except for a client earlier and she's left."

He glanced up at the house. "You're not being held against your will, are you?"

The question was so preposterous, Zelda couldn't hold in her laughter. "Goodness, no! A very kind captor it would be if they let me go morel hunting. This is my sanctuary, Officer, and I take great precautions to keep everyone out." So why hadn't the security system alerted her to Novak?

He shrugged. "That's good to hear. If you see or hear anything out of the ordinary, call 911 immediately."

"I absolutely will. If that's all, I must get back to my work."
They didn't want to leave, that was obvious.

"Thank you for your time, ma'am. Two Minneapolis police are on their way here, Detectives Magozzi and Rolseth. They need to speak with you too."

The blood drained from her face and she hoped they hadn't noticed. "I'll watch for them. Have a good day, gentlemen."

44

Gino tossed his phone in the console, then accelerated into a curve on the twisting country road, slingshotting into a straightaway. "Covina didn't see anything suspicious. No sign of the Rover or anybody else but Zelda, who said Annie left."

"That doesn't mean shit."

"Don't go where you're going, Leo."

Magozzi scraped his hands through his hair, wanting to tear it out because the pain would distract him from one far worse. "If they already left, their phones would be working by now. Christ. What's our ETA?"

"Ten minutes."

Not soon enough, Magozzi thought, frantically stabbing at his phone, pleading to anybody or anything that might be listening that Grace would finally answer. That hope was the only thing keeping him from spiraling into insanity. He was so deep down the rabbit hole of despair, he nearly hit the ceiling when the phone blatted out Grace's ringtone.

"Grace! Where are you?"

"We're headed back, we just got cell service—"

"Thank God." Magozzi released a huge blast of air and collapsed against the seat. "You're on the freeway?"

"Yes. You called about a thousand times, what's wrong?"

"Roadrunner traced the IP to Zelda's."

She was silent for a long moment. "That can't be a mistake."

"I don't think so, either. We're on our way, almost there."

Grace relayed the information to Annie, who yelped in disbelief. "I'm putting you on speaker. Tell us everything."

"Not much to tell. Covina PD just left Zelda's and they didn't see anything unusual. But if Mauer's there, he's not going to be outside playing croquet."

"Did Harley and Roadrunner find a connection between the two of them?"

Why did Grace sound so unbelievably calm when his voice was shaking like aspen leaves in a stiff wind? "They haven't found one yet. Annie, text them right away and let them know you're okay. They're as freaked out as we are."

"I just did. We're safe, Magozzi, so you and Gino can turn right around. You've got a whole platoon of folks hunting him, so let them handle it."

"You know we can't, not if there's a chance Mauer is there."

"Just wishful thinking that you two weren't stubborn asses like every other man I've ever met. Tell me this, how will you know if he's there? Like you just said, he's not going to be lollygagging outside playing lawn sports, he'll be holed up in the house, out of sight and out of reach without a warrant. And an IP isn't enough to get you one."

"They'll know," Grace said resolutely, trying to allay some of the panic on the other end of the line. "The best detectives on the planet, right, Gino?"

"Damn right."

Magozzi was thinking how great it was to feel a smile on his lips again, even though it was totally inappropriate, considering the fact that they might end up in a gunfight with Mauer soon. "How is Elizabeth?"

"Fine. I'm sure she'd love to say hi, but she's having a deep philosophical discussion with Charlie about swans. More on that when I see you."

"Did the boys crack into the flash drive?" Annie asked.

"Info on a Bitcoin account, presumably Mauer's secret cache, but they don't have a username or password. They're working on hacking it right now. Annie, have you known Zelda for a long time?"

"Only two years. I don't know her personally, but I've spent plenty of time with her."

Magozzi felt a cautionary tingle in his spine. Two years ago, they'd busted Praljik and Mauer. "I don't like the timing. Did you seek her out?"

"No, she approached me at New York Fashion Week. I couldn't believe it, I almost fainted . . ." Annie paused. "Oh, sweet baby Jesus, you think it was a setup."

"Was she acting unusual today?" Magozzi asked through gritted teeth.

"Not one bit."

"Did either of you see or hear *anything* strange?"

Grace answered tensely. "I thought I heard a scream as we were leaving, but Annie says it was a peacock."

"I didn't hear it myself," Annie clarified, "but Zelda has scads of them."

"Was there anybody else on the property?"

"I saw an old gardener with the most amazing gray dreadlocks pushing a wheelbarrow full of mulch. That's it," Grace said.

"You didn't tell me that, sugar."

"It wasn't worth mentioning. I'm sure Zelda has more staff than the White House."

Gino jumped in. "Anything else we should know? We're going in blind."

"It's a huge property. Lots of cottages scattered around and thick wooded areas."

Grace didn't sound so calm anymore, and the strain in her voice was killing Magozzi. *My fault.* "Be careful and pay attention to every single vehicle you see. I want regular texts until you get back to Harley's. We'll meet you there when we're done."

"You be careful too. Both of you."

It was the second time today she'd said that. "Always. Kiss Elizabeth for me." He panicked when the connection cut out briefly. "We're losing you. I love you, Grace."

But he didn't hear her response because his phone dropped service.

45

T RAVIS HELD HIS breath the entire time it took Wolfie to carry
him upstairs. When he placed him gently on a sofa and covered him with a fleece blanket, he curled into a ball like woolly
caterpillars did when you touched them. He was numb with terror,
so all the boxes and computers and guns in the otherwise bare room
didn't really register. But he knew this was all serious trouble.

"Drink this water, Travis. I don't want you to get dehydrated
or you'll get sick."

He eyed the bottle. "I'm not thirsty."

"That's the first sign of dehydration. Drink."

He took the bottle reluctantly. When the water hit his parched
tongue, he realized he was incredibly thirsty and gulped until it
was almost empty.

"Good boy. Now take a little rest."

"I'm still cold."

"I'll have Zelda get you a jacket when she comes back."

He nodded and pulled the blanket over his head because
cocoons kept caterpillars safe. He'd known that for most of his
life, even before he'd learned about it in school.

"Everything's going to be okay when you wake up."

But everything *wasn't* going to be okay because there was a
bloody dead man in the woods and bad people were after Wolfie.

And maybe he was bad too. He definitely wasn't his big brother anymore. Big brothers didn't lie to you about going swimming and watching movies, and they didn't hurt you. He wasn't at all what he pretended to be—he probably didn't repossess cars for a living—and it scared him. And Zelda wasn't so nice after all either. They were both fakers. His parents were drunks and mean sometimes, but at least he knew what to expect.

He peeked out cautiously. Wolfie was unpacking boxes and laying the contents out on a long table. "What's going to happen now?"

"We're going to leave soon."

"Where are we going?" Travis cringed when he saw anger in his eyes.

"To the Cities. No more questions, I have work to do."

The tears started again, tickling as they crawled down his cheeks. "I want to go home."

"I'll take you home, Travis, just not now, okay?"

His body shook with sobs, and he stuffed the blanket in his mouth to mute them. But still, he kept watching. Wolfie was now transferring the things from the table to a big suitcase with wheels. He didn't know what most of it was, but he recognized a bunch of phones in a clear plastic bag. And remembered his mom telling him one time she was on the wagon to call 911 if there was ever a time he didn't feel safe.

Don't call Malcolm or Grandma and Grandpa, call 911. Do you understand? This is important.

Zelda burst into the room, and he retreated back to his cocoon and played dead, which was easy, because he was suddenly feeling very sleepy.

"Out in the hall, Wolfgang, now! We need to talk in private."

He listened for the sound of the door closing, then waited until he heard their muffled voices on the other side before he sat up. He was alone now and was sure it was going to take a while for her to tell him about the dead man. All he needed was a few minutes.

He crawled toward the suitcase, holding his breath again so he could hear if they stopped talking or if the door suddenly opened.

If it did, he would play dead again or maybe fake a seizure like he'd seen a spy do in a movie to fool the bad guys. Now or never.

The only problem with his plan was that he was very dizzy now, the room suddenly blurry. His legs and arms were so heavy, he felt like he was trudging through thick sludge, like the mud at the farm when it rained hard like it had last night. But there were just a few more inches to go before he reached the bag with the phones . . . Just a few more inches . . . Be a strong and brave caterpillar . . .

*   *   *

Wolfie had never seen Zelda frightened, which frightened him. She was fierce, she was a warrior, she always had things under control. If she fell apart, the last link that held this chain together would snap.

"The local cops were just here. Looking for you. I got rid of them, but they said Magozzi and Rolseth are on their way."

Wolfie sagged against the wall because his legs weren't going to hold him without support. "Jesus—"

"How did they know to come here?"

"It has to be Aleksandar," he said dully. "He fucked up something and Monkeewrench traced the IP."

"That doesn't explain Novak."

"What are you talking about?"

"The dead body in the woods. It's Novak."

He pressed his hands to his head, trying to hold his mind together before it shattered into a million pieces. "Is he after you?"

"We parted on good terms over twenty years ago, so I imagine he's after *you*. And your money. What I don't know is how he found me, found out about you, or how he knew you would be here. But that doesn't matter now; he's dead. What does matter is who killed him and where they are now. You have to leave immediately. Load up what you can and take Aleksandar's car, it's in the shed on the far end of the property. Drive out the back way. Do you remember the trail through the woods that leads to the dirt farm road?"

Wolfie nodded woodenly, trying to comprehend how things had gone so bad so fast.

"Nobody knows about it." She withdrew a slip of paper from the pocket of her dress. "Here it is—all the account information in case something happens to me."

Wolfie sighed in relief. He hadn't *really* believed she'd withhold it, but even people you'd known your whole life could surprise you in the worst ways. "I'm sorry about before, Zelda. It was the stress."

She patted his cheek, appeased. "I believe you, Wolfie. I'll be in touch after the detectives leave. I've numbered all the burners and activated the first one. Get rid of it when we're finished talking and use the rest in order. The boy?"

"He drank most of the water. He'll be out soon."

"You're keeping him, then."

"It was never a question."

She reached out to clutch his hands. "I'm begging you one last time, Wolfie, get on a plane and leave. You won't find your revenge back in Gustavus or the grave. I don't want to lose you."

He felt the warmth of her sincerity and again regretted trying to kill her. She was his savior, his family, and she deserved the loyalty she'd given, the loyalty that he demanded from everybody else. How could he have thought any less of her? "Thank you for everything, Zelda. I mean that with my heart. Travis and I look forward to hosting you in Morocco. I've decided on that. Tangiers, I think. It's such a vibrant city."

46

M AGOZZI DIDN'T KNOW what to expect because Zelda, a
woman without a last name, had a very small online presence and there wasn't a single photo of her on the website. She let
the clothes do the talking, and to say her sensibility was eccentric
was like calling Mount Everest a hill.

As they approached the house, he saw a perfectly coiffed older
woman waiting on the broad front porch. Compared to the designs
he'd seen on the site, she looked downright demure. Still, her kaftan was loud enough to disturb the wildlife, and the gold jewelry
that weighed down her tiny body was probably worth more than
his pension. She smiled, waved, and gestured to a pitcher of lemonade and three glasses sitting on a cloth-covered table.

"This is really bizarre," Gino mumbled.

"Covina told her to expect us."

"Even unhinged people don't roll out the Welcome Wagon for
the cops."

"I think she's just forestalling the possibility that we would invite
ourselves in so she doesn't have to tell us to go fuck ourselves."

"That's a damn big house, Leo. Mauer could be anywhere in
there. Eyes wide open."

Magozzi got out first, eyes definitely wide open as he assessed
the windows. Most of them were shuttered, which required greater

scrutiny. Gun barrels were small enough to fit between the louvers without notice unless you were paying close attention. He didn't see anything, but he didn't relax, not by a long shot. "Miss Zelda?"

"The one and only."

"I'm Detective Magozzi, this is my partner Detective Rolseth."

She clasped her hands together and her rings clattered. "It's a delight to meet you both, Annie Belinsky has told me much about you. All good things, of course," she tittered flirtatiously. "Come, join me. Lemonade?"

"No thanks," Gino said in bad cop gruff.

"You have a beautiful home, ma'am," Magozzi countered with good cop pleasant.

"Thank you, Detective Magozzi. It's my place of peace and serenity. New York can be so tiring. Please sit."

Magozzi was happy to get under the covered porch. This *was* weird, but she wasn't a hostile witness, at least not yet, so it wasn't unpleasant. Unless Mauer was lurking behind the front door ready to shoot them. "Covina told you we're looking for a fugitive?"

"Yes, very frightening, but as I explained to them, I haven't seen a soul for days. Except Annie earlier."

"Wolfgang Mauer. Do you know him?" He waited for a tell, but she just stared at them blankly. It was convincing.

"He's not in the fashion business so I don't know the name. Should I?"

"He's the fugitive," Gino said brusquely. "You don't watch the news?"

"Never. It's far too depressing these days."

"He escaped from Gustavus Adolphus Security Hospital this morning. He's a killer and extremely dangerous."

"That's precisely why I have the best security money can buy. The world is on fire. If he's in the vicinity, he won't get in. Although I don't know why he would be. If he was smart, he'd be out of the state by now or out of the country."

A deflection? Magozzi wondered. Or simply an observation? She was hard to read.

Gino folded his hands on the table. "That's kind of what we were thinking, but the thing is, we just got some information that traces him to this address."

She looked truly befuddled. "Then I'm afraid you have bad information. Only a very select few of my clients know this place even exists. No one else, and certainly not a killer."

"You have a lot of buildings on the property—you ever rent out to anybody?"

"Heavens, no, I would never violate my haven. And to what end? I certainly don't need the money." She leaned forward conspiratorially. "My vocation requires me to be a social butterfly, but truth be told, detectives, I don't like people very much. I like them less on my property."

Touché. "You could have fooled us, you're a great hostess. Or are you just a good actress?" Gino needled her.

"That's exactly what I am, Detective Rolseth, as are all good hostesses and business people. And as long as we're on the topic, are you sure I can't pour you some lemonade?"

Whatever she might be, Magozzi had to admire her wile. "We're sure, but thank you. Do you know Aleksandar Nichols?"

"I've never heard that name either. Is he also a dangerous fugitive?"

"We believe he helped Mauer escape," Gino grumbled.

"I'm sorry I can't help you."

She was getting a little snippy, so Magozzi changed tack. "Your accent. French?"

She beamed. "I'm from Beaune, the wine capital of Burgundy, a magical place. French accents give you automatic credibility in the fashion industry, so I never endeavored to get rid of it."

"Mind if we take a look around while we're here?"

She smiled slyly. "Of course I mind, Detective Magozzi. This is private property."

"I had to try."

"I understand. Now, if you were to come back with a warrant, I would be more than happy to show you around, but I don't think your information is that good."

Gino was pissed because she was as guilty as hell in his opinion, but she was right about the warrant. He scanned the grounds. "This is a big place. It must take a lot of staff to keep it up."

"It does, you wouldn't believe."

"We'd like to talk to them. They may have seen something you didn't, especially any outdoor workers. You don't seem concerned about your safety, but we are."

Magozzi thought he saw a flicker in her eyes, the slightest fracture in her veneer, but then it was gone.

"Nobody is here today. I give them Fridays and Saturdays off."

"All of them?"

"Yes. They deserve time with their families, especially on the weekends."

That was a mistake, and Magozzi wondered if she realized it. One thing was certain—they wouldn't be getting any more out of her. He didn't want to tip their hand by mentioning the gardener, who was probably Mauer, although he couldn't fathom why he'd be posing as a worker. "Well, I guess that's about it, then. Thanks for speaking with us, Miss Zelda."

"It was a pleasure. I certainly hope you find this person quickly. I'm a bit on edge now after our conversation."

"Be very vigilant."

Gino stood and gestured to the swan pond. "Gorgeous birds. Only ones prettier are peacocks in my opinion."

"I agree. I used to have several peacocks, but unfortunately, they all contracted avian flu last summer and they had to be destroyed. Very sad."

"I'm sorry about that. You take care, ma'am."

47

G INO AS FUMING as he piloted down Zelda's mile-long driveway. "Oh, she was good. And lying through her teeth."

"Yeah, but we're not going to get a warrant based on a gardener and peacocks. And even Tolstoy couldn't come up with a
story that justified exigent circumstances."

"You know goddamned well she's the nun too. That could get
us a warrant."

"We can't prove it with a crappy video that doesn't even show
half her face, and that's all we've got."

Gino grunted in frustration. "What I don't get is how she
could be tangled up with Mauer. It doesn't make any sense."

Magozzi had been thinking about that too, and her kaftan
and the designs on her site had sparked something. "Maybe he's a
client. Or Praljik was. You remember how flamboyant that bastard
was, in his furs and crazy suits."

"I can see that, but no way a woman of her stature is going to
put her head on the chopping block and risk everything for a killer
client's killer son."

"You have a point. We're missing something." He scrolled
through his missed calls and saw Iris Rikker had pinged him almost
an hour ago. He didn't feel like talking to her or anyone else, so he
accessed his voicemail and put it on speaker so Gino could listen.

"Detective Magozzi, this is Iris Rikker. Lieutenant Sampson and I identified the vehicle the nun drove to Gustavus. A black Hyundai sedan with California plates registered to Aleksandar Nichols. I emailed the details and we put out a BOLO. We'll talk soon."

"Huh. That was some sharp work," Gino said.

"Very. But no hits yet or otherwise my phone would be on fire. That son of bitch has been one step ahead of us this whole time."

"His luck can't last forever, Leo. You better call Rikker back and give her an update. It's her case, after all."

"It feels an awful lot like ours."

"It's a tandem." He glanced over at Magozzi. "You look like you need a stiff drink and a nap."

"All I need is to see Grace and Elizabeth."

"You just talked to her. They're okay."

"I know, but I'm still scared shitless. I can't get rid of it."

Gino nodded in understanding. "There are canned margaritas in the cooler behind my seat. Wash the adrenaline out of your system and I'll call the sheriff."

"You brought margaritas to work?"

"It wasn't supposed to be a work day, remember? And I'm pretty pissed about it. I didn't even get any cake."

Magozzi winced at a sharp pain in his stomach, reminding him that he hadn't eaten since the Pig's Eye. And he didn't care. "You know where this is going, Gino. Mauer should have been long gone by now. Instead, he was parading around dressed like a gardener less than an hour ago."

"The dumbass is actually coming for us."

"Right. I'm calling the chief and ask him to pull every cop in the metro to form a cordon so tight around Harley's they can hold hands."

"Call McLaren while you're at it. He'll have every person from your party marching Summit Avenue with slings and arrows. Go all Braveheart on Mauer's ass."

"He's Irish, not Scottish."

"Same neighborhood, close enough."

48

GORAN CAME ACROSS the trail by chance. When he'd seen the cop car through the trees, he'd bolted like a startled deer and gotten disoriented, then hopelessly lost in what seemed like an endless forest. With no sense of direction and no idea where Novak's truck was parked, he'd wandered aimlessly, trying to keep his mounting panic at bay. He was bloody, he was armed, and he was probably one of the most wanted men in the world by now. Contact with anyone would be a death knell.

And then providence smiled on him. He stumbled onto a creek, a tiny, squiggly thing, purling over rocks and deadfall. He stripped off his bloody camo jacket and shoved it under some brush and leaves. Then he scrubbed his face and hands in the frigid water and washed off the knife. Not perfect, but it was good enough to pass cursory scrutiny. He took the creek as a portent, so he let it be his guide. As long as he kept it in sight at all times, he had bearing. That's what led him to the trail—two muddy tracks with a strip of greening grass between them. It led somewhere, and he hoped it was to the truck. He had plenty of problems—how to get to Mauer and what to tell Novak's people were chief among them—but you had to solve problems one at a time, just like you climbed a ladder one rung at a time.

When he heard the unexpected purr of an engine behind him, he dove into the underbrush and hid behind the trunk of a mature oak. It was getting closer, and it wasn't an ATV, the only thing that should have been on a trail like this one. He watched and waited, then caught a flash as sun hit chrome. Through Novak's excellent binoculars, he saw a black sedan, slowing bumping along the rutted track right toward him.

Praise Jesus. Mauer was behind the wheel, the boy in the passenger's seat. Novak's balls had been right. He stayed parallel and out of sight, dodging brambles and trees until the path terminated at a narrow dirt road that cleaved fields of stubbly green shoots. He knew this road because Novak had parked somewhere around here.

Mauer turned right, and ironically, let Goran know exactly where the truck was by pausing near a cluster of birch. He remembered it well because the brilliant white bark and all-seeing eyes had evoked vivid memories of the forests of his youth. After a few moments, Mauer goosed the accelerator, tires spewing rooster tails of mud, and Goran stumbled through the cover of woods toward the Suburban.

*   *   *

The country roads were mostly empty, so Goran hung far back as he followed and almost lost Mauer a few times. He seriously considered running him off the road and taking care of business out here, but it would only take a single passing car to see the accident and call 911. And if Mauer was stubborn, it might take a while to torture the username and password out of him, which increased the likelihood of a passerby and he really didn't want to kill an innocent. No, it was better to wait until Mauer got to his next destination and take things from there. Contingencies were also his specialty.

It surprised him a little that Mauer chose the freeway instead of staying on back roads, but once they were on 35, things got easier. Traffic became his blind, and he was able to stay close without risk by keeping at least two cars between them. It was tense driving, but he had experience tailing people and he knew the techniques and maneuvers that would ensure success.

Eventually, the Minneapolis skyline came into view, and he checked the gas gauge, relieved that there was still over half a tank. He had no way of knowing where Mauer was headed, but he figured he could make it at least two hundred miles, even in this petrol-guzzling monster.

Fifteen minutes later, Mauer surprised him again by merging onto a crowded freeway that would bring him right into the heart of St. Paul. The idiot should be driving as fast and as far as he could away from civilization, yet he was driving straight into it. Which meant he had another safe house. A perfect place for Goran to complete his task.

Novak had left him with many weapons to choose from, but a simple .22 to the knee would accomplish exactly what he needed. He didn't expect trouble from the boy, but if he did cause a problem, he would have to neutralize him. Generally, he tried to avoid harming or killing children, but sometimes they just didn't listen.

CHAPTER

49

IRIS WAS HUNCHED over a map, marking it with red Xs. "These are the locations we think Mauer has been. Gino said Covina is working with State to cover the perimeter around Zelda's, but they haven't seen any action since Magozzi and Gino left."

Sampson drew his own X over Summit Avenue. "He slipped out, and this is where he's going. I'd bet anything, otherwise he would be in Timbuktu by now."

"That's what they think, and they're mobilizing a presence to cover Monkeewrench and probably half of St. Paul." She sank into her chair and rubbed her eyes, which was a big mistake, because someone had dumped a bucket of sand in them when she wasn't paying attention. "We need to be there, Sampson. Monkeewrench and Magozzi and Gino have done us a whole lot of favors over the years and I want to repay that. Are you going to argue with me this time?"

"No, and they won't, either. But what about the presser tonight?"

"Fuck the presser. I'm not doing it until I have something good to say." She clapped her hand over her mouth.

He gave her a lopsided smile. "Never heard you drop the F-bomb before."

Had she ever dropped the F-bomb? She couldn't remember. "If there was ever a time, it's now."

Rachel wasn't happy about their impending departure, but she didn't criticize the decision. "Things are slowing down here, anyhow; even the tipline is dead. Some of the media left to cover a bridge collapse near Winona, but still smart you came in through the back."

"Forward anything that comes in."

She sniffed irritably. "I suppose there isn't anything you can't do from the car. And how do I explain to everybody that the sheriff isn't here for the multiagency press conference?"

"Don't explain anything, just tell them to go ahead as planned without me. We're acting on a credible tip."

"Is that true, or will I be lying?"

"A little of both. But it's too complicated to explain now. Thanks, Rachel."

"Watch yourselves. And never mind me, stuck here worrying about you."

Sampson smiled. "We won't."

"You're such a putz."

*   *   *

Magozzi sprinted up Harley's walk and pushed open the monstrous double doors that had once hung in a Medici fortress. All of Monkeewrench was waiting in the foyer, but he ignored everybody but Grace, and didn't give a damn about her opinion on public displays of affection. He squeezed her hard and refused to let go. And, surprisingly, she hugged him back just as tightly before she started squirming.

"I was so scared, Grace," he murmured in her hair.

She finally pushed him away gently and gifted him a small smile. "We were a little worried ourselves."

"Just a little?"

"Don't look so wounded."

Annie was pacing tiny circles, utterly stricken. "Lord almighty, I just can't believe this. I couldn't come up with a single red flag in the two years Zelda has been designing for me, and believe me, I tried. And now I'm going to have to burn that damn dress *and* most of my wardrobe."

"I haven't been able to either," Petra said. "There is absolutely nothing in my files that links her to Mauer or Praljik, at least in the U.S. I'm looking farther back into the past now. There has to be a connection there, maybe from the war. It's not widely known, but there were women in the militias, some of them officers."

Gino raised his brows. "That makes sense. Why else would she stick her neck out like that?"

"She said she was from France," Magozzi said. "You don't think so, Petra?"

"Everybody knows who and what Mauer is. Why would a French woman help him? Roadrunner, tell them what you discovered."

He consulted his notes. "She has a French birth certificate and her documentation looks legit. She entered the U.S. in 2004 as Zelda Rousseau, legally changed her to name to just Zelda in New York after she became a citizen in 2006. U.S. passport is legit too, I called a guy I know in the State Department. But her early history in Europe is almost nonexistent. She was basically a shadow until the early aughts."

"After the war ended," Petra clarified.

Magozzi thought about how wars never really ended when the fighting was over. Not long ago, he and Gino were chasing old Nazis and Jews who were still killing each other right in Minneapolis. Benjamin Franklin had said nothing was certain but death and taxes. He should have added hatred to the list.

"Come up to the office. We're a frog's hair from cracking into Mauer's Bitcoin account." Harley smiled wickedly. "When he sees big fat zeroes there, he's going to self-destruct. Then we can reel him in with a fake notification and BOOM, the honey trap slams shut."

Gino looked wistful. "Wish we could watch the magic happen, but Malcherson called in every cop St. Paul and Minneapolis has to spare. They'll watch this place for as long as it takes, and Leo and I need to get out there and see what the plan is. Rikker and Sampson are on their way too. And they're not coming because they want a piece of this; they're coming to support you."

"That's a big warm fuzzy. I love those guys." Harley cracked his knuckles. "Alright, let's everybody get to it."

"What if Mauer already moved the funds?" Magozzi asked.

"Not sure why he would. He doesn't have a reason to think it's vulnerable because we couldn't find it before and neither could the feds. But even if he did move the money, it doesn't matter because once we get in we'll have all the bank transfer information. He's fucked seven ways to Sunday any way you slice it."

50

ANNABELLE CHECKED HER phone, shocked to see that three hours had passed since she'd settled in at a table in the law library. Most of the time—actually, all of it, if she was truthful—had been spent online, scouring the news instead of studying. She'd devoured every single story about Mauer's escape, the three people he'd murdered, and Travis Dunbar's kidnapping, approaching it like an assignment. Perhaps with even more ardor. She was sure she now knew more about the events than anybody but the cops and Monkeewrench. But they hadn't experienced Mauer personally, felt his breath on their necks or faces or the tip of his knife against their flesh.

Was there something in all those nightmare memories that could help them? Could she even access them objectively after spending so much time pushing the past away? She closed her laptop and stared out a window at the late afternoon sun painting gold bars of light on the lawn and trees, infusing them with life for their next season. New beginnings were symbolic to her on an entirely different level, and that gave her resolve.

She had to try. Petra had been right—helping those who could no longer help themselves was now her passion, her mission. She owed it to the lost ones, to herself, and to Delia. And to the people who'd saved her life. With all the festering splinters in her psyche dislodged, it would be good to spend time with Monkeewrench, and hopefully make herself useful.

Annabelle took her usual route from Portland Avenue to her studio apartment on Oxford Street. There were lots of ways she could go, some shorter or more convenient if she needed groceries, but Portland was her favorite way because there were so many beautifully restored Victorians. As she strolled home, she admired all the gingerbread details, the turrets and ironwork, the diverse color palettes unique to each house. Maybe some of the schemes weren't authentic to the period, but only an architect or historical pedant would care. She certainly didn't.

She imagined herself living in every single one she passed, planting showcase gardens and decorating for all the seasons and holidays, especially Christmas. But right now she couldn't even afford to rent a duplex or guest house anywhere near this Summit Avenue–adjacent neighborhood. She had a lot of work to do before she could live her fantasy.

Success is just a manifestation of dreams, Annabelle. Without them, life happens to you instead of you making it happen.

Delia, who didn't have a future anymore, had taught her to dream about hers. She was dreaming for both of them now, and that kept her focused and motivated.

*   *   *

Wolfie was pleased with the guest house Zelda had purchased, mainly because the neighborhood wasn't just quiet, it was practically deserted. He hadn't seen a single soul except for a counterculture poser with thrift store clothes and ridiculous red hair. She was ambling down the sidewalk, shamelessly gawking at all the houses she'd never be able to afford. Who would employ somebody with hair the color of a fire engine?

He knew the type—they were the people who would confront you on the street and ask about your sustainable living practices or beg you to donate to some charity that turned composted sewage into anti-aging face masks. He'd killed for less. On any other day, he might have considered eliminating her from the gene pool.

Wolfie was rolling the bag of goodies up the front walk when he heard the burner ring. He scrambled to unzip the suitcase, then froze in confusion when he realized the sound was coming from someplace else. He looked around frantically, then a white-hot rage scorched through his body as he tracked the ringing to the car where Travis was passed out. That sneaky fucker.

He stalked over, yanked open the door, and found the phone inside the jacket Zelda had given him. If Travis had called 911, he was going to tear off his arms.

"You made a big goddamned mistake," Wolfie seethed, shoving Travis's limp body against the door as he answered. "I just got here, Zelda."

"Good. The police have nothing, but they're suspicious. Don't come back here."

"What about Novak?"

"Silas buried him in the woods."

"That's not good enough—"

"Novak is in the middle of a hundred acres of private property, nobody will ever find him. Worry about yourself."

Wolfie mopped the sweat that was suddenly dripping from his forehead even though there was a biting chill in the air. "Do you know who killed him?"

"How would I know that? Go. And don't you dare call me from jail."

"I'm not going to jail," he snapped to a dial tone.

*   *   *

Goran sat low in the driver's seat of the Suburban, watching Mauer lose it. Something was going wrong for him, something to do with the boy. And with his attention now focused on his call—Zelda, he was sure—it was time to strike. Crack his head, push him back into the car . . . no. He might see him coming in his peripheral vision and he couldn't disable him out in the open in broad daylight. He had to marshal his patience and wait for him to enter the house. Then he could launch his attack from behind, and the advantage would belong to him. Easy, especially since he was taller, heavier, and had put on thirty pounds of muscle in prison, something that weasel obviously hadn't.

He smiled as Mauer pocketed the phone and walked his suitcase to the house. Unlocked the door and pushed it open. The boy was still in the car, leverage that meant he wouldn't need to make noise or a mess by shooting Mauer. Things were going very well.

51

Gino and Magozzi stood outside Harley's gate, confabbing with Sergeant Amos Corwyn from St. Paul, a colossus with a deep, rolling voice that was astonishingly soft. But Magozzi knew he could shatter glass if he really let loose—he and Gino had seen the man in action in a joint MPD/SPPD operation. He had the pipes to be an opera singer or a stage actor, and Magozzi had heard rumors that he did improv at the Shakespeare Shack on open mic nights. But he wasn't going to ask in case it was a touchy subject.

After pleasantries and a brief discussion about next winter's police broom ball teams, Corwyn got to business. "We had a department-wide Zoom at headquarters with your chief and mine and we're all squared. Plainclothes officers on foot, unmarkeds trolling the neighborhood in a grid, and we'll have a utility van parked across the street as a command-slash-watch post. Regular patrols already assigned to the area will proceed as usual. Are we missing any angles?"

"Hell, no, this sounds like better planning than D-Day," Gino said. "Really appreciate this, Sergeant."

"We're all happy to do it. Monkeewrench has done a lot for us over the years, and it's an honor to be on the giving end. I understand they have some pretty impressive security themselves."

"The Pentagon could learn a thing or two from them. But nothing matches people on the ground, especially since we have no idea where he'll be coming from. And we're sure he's coming."

Corwyn nodded sagely. "The perfect op is when the bad guy gets taken down before he's anywhere near his target. Does Monkeewrench have a death laser too?"

Gino snuffled. "Not last time we checked. Where do you want us?"

"You're both targets, so we want you out of harm's way. And it would be valuable to have you inside watching their cameras in case you see things we don't. But nobody's going to argue with you if you're not cool with that."

Magozzi's instinct was to get out there and be a warrior, a hero, save lives. But some of the lives he was planning to save belonged to Grace and Elizabeth, and he wasn't going to leave them alone. He and Gino would stay inside with Monkeewrench, help monitor, and if things went south, they would be the last line of defense. Which was laughable with the army covering the outside and Harley's armory stashed in his wine cellar. He was pretty sure all of them could probably shoot better than him and Gino combined. "We're on board, Sergeant, but we need a portable. Phones aren't going to cut it."

"Way ahead of you, I've got a radio tuned to the ops-dedicated frequency so you'll be in constant contact." He gave them a pearly white grin. "Plus you'll have play-by-play action of the stakeout."

Gino grinned back at his joke. Stakeouts were ninety-nine percent boredom, one percent terror. That is, if anything happened at all. "We'll grab a twelve-pack and make some popcorn."

Corwyn liked that. "We've got this covered, detectives. Hang tight, I'll get the radio."

The visual of him walking back to his squad made his footsteps sound like thunder. "I swear I hear the sidewalk cracking. He's got to be bigger than Freedman by at least fifty." Gino gave his partner a circumspect side-eye. "Did you actually have a brain freeze back there, thinking you were going to be a dumbass street cowboy?"

"Briefly. Can't help it."

"Get back inside, Leo. I'll be right behind you, I just have to call Angela—"

"Hey, guys!" McLaren was hurrying down the sidewalk, looking almost normal in a polo shirt, windbreaker, and jeans.

Gino was obnoxious enough to ask what Magozzi was trying hard not to think about. "Got your tighty-whities back on or are thongs a regular thing with you?"

McLaren gave him his best Johnny Rotten/Billy Idol sneer. "Fuck you, Rolseth, I'm a boxer man all the way."

Magozzi clapped him on the shoulder. "Thanks for your sacrifice, Johnny. You permanently blew the images of all the corpses I've ever seen right out of my mind. I'll be forever grateful."

He snorted. "Anything for you, Leo."

"Was it really Gloria's idea?"

He buffed his nails on his windbreaker. "'Course it was; she's always looking for ways to see me naked without committing to marriage."

"Humiliate you," Gino said, covering with a cough.

McLaren ignored him. "Freedman's on his way. What can we do?"

"Corwyn's running the show, but honest to God, he's got this thing so dialed in, you really don't need to be here." But Magozzi knew he did—MPD and Monkeewrench were McLaren's family, and he'd take a storm of bullets for any one of them and die with a smile on his lips.

"Are you kidding me? Hell if I'd miss out on this, and I'm even sober. Well, almost. You guys okay? I mean, this is some crazy, scary shit."

"We are now that you're here," Gino said, meaning it.

52

MAGOZZI FOUND GRACE, Elizabeth, and Charlie in the kitchen. The humans sat at the massive walnut table eating chicken nuggets; the canine party of one was drooling at their feet, working his pathetic-starving-dog con hard. He had to give Charlie props for believability.

"Dah!" Elizabeth squealed, greeting him with chubby, flailing arms.

"Hey, sweet pumpkin." He planted a kiss on her cheek. In response, she patted his and he felt his heart go all squishy.

"Ouch. Dah need shave."

He laughed. "Yep, Dah need shave. I'm a human Chia Pet on steroids."

"Dick suit!"

God, Gino was in so much trouble. Or maybe not, because amusement tugged at Grace's mouth. "Might I interest you in a chicken nugget, Detective?"

"Absolutely." He sat down and plucked one off her plate. Surprisingly, they were excellent for preformed mystery meat cloaked in deep-fried breading, but then again, he was starving. "Would it be rude to point out that your culinary standards have slipped?"

"This is an upgrade from the peanut butter and jelly sandwich she mutilated earlier."

"It must kill you to be reduced to frozen food."

"These are homemade," she said indignantly.

"*That's* why they're so damn . . . darn good." He continued poaching her nuggets, then nearly choked when he saw Grace toss one to Charlie. "You are a total hypocrite."

"Sausage upsets his stomach and the nitrates make him scratch. What's happening outside?"

"You have your own army. A photon of light couldn't get in here. But I'd still like you and Elizabeth to go to the safe room."

"One insane man against an army, our security system, and bullet-resistant windows? I think you've elevated Mauer to divine status."

Magozzi knew she was right, which did nothing to assuage his anxiety. "Better to overreact than underreact."

"We need all hands on deck. But I'll compromise and put Elizabeth down there. Where are you and Gino going to be?"

"We're staying inside to monitor the security feeds and the radio."

She looked at him with those intense Caribbean-blue eyes. "It's driving you crazy, though, isn't it?"

"What?"

"Not being out there."

"I'm retired. Well, almost. Besides, I'm a homicide detective, I only show up for dead bodies." Magozzi didn't like the direction her mind was going so he changed the subject. "Is everybody else in the office?"

"Roadrunner and Petra. They finally got into Mauer's account, and they're monitoring for activity. He doesn't have any money now. That's a big problem for him."

"How much was in the account?"

"Over thirty million."

He whistled. "Wow. Where did they stash it?"

"It's safe. We'll turn it over to the feds when this is finished."

"Minus a commission?"

Grace smirked at him. "I'm glad to see you're retaining your sense of humor."

"It's keeping me from losing my mind. Where are Harley and Annie?"

"In the wine cellar getting the heavy artillery just in case."

"*Annie?*"

"She's very angry; she needs to handle some weaponry and blow off a little steam. You know she's not the fragile Southern magnolia she puts on."

Magozzi did know. "I'll get up to the office. Gino should be here shortly, so I'd recommend hiding all comestibles."

"He's welcome to share our three-star Michelin feast. I have another tray of nuggets in the warming oven."

"It will be the highlight of his year. Well, second best, after the strudel." He leaned over and looked into Elizabeth's big, wondering eyes, the same color as Grace's, but with a slash of brown in the right one—one of his genetic contributions. "Don't let your mother feed Charlie any more chicken."

Elizabeth giggled and threw a piece on the floor, directing contravening his parental authority. Right in front of him. "Chawrie is hungry."

He glanced at Grace. "Already a rebel. Puberty is all on you."

"If you're not ready to give up the job, I'm okay with that."

Busted. How had he been so stupid to think that she wouldn't pick up on his uncertainty? "Are you kidding? I can't wait to sit on my butt all day, eating homemade chicken nuggets and drinking scotch."

"You're a terrible liar, Magozzi."

* * *

Harley tossed Annie another AK-47. "This one should be good and clean, I just used it at the range, but check the magazine and the firing pin, I might have taken it out—"

"I know exactly what to do, fool."

"It's just kind of hard to take you seriously in four-inch heels. Stilettoes and guns, it's like a calendar I had once—"

"Shut up, Harley."

"I love a woman who can't take a compliment, it's challenging. Have you thought any more about kids? I don't want to deprive the world of my DNA before I die. All this handsomeness and brilliance? It would be a crime against humanity."

Annie checked the firing pin and slammed the magazine into place. "Good to go," she snapped, tossing it back with enough force to set him on his heels.

"Did I forget to mention that it would be equally felonious to deprive the world of your DNA? I mean, our genes combined could launch a thousand rockets . . . Annie? Annie, what's wrong?"

She wiped a tear from her eye, dislodging a rhinestone. "I almost got us killed over a stupid dress."

"Hey, hey, come here." He wrapped his gargantuan tattooed arms around her and she didn't resist. "You didn't do anything. How were you supposed to know your designer was stashing a psychopath in her house?" He lifted her chin. "Guilt is the most worthless emotion in the human repertoire. And you're wrecking your makeup. The hottest babe in the world can't go around looking like a raccoon."

Annie sniffled. "It's waterproof."

"You might want to ask for a refund. I don't think I've ever seen you cry before, Annie."

"Tears aren't the same as crying."

"Whatever you say. You have to admit, this feels pretty good, you in my arms." He braced for a rejoinder while crafting potential parries.

"Actually, it's not horrible."

Harley beamed down at her. "It's about time you figured that out, woman."

53

GORAN THOUGHT THE kid was going to be easy because he looked unconscious, slumped against the car door like a pile of rags. But when he grabbed him, he reanimated and fought like a Tasmanian devil.

"You shit," Goran hissed, putting him in a headlock and pressing Novak's Grach against his temple. "Make a sound and you're dead."

Travis was still groggy and disoriented, but a higher level of terror than he'd ever known cleared the cobwebs fast. He now understood that he'd been drugged twice by Wolfie, who'd slammed him against the door when he'd found the phone. And now this new bad man was strangling him and had a gun to his head and he couldn't comprehend what was happening or why. But even though his mind wasn't right, his body felt like a hot wire. He couldn't run, he couldn't speak, so he struggled.

A bad idea, he realized too late as the vise of the beefy arm closed tighter around his neck until he couldn't breathe. Warm urine trickled down his leg as black spots swam in his eyes. With no other options, he went floppy and played dead again, hoping dead wouldn't be for real this time.

The man scooped him up and eased the pressure on his throat, but the gun was still firm against his temple. Travis desperately wanted to relinquish control to the drugs and hopelessness and fear, but he willed his eyes to open a slit—if there was a chance to escape, he wouldn't see it with them closed.

With each heavy footstep, a wavering, dark green door grew larger in his impaired field of vision, and he flinched when the man kicked it open. Wolfie was sitting at a desk in front of a laptop computer, fingers dancing over the keys. He looked up abruptly and spun in his chair, raising a big handgun with a long barrel and a funny thing on the end. But it drooped in his hand as his face went white as snow. His gaze jittered manically, disbelievingly, between him and the new bad man. "*Goran?*"

Travis couldn't believe how quickly the man's foot lashed out in a high kick that connected with Wolfie's wrist and made him yelp in pain. The long gun with the funny end flew from his hand and slid across the floor. He committed to memory exactly where it had come to a stop.

"Wolfgang, it's been a long time," Goran purred. "So nice to see you again. I think you know the reason for my visit."

"How is this *possible*? How are you here?"

"Technically, I drove, but the rest is a longer story and I don't have time for idle chat."

"Novak. You killed him."

Goran wasn't surprised that Mauer didn't need the rest of the story. "Ah, you found him. Yes, he was a very good friend, but he outlived his utility. I have many helpful friends, including Aleksandar, but I suspect he is no longer with us either." He chuckled. "Don't look so crushed. He was a parasite who took advantage of you. Betrayed you. He was the one who sold me the account information. He came quite cheap too." Goran clucked his tongue. "Don't beat yourself up, we don't always make the best judgments when it comes to matters of the heart. If it makes you feel any better, he betrayed me too. Now, let's settle our affairs, shall we?"

"You'll never get the money! Your information is worthless without—"

Goran shoved the gun harder against the boy's head and tightened the headlock. "Perhaps you don't understand. Get me my money NOW and he lives, otherwise I'm going to paint this room with his blood."

"Don't you dare hurt him or I'll—"

"What? Kill me? I don't think so. I'm in control now and you are totally fucked. Even Zelda can't save you, although I'm sure she tried. Why you didn't disappear when you had the chance is beyond me."

He followed Mauer's nervous eyes toward the array of weapons and gear spread out on the floor. "Ah, I see. Impressive. Explosives too? But I guess it makes sense, you being a one-man band, you need the extra juice. And just who is this exciting party for? The people who caught you?"

"The people who killed my father!"

"Peter died of a heart attack. We were cordial a long time ago as you know, and even then I warned him about his excesses."

"They KILLED him."

"And I'm going to kill this pet of yours unless you get on that computer right now and give me back what you stole from me." He readjusted, jamming the gun under Travis's chin while he slid his knife from its sheath. "Maybe I'll cut some important parts off first, would that be motivating? I think it might be. You have three seconds before I slice off his ear." The boy whimpered, and Goran smashed a hand over his mouth. "Shut the fuck up."

Wolfie was shaking with fury so incapacitating that he had to remind himself to breathe. Goran didn't bluff, so he had to ride this out, save Travis, then rip Goran's guts out and cut off his head. That bastard wasn't the only one with a big knife. Wolfie ultimately had the upper hand, just not right at the moment.

It was agonizing to type his username and password into the Bitcoin exchange, but he had no choice. And in a way, it made him feel noble, making a sacrifice any good parent would make for their child. He could smell Goran's foul breath and his heart seized, thinking of how frightened Travis must be. "Get back."

"You're not in any position to give orders." His gun connected with Mauer's skull with a satisfying crack. "I had a different idea how this would all play out, but I like this better. Or maybe I should try a hybrid approach and cut off *your* ear first."

Wolfie slammed his finger on the Enter key, and his account populated the screen. A moment later, he gasped in horror. Zeroes. *Zeroes.* Nada, nothing. He threw the wireless keyboard across the room and wailed in rage.

"What the fuck is this, Wolfgang? A trick?"

"No, it's not a goddamned trick! It's gone."

"You fucking liar!" Goran hit him again, this time between the shoulders.

Wolfie bent over and vomited McDonald's and caviar onto the floor. "Monkeewrench. Goddamned, fucking Monkeewrench."

Goran's grip loosened on the boy as he felt the ground falling away beneath his feet. He knew Mauer wasn't lying. And where did that leave him? No-fucking-where. "You're so smart, GET IT BACK!" he screamed.

Travis wasn't really in his body anymore, but he still had loose fragments of thoughts that seeped in through the shock. Wolfie was bad, but he hadn't held a gun to his head or threatened to cut off his ear or kill him. And he'd been nice to him at first. He was the lesser of two evils, a choice he'd had to make his entire life.

With every ounce of energy he could muster, his teeth clamped down hard on the thick, hairy arm around his throat. Heard him scream. Saw a knife flash in Wolfie's hand as he moved fast as a cat. Felt the sticky heat of blood on his face as the new bad man dropped to the floor, releasing him.

And then he ran.

54

THE DARK AND ugly thing he'd been fighting had finally taken over. Wolfie no longer existed, so he wasn't truly cognizant of his hand slashing and sawing and plunging the knife into the carnage that used to be Goran over and over and over again. Twenty, thirty, forty times. He couldn't stop. He *didn't* stop until exhaustion forced him to his knees. He collapsed in a lake of blood, not caring that it was seeping into his clothes and blurring his vision, not caring that there were chunks of tissue and shards of bone clinging to his arms and face.

When the dark and ugly thing finally got bored and receded, he looked down at what he'd done, trying to remember how it had all started.

Goran. The zeroes on his computer screen. His brave boy, biting Goran's arm and giving him the opening he needed to save them both.

He jumped to his feet. "Travis?!"

No answer.

"It's safe now, come out. Travis?" Impelled by mounting panic, he thundered through the small rooms of the guest house. And then he saw the open door and knew he was gone, just like the money. All his beautiful plans had turned to shit. Travis was just another traitor, and because of him, he couldn't stay here. Because of Monkeewrench, he couldn't go back to Zelda's. Nowhere to run, nowhere to hide.

This is your fault. If you'd paid more attention to that Suburban so suspiciously parked off the road, none of this would be happening. You know what you have to do now, son. There's still time to make things right.

Peter didn't speak to him often or at length, but when he did, it was always the truth.

*   *   *

Annabelle stopped at Whole Foods and charged a premade charcuterie tray and a bouquet of Stargazer lilies on her only credit card that wasn't maxed out. It was the least she could do for Monkeewrench, and it was well worth a few extra shifts at Sweeney's. It was such sorry recompense for saving her life, but her mother always told her it was the thought that counted.

She decided to take Portland to Harley's so she could focus on the north side houses this time. You couldn't fully appreciate them if your gaze was constantly darting back and forth from side to side. The street was especially quiet at this time of day, well before people made their way home from work, and she could almost make herself believe it was hers alone. It was a dream too big even for Delia, but that didn't diminish the pleasure of the illusion.

The fantasy shattered when she saw a small figure in the distance, weaving down the sidewalk toward her, covered in blood.

"Will you help me?" he choked before collapsing on the sidewalk.

Annabelle dropped the tray of charcuterie and the flowers and ran like hell. She was going to help somebody while they still had a voice. She was going to save somebody before they were dead.

She crashed down on her knees beside him, oblivious to the pain of concrete against bone as she fumbled her phone out of her tote and punched 911. "What happened? Where are you hurt?" His eyes were empty, the flesh of his face that wasn't bloody the purest white she'd ever seen. He was in shock.

"It's . . . it's not my blood."

"My name's Annabelle and I'm calling 911. Help will be here soon, okay?"

He stared at her blankly for a moment, then raised his arms in a heartbreaking, desperate plea for comfort. She lifted him up to her chest and started rocking, murmuring soothing nonsense into his ear. And then she cried, remembering Detective Gino Rolseth telling her everything was going to be okay, and how much those words had mattered. "It's going to be okay, sweetheart, shh. What's your name, honey?"

"T . . . T . . . Travis . . . he killed a man . . . with a knife . . . blood . . ."

Annabelle gasped sharply. "Are you Travis Dunbar?"

He nodded against her chest.

"Where is the man who took you? Is he alive?"

"Please don't let him get me."

Oh, God. What had he done to him? And why wasn't 911 picking up? "I promise I won't, Travis. Can you tell me where he is?"

"B . . . back there . . . I think . . . I don't know . . ."

Annabelle looked over his shoulder and saw plumes of smoke billowing up into the cloudless sky. A house fire—the smoke was too black to be anything else. Mauer had to be behind it, and if there was any justice in the world, he would be frying to a cinder right now.

Finally, a tinny voice came over her phone speaker. "Nine-one-one, what's your emergency?"

CHAPTER

55

IRIS HAD JUST merged onto 94 East when the all-units callout came over the radio—police, ambulance, and fire. And then the dispatcher relayed the thrilling news that Travis Dunbar had been found. Her heart was in her throat as she stomped on the accelerator and flipped on the lights and siren. Travis was safe, but Mauer was still on the loose. "That bastard is really here. A part of me thought he would cut his losses."

Sampson punched frantically at Google Maps. "Me too. Magozzi and Gino were right."

"Where am I going?"

"Take the Lexington exit in two miles, right, then a left on Portland. Says we're eight minutes out."

She pointed at a black smudge in the sky. "There's the fire. Think it's related? A diversion, maybe?"

"If Mauer started a fire, that means he's at the end of his rope. And even more dangerous."

She straight-armed the steering wheel as she veered onto the exit and squealed through the intersection, almost sideswiping some moron in a white minivan who didn't notice the lights or the one-twenty-decibel siren. "Tell me when you see Portland, I'm busy trying not to get us killed."

"Next light."

Iris wasn't sure if she'd two-wheeled it onto Portland, but it felt like it. Seconds or maybe hours passed before she saw a dizzying kaleidoscope of flashing blue and red. Firehoses spouted water into the smoke a few blocks up; closer, EMTs were guiding a stretcher and an IV pole to the open back doors of an ambulance. Cops were already setting up a makeshift barricade. She stopped just short of running over a uniform who was struggling with an orange barrel and thrust her star out the window. "Sheriff Rikker, Dundas County. Do you know if Travis Dunbar is okay?"

"He was standing on his own two feet when I got here, so that's good."

"Mauer?"

"No sign of him, but there are probably more cops here than residents right now." He rolled the barrel away to give her space. "Go on through, Sheriff. Ask for Sergeant Corwyn, he's running the show and he'll fill you in."

Iris was shaking with systemic overload as she drove past the barrels, parked next to the ambulance, and vaulted out of the car. The woman hovering over Travis looked worse than he did. Her flocked yellow dress was smeared with blood and her lips were compressed in a white line as she held back tears. "I'm Iris Rikker, Dundas County Sheriff, and this is Lieutenant Sampson. Were you the one who called 911?"

Annabelle nodded and reluctantly released Travis's arm so the EMT could load him. "Is he going to be okay?" she asked him.

"He's in shock, but not injured physically that we can tell, just dehydrated. Are you family?"

"We are now," she mumbled, and Iris thought that was a mysterious answer. She took the woman's arm gently and moved her to the sidewalk to give the ambulance room as it yelped its way out of the bedlam.

"What's your name, ma'am?"

"Annabelle Sellman."

"That sounds familiar."

Her pale, stricken face clouded. "I'm one of Mauer's victims. Survivors," she corrected herself as she looked down at her bloodied dress.

Iris had to temporarily suspend her disbelief—what machination of the universe had entangled this woman once again with her tormentor to save another? Thinking about it made her head hurt, but the "family" comment made sense now—she and Travis had an ignominious bond of shared horror. "Tell us how you found him."

She took a deep, quivering breath and looked at them with vacant eyes. "He found me. I live near here and I was walking to the Monkeewrench house, they invited me to visit. Do you know them?"

"We were on our way there when the call came in. Go ahead."

"I saw Travis stumbling down the street, drenched in blood . . . I didn't know who he was until I asked his name . . . he could barely speak, he was so terrorized, but he managed to say, 'He killed a man.' And then, 'Don't let him get me.' And he mentioned a knife. He was so brave to get away. God, I hope he's going to be okay, but how could he be? Does he even know his parents are dead?" The tears she'd been holding in spilled.

Iris had been so busy with the present, she hadn't even thought of the aftermath. The trauma, the unknown damage likely far beyond anything Travis Dunbar had experienced at home. He was alive, but at ten years old, his life was scorched earth. Her throat closed and she teared up too. "He's safe now because of you, hold on to that, Annabelle. And go see him at the hospital, he needs good people surrounding him."

"I plan to as soon as we're finished here. Take care of him when he gets back to Dundas County. He needs good people there too."

Iris swallowed hard and looked at Sampson. He was biting his lower lip. "We promise."

Sampson cleared the emotion from his throat. "Did Travis say anything else about Mauer?"

"No." Annabelle raised her face to the smoke-smudged sky. "It's really amazing, isn't it?"

Iris raised a brow. "What is?"

"I moved to this neighborhood from Minneapolis because I go to Hamline Mitchell on Summit Avenue. I enrolled in law school because of what Mauer did to me. And if Mauer hadn't come after Monkeewrench I never would have run into Travis. Not a coincidence, just a long chain of cause and effect. Mauer set it all into motion and it's going to bring him down."

"Mauer's bad karma finally caught up with him," Sampson said.

Annabelle looked down at her bloody dress again and shivered. "Find him. Find him and kill him. He doesn't deserve to live."

Iris had no argument, but it wasn't up to her to decide.

56

EVERYBODY HAD BEEN in the third-floor Monkeewrench office watching camera feeds and listening to the police radio when all hell broke loose on Portland Avenue and sirens started wailing. The tension in the room went from palpable to suffocating.

"He's here." Petra spoke quietly. It was barely a whisper, but her voice resonated like an explosion.

"But Travis Dunbar is safe, thank the good Lord," Annie murmured.

Magozzi was at Grace's computer station, shifting back and forth on his feet like a racehorse in the gate, trying to distribute the influx of adrenaline in his bloodstream. He wanted desperately to lock her in the safe room where Elizabeth and Charlie were playing, but that wasn't going to happen.

She touched his arm. "We've all got this, Magozzi."

He hoped to hell she was right. "Roadrunner, did you get your computer synched with the radio frequency so you can hear everything?"

"A long time ago."

"Sorry for the stupid question, I'm a little tweaked. Gino and I are going downstairs, we're the eyes on ground level."

Harley was kind enough to preempt his next stupid question. "I just rechecked the security system, it's a hundred percent, running smooth as my Fat Boy on the way to Sturgis."

"The intercom?"

"All systems go. We're going to be fine, Leo. Now get out of here and do your thing, we'll do ours."

"Yeah." Gino pulled him out of the office and into the elevator. "They're Monkeewrench, for God's sake."

"I know, but don't tell me you're not too wired to think straight."

"Of course I'm wired, but this nightmare is going to be over soon one way or the other, and that puts me in a Zen frame of mind."

"Chianti and Angela's manicotti are the only things that put you in a Zen frame of mind."

"Exactly. Nightmare over, chianti and manicotti begins. Heaven and hell in reverse."

Magozzi closed his eyes briefly, trying to absorb some of Gino's poise. His partner actually did have a lot of Zen in him that had nothing to do with food or drink. He had a ferocious temper on the job and could go from zero to eleven in a heartbeat, but he had the extraordinary gifts of intuitiveness and empathy. Whatever he was feeling, he could reel it in and calm you down when you needed a reset, even if he was freaking out too. That was Gino. His best friend. And the whole reason retirement was looking like a bad idea. They'd be friends until somebody ended up in a grave or an urn, but a partnership was different than barbeque and beers in the backyard on weekends.

The elevator pinged and the doors slid open. Magozzi hurried down the front hall. "You scope out the back and west side, I'll take the front and east."

Gino looked around, trying to figure out which direction was west. "Okay, see you in about an hour. If you get lost, just ask the Minotaur."

They went from window to window, weapons drawn. They both knew it was overkill, but it was kneejerk and made them both feel better. It didn't take an hour, but the size of the house was truly daunting. Magozzi always forgot about that because most of his time spent here was in the kitchen or office.

Gino came back from his recon and plopped down on a window seat that looked out on Summit Avenue. "Clear."

"Likewise."

"I think I was born too late."

"What do you mean?"

"Look at all those mansions from another century, Leo. The people who built them couldn't even imagine all the bad shit in this world today."

Magozzi followed his gaze. Crime, cruelty, and depravity had existed since the dawn of time, and technology had a dark side because humans had a dark side. But this century had proliferated violence and brutality that didn't exist in 1891 when Harley's house was built. Now a hideous crime was just another news story that would instantly be forgotten because there were a hundred more to take its place. "I'm right there with you."

"We're living in a sick society. Anarchy isn't a philosophical joke anymore, it's a threat."

Magozzi jumped when his phone chimed. It was Corwyn, which meant he had information he didn't want to go out over the radio. "Gino, keep the intercom open so Monkeewrench can hear this call. Sergeant, what's the status?"

"Travis Dunbar is on the way to Regions. Sounds like he's going to be fine."

"Thank God."

"But he's covered in somebody else's blood. He told the woman who found him that Mauer killed a man with a knife. No sign of that shithead, but we found the black Hyundai—it's parked in the driveway of the house that's on fire so he was definitely there. K-9 and airship are on the way."

Magozzi shuddered. "Mauer's safehouse was right here all the time. Jesus."

"Is Dundas County around?" Gino asked. "They were coming up here, but we haven't heard from them in a while."

Corwyn grunted. "Because they drove right into this mess. Sheriff Rikker is talking to the woman who saved that poor kid. Name's Annabelle Sellman. She said she was on her way to Harley's when she saw him. You know her?"

Magozzi and Gino gasped simultaneously. "She almost didn't survive Mauer two years ago."

"Wow. Well, she lived to be a hero and flushed him out in the process. That's poetic justice in my book."

Magozzi thought about Grace's description of the gardener she saw at Zelda's. "Tell your people that Mauer might be wearing a gray dreadlock wig."

Corwyn was silent for a moment. "You'll have to tell me later how you know that."

"The house that's on fire. Can you confirm the address?"

"Sixteen-two-fifty Portland Avenue."

Magozzi heard voices on the other end of the line, shouting in the background.

"Yeah, yeah, I'll be right there," Corwyn snapped. "Look, I gotta run, detectives, but I'll be in touch."

Magozzi hung up and spoke into the intercom. "You got the address?"

"Roger that, we're on it," Harley said.

He looked at Gino and answered his unspoken question. "If there's a connection between those property records and Zelda, Monkeewrench will find it."

Gino raised his brows. "*That* would be enough for a warrant."

57

WOLFIE HAD MADE peace with his decision, and in his state of equanimity, he was able to relish the chaos he'd created. He particularly enjoyed watching the scattered, frantic cops racing around on foot like loose horses because they assumed he was too. They had no idea he was hiding in plain sight in the Suburban, trolling the neighborhood like every other person gawping at the mayhem.

In spite of all the setbacks he'd suffered, things were going to work out. Not as he'd imagined, but even better now that fate had again intervened on his behalf. He'd always been skeptical of his father's conviction that everything, good and bad, was part of a greater cosmic plan, but now he was a true believer.

The only thing missing was Travis, but it obviously wasn't meant to be. Wolfie's anger and disappointment were deep, yet the loss was still profoundly painful. They could have had such an amazing life together if only the boy had trusted him. Of course, with his background, trust would be a very difficult thing to give. He should have recognized that earlier.

He turned right on Summit Avenue and made his second and last pass. With most law enforcement diverted to Portland Avenue and the foot pursuit, the street wasn't as busy as it had been earlier. Some of the plainclothes cops were still hanging around, trying unsuccessfully to look innocuous, and the white van was still parked across the street, but they wouldn't be a problem. This was going to be quick and dirty. Shock and awe. The greatest show on Earth.

He turned onto Oakland Avenue and parked in front of a brick apartment building to go through his punch list one last time. As he approached the house, he would toss the signal jammer over the fence. It wouldn't take out everything, but it would make a good dent in communication. It might even bring one or more of them outside, which would be a deadly mistake on their part. Then it was full speed ahead. Gates were merely deterrents, only as strong as their hinges. No way would they hold against the brute force of the Suburban and its massive engine. He checked the detonator wiring one last time and smiled. Time to hit the lights.

*   *   *

On the west side camera feed, Grace noticed a black Suburban slowing as it approached the farthest perimeter of the fence. "Do you see that, everybody?"

"Yeah. I don't like it." Harley called down. "Heads up, guys, black Suburban approaching on Summit from the east . . . shit, they just threw something in the yard! That's gotta be him!" He leapt out of his chair like an Olympic high jumper, grabbed his AK and tablet, and thundered down the stairs. The elevator was too slow.

At the front window, Magozzi watched the truck as he punched the call button on the radio over and over again. "Goddammit, Gino, it isn't working! Call Corwyn!"

"Can't, my phone is fucked up too!"

"It's a signal jammer," Harley was almost on top of them before they were aware of his presence. "That fucker is here—oh, shit. He's picking up speed!"

*   *   *

Iris had just parked in front of Harley's when a Suburban roared past them in a blur of black. "What the hell?"

"He's going to crash it!" Sampson shouted, jumping out of the car and ducking behind the door as the truck made a hard right and plowed straight through Harley's gate like it was made of toothpicks. Sampson emptied his gun and shredded two of the tires, but it was too little, too late.

*   *   *

"Back, back, get down!" Magozzi shouted as gunshots pierced the air and the leering grill of the Suburban bore down on them. They all braced for the impact as the truck smashed into the front doors with an ungodly sound loud enough to rupture eardrums. Splinters shot through the air like miniature spears, but the ancient wood that had seen battering rams and battle-axes held strong. There was a brief, eerie silence before Iris Rikker's voice boomed through a bullhorn, stunning them all.

"It's over, Mauer, hands out the window where we can see them!"

A distant part of Magozzi's brain wanted to believe this was over, but his frontal lobes were clamoring an ominous warning. "Harley, what do the cameras show?!"

He tapped frantically at his tablet. "He's too close for the front cameras to pick him up, checking east and west side panoramics . . . okay, okay, I got him! Airbag is deployed, he's fighting with it. I count eight cops on the street, including Rikker and Sampson."

"Does Mauer have any visible weapons?"

"Don't see any, he's too busy with the airbag."

"Get to the stairwell, I'll be back."

Gino grabbed his arm. "Where the fuck do you think you're going?"

"Mauer is preoccupied, I'll come at him from the side. The cops out there can't shoot toward the house, and approach is too risky—"

"Don't be stupid, they're not Cub Scouts, let them handle it—"

Magozzi batted his hand away. "They're street cops and detectives, not SWAT, they don't have the experience or the gear to—"

"And neither do you, goddammit!"

"I'm going, Gino."

Harley blocked him with his bulk and Magozzi was ready to fight this boulder with everything he had. Instead, Harley shoved the AK into his hands.

"You're not going anywhere without this, you stubborn asshole."

*   *   *

Wolfie should have thought of the fucking airbag and the damage it could do. But the pain and the powdery shit burning his mouth and eyes didn't matter, only the detonator did. But he had no idea where it was. The goddamn airbag had knocked it away. He pulled his knife and started shredding the inflated fabric with the same brutality he'd exerted on Goran.

And then he saw the detonator on the passenger side floor, just an arm's length away.

*   *   *

Magozzi didn't hear any ambient noise; he was only aware of his ragged breath as he crab-walked along the side of the mansion, the unfamiliar weight of the big gun killing his shoulder. He gestured to the officers on the street just in case they decided an idiot in a suit wallowing in mud with an assault rifle was a clear and present danger . . .

FOCUS.

He took a deep breath, cleared his mind, then dropped to his belly when he reached the flowerbed where lilies of the valley would be blooming in a few weeks, the peonies a month after that. He raised the gun and peered around the corner.

Perfect line of sight. He could see Mauer slashing at the air bag with a knife. He raised the AK and prepared to fire because this was a righteous shooting whether or not the evil bastard was holding a gun. As his finger twitched, Mauer suddenly ducked out of sight.

There was no flash of sudden clarity. No mental or moral calculations assessing pros and cons or consequences. There was no decision at all. He just pulled the trigger and watched a succession of beautiful orange flowers that didn't belong in any garden bloom from the muzzle as glass shattered and bullets turned the Suburban's door to filigree. When the magazine was spent, the world was quiet again. Except for the thunder of his heart.

58

M AGOZZI HAD THE mother of all headaches, and his ears were numb and buzzing. He was positive that he was delirious *and* deaf because everything that followed seemed syrupy and surreal. The movements of the cops fanning across the lawn and surrounding the truck seemed like an underwater ballet. Johnny McLaren, who was already surreal on the best of days, was running toward him in slow motion, spiky orange hair reminding him of the muzzle flashes. Then there was another voice shouting, muffled and warped like it was a record set to the wrong RPM.

"HE'S DEAD!"

Johnny dropped to his knees next to him. "Goddamn, you're the man, way to get the bad guy. You okay, Leo?"

Magozzi remembered to breathe. "What did you say?"

"Next time, don't play with that shit without ear protection."

It suddenly all synched. No wonder everything seemed so weird. He'd felt the same disorientation after an AC/DC concert where he'd been sitting in front of Angus Young's Marshall stack of hell-power. When your faculties were screwed up, everything else seemed screwed up. He rose on wobbling legs with Johnny's assistance, dripping clots of mud from his ruined suit onto his ruined shoes. "You ever shoot an AK, Johnny?"

"Not without muffs."

"Lesson learned."

"You didn't exactly have the luxury of time. Who knows what that asshole had planned?"

Magozzi's pain receptors suddenly kicked into high gear. His adrenaline buzz was wearing off. "I can feel my heart pounding in my shoulder."

McLaren nodded in sympathy. "It'll get worse before it gets better, AKs kick like mules. But with a little practice and the right technique—"

"I'm never shooting one again."

Gino was suddenly by his side. "Way to go, you jackass, never mind that I almost stroked out a half dozen times. Jesus, you're a mess."

"I can't hear you."

"Now you actually have an excuse to say that. I hope you have clothes in the trunk."

"I do." He saw Iris Rikker hurrying toward him, Sampson right behind her.

"Sharp shooting, Detective."

"Nothing sharp about it, Sheriff, you don't need to aim with that thing."

"You did what all of us wanted to."

God, his shoulder hurt. It was the same one Mauer had shot. How fucking ironic. "Did you run the plates on the Suburban?"

"Always a cop first," Iris smiled. "Stolen plates, we'll chase it down. The back is stuffed with guns and militia gear. You prevented what could have been a real tragedy."

Magozzi cringed, thinking about what might have happened if he hadn't pulled the trigger. That impulsive, heedless action wasn't his proudest moment, because he'd lost control for the first time on the job and it had been personal. But it had ended things without collateral damage. The mandatory investigation of an officer-involved shooting would hopefully be a formality, but the AK might be a real problem. He would never regret his actions, but there was a possibility he wouldn't have the luxury of choosing his retirement date anymore.

Iris saw the myriad of emotions play out on his face, and she touched his arm gently. "You did the right thing, everybody knows it. Sampson and I are stopping at the hospital to see Travis, then we have to get back to Dundas, but we'll be seeing you again soon. And you know we'll keep an eagle eye on him and make sure he gets all the resources he needs."

"Thank you, Sheriff. And you did a damn fine job with all of this." He looked at Sampson. "Both of you."

She and Sampson nodded their thanks, then Iris turned to Gino with a raised brow and a sly smile. "And Detective Rolseth, it's been a pleasure, as always."

His mouth twitched. "I'm Gino to you, and kick me in the balls if I ever get salty with you again."

Iris's eyes widened, and Sampson started laughing.

Magozzi wanted to feel the manic elation everyone else did, but he just felt hollow and disconnected from everything happening around him. Part of it was the lingering effect of the adrenaline washing out of his system, but he suspected another part was the onerous burden of taking a life, even a worthless, evil one.

But then Grace, Harley, Annie, Roadrunner, and Petra surrounded him and that made everything better. They all expressed their love and relief in their own ways, but Grace's was the best greeting of all because she hugged him before he had a chance to. It was the first time she'd ever done that. It was a watershed moment, but his head was too messed up to fully appreciate it. That would come later.

He inhaled the lemony scent of her hair and he was instantly in the place he was always meant to be. Home wasn't sticks and bricks, it was people, and he was so glad he'd figured that out. "I'm getting you all muddy."

"I don't care."

"Are Elizabeth and Charlie still in the safe room?"

"Believe it or not, they slept through everything—" She jerked her head when she saw cops scattering, running toward the street.

He followed her gaze and felt a wave of nausea crash down on him. Something was very wrong . . .

"BOMB! BOMB! Get everyone out of the house NOW!" someone screamed.

Magozzi and Grace ran for their daughter's life. He flew up the stairs to the third level, certain his feet never even touched the risers. He misjudged his speed and almost smashed into the safe room door. *There's time, there's time, everything is going to be okay except my* FUCKING FINGERS don't work and I can't punch in the code—

Grace was suddenly next to him, working the keypad.

When he burst into the room, he didn't see anything except his little girl, wide-eyed on the sofa. Charlie started barking in panic. Elizabeth started crying. Kids and animals knew when something was wrong with their people. He swept her up off the sofa and ran, Grace right behind him, the dog at their heels, silent now, because he knew he had a job to do.

"Dah! Momma, what wrong?!" Elizabeth's voice climbed the scale of terror.

His heart crumbled as he felt her terrified tears dripping down his neck. What should have been one of the happiest days of his life was turning out to be the worst. "It's okay, pumpkin," he panted as he burst out the back door. "We're just running a race, it's a fun new game—"

"No, Dah, scary!"

"It's okay, honey, Momma is going to take you home with your aunties and uncles. See? They're waiting for you in the car and you're going to have so much fun."

"NO! NO, DAH, NO!"

Magozzi would never forget the sound of Elizabeth's terrified screams as long as he lived. He kissed her hot, wet cheek and passed her to Grace. "Go!"

59

MAGOZZI WAS STILL trembling an hour later as he and Gino sat in the sedan behind the back perimeter of the barricade. He would be forever grateful his Zen partner knew the value in pretending everything was normal. If Gino had tried to make him feel better, he would have been forced to punch his lights out.

The neighborhood evacuation had been fast and efficient because there were so many police already present and a lot of residents were still at work. Corwyn had pulled the evac to four square blocks just to be safe, but also to make sure the media couldn't film it—a bomb threat at a Summit Avenue mansion was gold for those vultures. But nobody could do anything about the helicopters.

Bloomington Bomb Squad had arrived forty-five minutes ago. They wouldn't know anything until Barney Wollmeyer gave the all-clear. Magozzi wouldn't even consider the alternative. It was a gut-wrenching waiting game, but a hell of a lot better than defusing a bomb. Barney was his hero.

Gino, a seasoned stress eater, was inhaling a bag of Cheezy Puffs. Magozzi, a stress starver, couldn't even contemplate putting food in his mouth.

"Is that from the stash Tommy gave me?"

"I may have helped myself to a couple bags when you weren't looking."

Unlike anything else about this horrific Friday, *that* was normal, and it made Magozzi unreasonably happy. He would get over this soon, feel great about it, because Mauer was gone for good, but that bastard had stained all of their lives and it was going to take time.

He looked out his window, this time not at all surprised to see Chief Malcherson walking toward them. As fastidious as he was, he'd gladly slog through sewage to be there for his men and women in the field. He would always be a cop first, chief of police second.

Gino rolled down his window. "Chief, seeing you just made a really bad day better."

"My very sentiments. This has taken some years off my life, but it's nothing compared to what you two have been through. How is Monkeewrench, Detective Magozzi?"

The question was earnest, but a courtesy because Malcherson knew the cost of trauma as well as any of them. "They're safe."

He nodded his understanding. "Bloomington just cleared the truck, and I wanted you to know immediately as it's not going over the radio. I will be giving a joint statement with St. Paul soon."

Magozzi and Gino both let out a million cubic feet of air and sank back in their seats.

"Crime Scene is waiting to take over," Malcherson continued, "but Jimmy Grimm told me Harley can go home anytime as long as he goes in through the back and stays inside."

God bless Jimmy Grimm. "What's the story on the bomb?" Magozzi asked. "Was it even real?"

The chief's face remained impassive as usual, but it got very dark, like a storm cloud had just passed over and sucked up all the light in the world. "There was enough C-4 inside the Suburban to decimate a city block, according to Barney. And the detonator was perfectly wired and functional. Detective Magozzi, if you hadn't killed Mauer when you did, many lives would have been lost."

"Sweet Jesus," Gino whispered.

Magozzi took a shaky breath. "This was a joint effort, Chief. Dundas County played a huge role, and so did Monkeewrench."

"Of course, that's a given. I'll reach out to both parties."

Magozzi chose to remain fixated on the case because if he had that to focus on, he wouldn't have to think about what might have happened if one tiny breath had disturbed a fragile house of cards. "Monkeewrench is going to look into property records for the Portland house, we're hoping we can link it to Zelda—"

"Don't worry about anything except yourselves and your loved ones right now. We've been working all the angles with the assistance of the FBI. At this point, we know the home's owner of record is a rather sketchy LLC that was set up in Morocco and appears to exist only on paper. On top of Travis Dunbar's kidnapping, the FBI is also looking at wire fraud. We'll untangle this, it's just a matter of time."

Magozzi sighed in relief. "Great work."

The chief smiled wryly. "We can actually function without you, Detective Magozzi, although that is a worst-case scenario. It's going to be hard to lose you."

Magozzi was stunned by the blatant statement from a man who loved subterfuge. He was compelled to respond with equal sincerity. "It's going to be hard for me too, sir."

Malcherson braced his hand on the roof of the car and leaned into the window, speaking softly. The media were collectively foaming at the mouth, and directional microphones were incredibly sophisticated these days. "For your ears only—Arson found a body in the wreckage of the fire. The scene is still too hot to send in Crime Scene, but they said it will take some time to identify it once it goes to the morgue. Not only is it badly burned, it's not intact."

Magozzi tried to swallow, but the visual had sucked all the saliva out of his mouth. "Not intact?"

"The victim was decapitated and dismembered."

Magozzi was dumbfounded as he watched the chief check his watch casually, as if decapitation and dismemberment were just everyday occurrences unworthy of further consideration. "I'm late, gentlemen, but I have a request. Actually, an order."

"What's that, Chief?"

"Both of you go home to your families now. Be with them tonight. Turn off your phones. Everything else can wait."

"That is one class act," Gino commented after Malcherson had disappeared into the throng of cops guarding the barricade. "And no way I'm going to disobey a direct order. I'll drop you at Grace's, then I'm going home. Don't get too drunk—we have a shit-ton of paperwork to do tomorrow."

"Sorry I can't help, I'm on administrative leave."

Gino snorted. "Like that's going to stop you. Pick you up at ten tomorrow?"

"Earlier, I want a Pig's Eye redux. I liked the bartender almost as much as the cinnamon rolls."

"Might be tough to get reservations this late, but I'll pull some strings."

60

RIG JOHNSTON TOOK his three spaniels out for a run in the country every afternoon after his early shift at Blaisdell Construction. Not that Covina was a concrete jungle, but he and Solvig lived in town, and his fellas were a high-strung bunch who needed space to blow off the energy of youth. Bred to flush birds, they loved the ditches and fields, and his wife loved the fact that they came home too exhausted to dig up the lawn or knock over furniture. Trig loved the solitude and the camaraderie of his best friends.

They were lobbing down the dirt road a little too far ahead of him, so he blew the training whistle, confident they would stop in their tracks and wait for his order. Obedience was the difference between a working dog and a pet, and his goal was to have them ready for hunting season this fall.

But this time, they didn't mind him, didn't even balk. They'd caught scent of something irresistible and were in a fever, barking like maniacs as they veered off the road and into the woods of posted private property.

He blew the whistle again and again, shouted their names, then finally took off after them. Dogs couldn't read NO TRES-PASSING signs, but the rich city folk who came down here to their weekend places thought they should. They didn't take kindly to an animal lifting its leg on their trees or flowerbeds or chasing ducks off their lakes. Last year, one of those idiots had filled Lionel Kray's Irish setter full of BBs. The sorrowful thing was that Lionel had ended up in court for assault after he'd knocked the guy out, and the *real* assailant had gotten away with a slap on the wrist and a vet bill.

Trig was huffing and puffing by the time he found the dogs deep in the woods, digging furiously near a maple tree, clods of dirt flying from their paws. He could see a big house through the trees and he knew this could be real trouble for his boys.

"REX, RUMMY, RAFFIE, BAD DOGS! HEEL!"

Not even a whimper or a glance, like they were totally deaf. That had never happened before, and it never would again. You never beat an animal when it disobeyed because that degraded trust, but he would let them know who was boss.

He stormed up a shallow incline and yanked Rex away by the collar, then gently booted the other two. "Get back! Sit!" he shouted, and that broke their trance. They scrambled away and sank to their haunches, whining. "Good boys, stay. Now let's see what the hell got you in such a tizzy." Trig turned and saw the dead man in a shallow grave.

He jerked back in shock and revulsion, his heart a jackhammer in his chest. His instinct was to run, but he couldn't move, couldn't pull his eyes away from the gruesome, bloody, muddy visage. Those startled-looking, milky eyes mottled with dirt seemed to be staring straight into his soul, tugging at him. Dear God, it was like the corpse was trying to communicate with him, coax him into the grave.

He swallowed the hot acid that shot up his throat, but he still couldn't make himself turn away from the horror, from the gaping wound in the man's neck that looked like a larger, second mouth. He was wearing camouflage, and holy Mary, Mother of God, is this what happened to trespassing hunters here? What else could it be?

His bladder let loose and that finally knocked out his paralysis. He scrambled for his phone, but his hands were shaking so badly he could barely punch 911. After he finished his call, he dropped to his hands and knees and vomited. He was still retching when he heard a muted pop, then the whine of a bullet as it whizzed past his ear. A split second later, another bullet hit the maple's trunk a foot away from his head, spraying bark onto the dead man.

Trig jumped to his feet and ran as hard as he prayed, the dogs in the lead. They were as panicked as he was because they could tell the difference between a bird gun and a handgun. They knew this wasn't a field exercise.

He heard another pop and felt a scorching pain in his leg. He screamed and collapsed, thinking his life couldn't possibly end this way, it was too absurd. He'd just been taking his dogs for a run in the country, how could that get you killed?

He felt tears on his cheeks, heard frantic shouts. His vision was blurry, fading, but he was pretty sure he saw cops running toward him. How did they get here so fast?

"I'm hit," he groaned weakly. The last thing he registered before he passed out was Rex's tongue swiping his face.

61

G INO PARKED IN front of Grace's house and draped his arms over the steering wheel. "Well, that was one hell of a day."

The understatement of the millennium flipped a switch in Magozzi's brain and he started laughing. Couldn't stop. Gino's cackles fueled the fire of his hysteria, and soon they were both gasping and wiping their eyes. Damn, it felt good to let go.

Gino wheezed and finally caught his breath. "How's the shoulder?"

"It's an eleven on a scale of one to ten."

"Ice it and take four ibuprofen, you'll be good as new in the morning. And don't watch the news, you lived it. You don't need to hear some clueless dipshit's analysis." He started drumming his fingers on the dashboard. "I suppose this kind of seals the deal on retirement, huh? Talk about one last victory lap."

Magozzi stared out the windshield at the twilit street. A few kids in shorts and T-shirts were still playing in their yards, but the plummeting temperatures of an early spring night would send them all inside soon. That was thing about April in Minnesota. You could get a sunburn and frostbite in a twenty-four-hour period. "Actually, it's the opposite. You all need me. Desperately. Who else would have turned Mauer into oatmeal and saved the day?"

Gino rolled his head to look at his partner, in dire danger of laughing again. "Get your ass inside, your people are waiting for you."

*   *   *

Magozzi was greeted at the door by Charlie, who led him to the kitchen at a dignified pace like a hairy butler. All the people he loved—*his* people—were clustered together around the granite island, talking in low, subdued tones while they sipped wine. Circling the wagons was a primordial human instinct.

They all animated and beamed at him when he walked in— even his beautiful, reticent Grace. But every face was pale and drawn, every pair of eyes deeply troubled, reflecting the terror and trauma of the day. Maybe they'd talked about some things, but he doubted it. The postmortem would come later. Mauer had been tormenting them all day, had almost killed them, and wasting another thought on him right now was tantamount to keeping that fuck alive. It was time to be in the moment.

He went to Grace first and took her hands, squeezing them with an urgency that made her wince. "Is Elizabeth okay?"

"She calmed down once we got here and she's back to her old self. She ate, got an airplane ride from Uncle Harley, and Auntie Annie read her *Green Eggs and Ham* before bed."

"She's sound asleep," Annie promised. "Kids are resilient beyond adult understanding."

It was true, but he would never get over the guilt. He didn't want to think about that now either. "She's tough like her mother."

"Or like her badass dad." Harley hopped off his stool with a sly wink. "Here, take a load off, buddy, I'll pour you a glass."

"I thought you'd be back home by now."

"I was waiting for you. We all were." He sloshed a healthy dose of white into a waiting goblet. "Cheers to you, Leo."

Magozzi raised his glass. "Cheers to all of us." Nothing more needed to be said. He took an impolite gulp, hoping the wine had a high alcohol content. From the burn in his throat, he believed it did. "God, this is fantastic."

"Grace's taste in wine is *almost* as good as mine. Obviously, your party's isn't happening tomorrow, but let's get together anyhow and bask in the oenological glory of what I curated for the occasion. I don't know about the rest of you, but twenty-four hours from now, I'm going to be good and ready to get shit-faced and celebrate."

That necessitated another toast, and after the second gulp, Magozzi came crashing down from his all-day high and exhaustion came on hard and fast. Everyone noticed. But it felt good to be here, chatting about benign things that merely grazed the perimeter of the black events of the day. The mood wasn't exactly festive, but it was what they all needed.

When the bottle was empty, Roadrunner stretched and yawned. "Petra and I are going hit the road. We'll take an Uber."

Harley drained his glass. "I should get going too. My kickass, invincible doors are crying for some TLC."

"I'll drive everybody home in Grace's Rover," Magozzi offered. "I'm not drunk yet."

Petra smiled. "Stay home and work on that. Do you want to ride with us, Annie?"

"Thanks, sugar, but you two go on ahead, I'll catch a ride with Harley."

Roadrunner waved goodbye in his awkward way while Petra hugged everyone. She looked younger and happier than Magozzi had ever seen her, dark eyes somehow lighter. It was little wonder. The last living link to the horrors of her past was gone forever.

Annie nudged Harley. "Call us a ride, I'm fresh out of steam."

"Yes, ma'am."

"Honestly, it's no trouble," Magozzi started to say, but he was silenced by an admonishing, rainbow-tipped finger.

"You are staying put. The three of you need to be together. Well, four, counting Charlie."

Magozzi couldn't imagine going home to an empty house after this day, and it saddened him to think of Annie alone in her posh downtown condo, of Harley rattling around his big mansion like a restless ghost.

Harley pocketed his phone and gave Annie a nudge. "Ride will be here in five minutes. You ready, milady?"

"Ready to run a bubble bath and pour a bourbon."

"I don't have bubble bath."

"What's that got to do with anything?"

"You're not going home, you're staying with me tonight."

"Why would I do a fool thing like that?"

"Isn't it obvious? I need some help. There are splinters all over the damn foyer floor, and I don't know how to use a broom or a vacuum."

Annie folded her arms over her bosom and glared at him ferociously. "A lot of people work their whole lives at being as offensive as you are and they don't even come close."

He waggled his eyebrows. "And when you're finished cleaning, you can go up to your bedroom and slip into something more comfortable while I pour you a bourbon."

"What did I tell you this morning?"

"That I'm pretty much irresistible."

"I *told* you that it was an insult to farm animals to compare you to them."

Magozzi grinned at their blessedly normal banter. Even a near-death experience hadn't stifled it. But he sensed something different between them, barely perceptible, like a draft you felt from an opening door. Or maybe that was the wine and his overwrought imagination.

Harley waved impatiently. "Come on, sugarplum, let's go."

"What kind of bourbon do you have?"

"Anything you want. I have over a hundred bottles."

"Alright," she huffed. "I'll babysit you tonight, but I'm not happy about it."

* * *

Grace and Magozzi stood on her front stoop and waved Annie and Harley off into the chilly spring night like parents on prom night. The sky was sugared with stars, and a full moon hung low, icing the bare trees on the boulevard with cool white light.

He put his arm around her, hugging her close. "It's cold. We should share our body heat."

"Or go inside."

"Always the pragmatist."

She laid her head on his shoulder. "Why did you become a cop?"

Magozzi didn't hesitate. "To help people."

"You helped a lot of people today. Saved their lives. Including ours."

"But I put you all in danger again. *Because* I was on the job. That kind of diminishes the 'helping' part."

"We've been through this a dozen times, Magozzi. We choose to put *ourselves* in harm's way because we want to take down criminals, just like you and Gino. Danger is an occupational hazard. And if you hadn't been on the job, things might have turned out very differently. That's what you need to think about. That's what matters."

"Retirement makes sense in a lot of ways," he countered weakly.

Grace sighed in exasperation. "If you don't want it, it doesn't make any sense at all. Tell me the truth, Magozzi."

He looked into the extraordinary eyes of this extraordinary woman who was wiser than he could ever hope to be. She understood, and she was giving him permission. "I'm not ready." There was great relief in confessing.

Satisfied, she returned her gaze to the sky. "I knew that a long time ago."

"Then why didn't you tell me?" he teased.

"You had to come to the conclusion on your own."

He turned her to face him and cupped her cheeks. "I love you, Grace."

Her eyes sparkled in the celestial light bathing this part of the world and she smiled—a big, beautiful, joyful smile that transformed her face and showed her teeth. "I love you too, Magozzi. Were you afraid I didn't?"

"Maybe a little. I'm needy. Do you have any more wine?"

She pulled him into a warm house that was so much more than that.

62

I RIS HAD AVOIDED not just a joint press conference but another impromptu statement in the county courthouse parking lot because word traveled at the speed of 5G these days. At the whiff of the drama in St. Paul, the media had fled like a swarm of locusts long before she and Sampson made it back to Dundas. She wasn't off the hook entirely—at eight sharp tomorrow morning, she would take the podium along with many other devoted members of law enforcement who'd chased this case with equal zeal. Mauer had been taken down by a collective, each person and entity a cog in the wheel that had finally run him over. After a good night's sleep, she would express this more eloquently to the cameras without a single cliché, like the English teacher she used to be.

Unfortunately, neither she nor Sampson could avoid the paperwork. But that would take a full day at least, and they were both too exhausted and emotionally drained to spell their own names, let alone write cogent reports. They'd pick it up tomorrow, sheriff's orders.

They were sitting in the empty courthouse parking lot with the windows open and the heater blasting, listening to peepers sing from their homes on the banks of Lake Kittering. It was a beautiful night after an ugly day, more so for Travis than anybody.

He'd looked so tiny and frail in his hospital bed, staring mindlessly at the TV. The doctor had said he was mildly catatonic when he'd been admitted, and news of his parents' deaths had sent him all the way there. A protective mechanism against severe trauma. But he'd been surrounded by people who loved him and would be there when he snapped out of it. People who would take him into their lives and care for him. "I think Travis is going to be okay. He just needs time."

Sampson nodded. "Hopefully he won't just be okay, he'll thrive eventually. The grandparents are good, solid people, they'll step up and then some. And you know Annabelle will always be there for him. So will we. But emotionally, he's got a long road to recovery. The whole family does."

"Annabelle told me she's setting up a GoFundMe page. I'm sure that will bring in enough money to get Travis the best treatment for as long as he needs it."

"I'll be one of the first to donate."

Iris inhaled a deep breath of crisp fresh air that smelled like the purest distillation of a world coming back to life. "This is nice," she said softly. "Peaceful. I can't believe I lived in the city for so long."

"What made you move there in the first place?"

"The obvious reason. I was so sheltered growing up, I wanted to experience a different kind of life. A more exciting one. Different isn't always better, though. Were you ever tempted?"

"Every country kid is, but it never held my attention. The sounds of birds and frogs are more exciting to me than car alarms and sirens." He blew out a sigh. "It's been a hell of a long day. You must be worried about Puck. She's supposed to get that special food twice a day."

Iris smiled at his concern. "I had the neighbor girl go over and feed her. She loves Puck more than her own cat."

"Who wouldn't? Want to grab a bite and some coffee?"

"The café is closed."

"We could get greasy burgers at the Porterhouse."

"No thanks." She hedged, then after a lot of mental acrobatics, decided what the hell? She didn't want to be alone any more than he did. "But I have chicken soup in the freezer. And a fancy new coffee maker, some wine, and a bottle of gin. It was my ex's, which makes it five years old at least, but I don't think it goes bad, does it?"

"No. Is that an invite?"

Iris started driving.

* * *

Roadrunner had been in Petra's bathroom for too long, polishing her ring while he agonized. *The* ring. It would only be hers if she accepted it. Was this the right time or the wrong time after everything that had happened today? And if not now, when? Would there *ever* be a right time?

"*Dušo?* Are you okay?" she called.

"I'll be right out, I'm just . . . washing up." He splashed his face, then stepped out of the bathroom with a cartwheeling heart. Petra was in the living room, sitting on the hearth with a lowball of vodka and lime. The firelight danced in her hair and cast a golden penumbra on the side of her face. It reminded him of the amber in his hand.

"Come, sit next to me."

Roadrunner obeyed and looked into the dark eyes of a woman he felt like he'd known his entire life. "This feels great. Cozy. It's cold outside, I heard there might be frost. Maybe even a freeze," he rambled nervously.

Petra's glance was questioning. "That worries you?"

His cheeks started to burn and it wasn't from the heat of the fire. "Uh . . . well, kind of. Harley's flowers are coming up and maybe he should cover them tonight. You know how obsessed he is about his gardens, I should probably call—"

"A man obsessed with his gardens knows how to take care of them. Is everything okay?"

"Yeah. Yeah, great."

"Can I get you something to drink? Your favorite smoothie? I have some in the fridge left over from breakfast."

He tried to smile, but his lips weren't working. "Actually, I'd like what you're having."

"A *vodka*?"

"Yes."

She raised a brow doubtfully. "That's an interesting request from a man who rarely consumes alcohol."

"I'd like to start drinking now."

Her laughter sounded like the wind chimes that hung on her front porch. "I understand, it's been that kind of day. I'll be right back."

After she'd left, Roadrunner practiced getting down on one knee, but it felt stupid. Corny. Inauthentic. And he was having trouble balancing because his whole body was rubbery. God, this was a disaster . . .

He heard that wind chime laughter again. "That's an interesting yoga pose." Petra placed his vodka on the hearth next to hers.

"It's . . . a modification of Warrior Pose," he vamped lamely. "Something I'm experimenting with."

"Uh-huh. You clearly have something on your mind, *dušo*. Talk to me."

He rose on unsteady legs, then filled his lungs and took the step that spanned miles and decades—one that would kill him or cure him. He presented the ring on a sweaty, upturned palm that was shaking so badly he almost dropped it. "Will you marry me, Petra?"

She gazed down at the sparkling diamonds and glowing amber—past and present—and began to weep, something she hadn't done since she'd lost her family all those years ago. "I've been waiting, *dušo*."

63

MAGOZZI SLEPT LIKE an angel. He didn't exactly feel refreshed or alert when he crawled out of bed at six AM, but he felt somewhat human again. Except for his shoulder. Gino was a liar—four ibuprofen, ice packs, and several glasses of wine hadn't touched the pain. It was so bad this morning, he considered amputating the right half of his body with one of Grace's chef's knives. That couldn't possibly feel any worse.

He started a pot of coffee—surprisingly difficult to do one-handed—and turned on his phone. As he gaped at the astonishing number of missed alerts bloating his inbox, Gino called, sounding extremely overcaffeinated.

"About time you answered, Leo. Was your phone off or what?"

"Of course it was off. Wasn't yours?"

"Angela and I drank a bottle of Chianti last night and I forgot to mute it. The chief woke me up an hour ago. The shit really hit the fan last night."

"In a good way or bad way?"

"In a great way. Zelda's in custody and she's toast."

Magozzi was suddenly wide awake. "What happened?"

"She tried to kill a trespasser on her property. A bullet caught him in the leg real close to the femoral artery. He's damn lucky he got a call into 911 before she went psycho on him. Even luckier there were cops there already, watching the place."

Magozzi rubbed his temples, hoping it would stir the cornmeal mush of his brain back into a cohesive organ capable of forming rational thoughts. "Jesus. Why would she do something stupid like that? It's like setting off an 'arrest me' flare."

"Panic. Desperation. The guy's dogs dug up a fresh body in her woods. Pretty gruesome, his throat was slit ear to ear. Cops, techs, and the FBI were crawling all over the place the whole night. It's going to be a goldmine once the lab processes everything."

Magozzi heard a loud slurping on the other end of the line. Gino going in for another jolt of caffeine, which reminded him to pour himself a mug. "Did they ID the body?"

"Sure did, and this is where it gets mighty interesting. Name's Novak Kostić. A real bad, real slippery son of a bitch who's been on Interpol's Most Wanted for years. Known associates are none other than Peter Praljik, Goran Stanković, and a cavalcade of other dirtbags from the Balkan war. Petra called it—she knew Zelda or whoever she really is had to be connected to Mauer in the past, it was the only explanation that made sense."

Magozzi was paralyzed by astonishment for a moment, although he shouldn't have been. "I was thinking earlier that wars never really ended."

"You're right about that, but the war's finally over for these freaks. It's a thing of karmic beauty, isn't it? Somebody should have put them all in a room together years ago."

"It's going to take a long time to sort this mess out, Gino."

"Yeah. You cut a Gordian knot and end up with a bunch of loose ends to tie up. Like the crispy critter in the Portland house who hasn't been ID'd yet. But I'll bet you a hundred bucks it's Stanković."

"No bet, I'm with you on that."

"And I had you pegged as easy money. More's the pity. Damn, Leo, isn't this the greatest way to start the day? We got Zelda cold. As it stands now, she's looking at prison time for attempted murder of a trespasser and concealing a dead body. Once the lab processes everything from the house and property, I guarantee we'll be able to nail her for accessory to kidnapping, harboring a fugitive, and abetting a terrorist. She is never going to see the light of day."

Magozzi was ecstatic, but he also felt the familiar melancholy that always accompanied the wrap-up to a big case. When something—even a bad something—that had so completely consumed your life ended, you lost your mooring for a while. But the melancholy never lasted more than a couple days. This time, it was gone almost as fast as he'd acknowledged it. "I suppose this means breakfast at Pig's Eye is out."

Gino chuckled. "Rain check on that. Chief wants us in his office at our earliest convenience, and you know what that means."

"Yeah. Get our asses there right now."

"You got it."

* * *

They found the chief pacing in his spotless office where no speck of dust had ever dared to venture. He looked up anxiously, waved them in, and shut the door. His eyes were cupped with dark pouches, and his sallow, hangdog face was droopier than Magozzi had ever seen it. He knew the chief hadn't slept much, if at all.

"Thank you for coming in so promptly, detectives," he said wearily. "I was hoping to let you sleep in, but news is coming in at a brisk pace and I know you want to remain on top of this. Believe it or not, we've just begun to scratch the surface."

"Don't we know it," Gino said. "It's going to take about fifty whiteboards to get this all laid out and sewn up."

"Indeed. But it's only a matter of time, and I don't believe it will take as long as you might imagine. With the FBI and Interpol and Petra's organization working in tandem with us, there is significant progress happening by the minute."

Gino cocked a brow curiously. "How's it going, working with Shafer again?"

Malcherson gave him the long-suffering look of a parent with a chronically recalcitrant child. "I think you know the answer to that, Detective Rolseth. However, I'm happy to relinquish control to the FBI this time. I'd like your reports by noon."

"Absolutely," Magozzi promised, placing his shield and sidearm on the chief's desk. "I totally forgot about administrative leave protocol yesterday, my apologies."

"Understandable, and no apologies required." He placed them in a desk drawer and leaned back in his big leather chair, regarding them shrewdly. "Incidentally, there's a GoFundMe page for Travis Dunbar. I was on it this morning to donate, and the response has been remarkable. In fact, I noticed a rather large donation by an anonymous party. One hundred thousand dollars. I wonder who that generous soul or souls might be."

Magozzi knew nothing about the GoFundMe page, but Monkeewrench obviously did. And the chief knew that as well as he did. "Gee, I can't imagine."

"I guess we'll never know." He folded his hands on his pristine desk blotter, his eyes landing on Magozzi. "The complexity of the wrap-up will delay your retirement, Detective, but I will assign another detective to take your place if you wish. You've certainly earned it."

Magozzi felt a slow smile lift his mouth. "That's kind of you, Chief, but that won't be necessary."

He nodded. "I knew you'd want to see this through to the end."

"And beyond that, sir."

Malcherson raised a white brow. "Meaning?"

"Well, naturally, I've been looking ahead, thinking a lot about my future lately." Magozzi was tempted to milk the suspense, but he was classier than that. "I realized it's not my time yet, sir. It would be a privilege to stay on—that is, if you haven't already reworked the roster to reflect my absence."

Malcherson's granite face was unmoved, but his lips were seriously considering a smile. "As a matter of fact, Detective, I haven't gotten around to the paperwork." He reached into the credenza behind him and withdrew a very expensive bottle of scotch and three glasses. "From the expressions on your faces, you're both surprised to learn I keep this here. It's only for very special occasions." He dosed out three pours. "Welcome back, Detective Magozzi."

Gino was grinning so hard he thought his face might split. "He never left."

Malcherson couldn't control his smile any longer. "Perhaps another party is in order. I'm sure Detective McLaren would be happy to reprise his role."

For the first, and probably last, time ever, the three of them drank scotch in the chief's office at seven in the morning and laughed until their faces were red. Magozzi thought that Johnny would be proud to know most of the laughter was at his expense.

ACKNOWLEDGMENTS

WHEN I DECIDED to write an eleventh Monkeewrench novel years after the last one, I knew my most important job was to bring these beloved characters vividly back to life and do justice to their histories and their futures. In order to reanimate them in the way they deserved, I had to *become* them again. For you. For PJ. For myself. No pressure. Just like scaling Mount Everest, easy like Sunday morning.

As it turns out, I fretted for nothing. It *was* easy and as cozy as stepping into a favorite pair of slippers or going home for Christmas. I felt the gang unfurling and coming to life inside me like sea monkeys in water. The years of separation melted away. Some of it was muscle memory (yeah, I know the brain isn't a muscle, but you get the drift), Mostly it was dedication and a lot of hard work. I trained like a runner before a marathon.

After five years of "living" in Los Angeles with Detective Margaret Nolan and her supporting cast, I knew I had to do some serious recalibration in order to find my way back to Minneapolis and Monkee World. To that end, I reread the previous ten novels, some of them several times. Once my due diligence was completed, I decided to do something I've never done before: follow up on the storyline of its predecessor, *Ice Cold Heart*. I felt like I had a lot more to say about that book, and I wanted to expand on the character arcs I'd set up. In this instance, picking up where I left off was a good choice that gave me sure footing on my reentry.

It's more a continuation than a sequel, and once I got started, the writing was an odyssey of rebirth and rediscovery. It felt more like a party than work, in large part because it brought me right back to the grand days of writing with PJ. Every minute I spent with my mother while she was still here was the best party I've ever been to.

Another source of fun was sprinkling Easter eggs throughout the manuscript—sly nods to previous books in both series. It wasn't intentional, it just happened, and it gave me plenty of chuckles along the way.

Many, many thanks to Matt Martz and everyone at Crooked Lane for your continued support of the Monkeewrench series. You gave me the great gift of letting the gang breathe new life, and you have my gratitude.

To my longtime agent and dear friend, Ellen Geiger. "Forever on and at your side." That goes both ways, honey. I love you. And to the rest of the dream team at Frances Goldin Literary Agency, a thousand thanks. You rock.

To my incredible friends, who are also family. You are my solid foundation and my joy.

Sending big hugs to Carole Anne Burgess, a wonderful U.K. fan who has been there from the very beginning. My very best and love to you.

And thanks to you, dear readers. I'm endlessly grateful that you let me speak to you 80,000 words at a time. I hope you enjoyed this latest adventure in Monkee World!